Somewhere, a night bird cried

Hunching deeper into her coat, Cora tried to ignore the snap of branches and the rustle of leaves deep within the bordering pathway. She rounded a bend and stopped short. She stood in a small clearing, the castle several yards ahead up a steep hill.

At the top of the rise, a terrace extended out from the southern end of the castle. Bright light flooded the area, bathing it in brilliant white. A man stood just outside the rim of light—a dark, brooding figure flanked on either side by two huge dogs.

All three seemed unaware of her presence, their heads raised skyward. The wind whipping off the water was brisker on top of the hill, and the man's heavy overcoat blew open to the elements. His body was long and powerful, and he was clothed almost entirely in black. His hair was dark, and he wore it long and untrimmed.

Cora tried to get a glimpse of his face. Something told her that it would be worth the effort. But the shadows from the castle walls kept him safely hidden....

Dear Harlequin Intrigue Reader,

To chase away those end-of-summer blues, we have an explosive lineup that's guaranteed to please!

Joanna Wayne leaves goosebumps with *A Father's Duty*, the third book in NEW ORLEANS CONFIDENTIAL. In this riveting conclusion, murder, mayhem…and mystique are unleashed in the Big Easy. And that's just the beginning! *Unauthorized Passion*, which marks the beginning of Amanda Stevens's new action-packed miniseries, MATCHMAKERS UNDERGROUND, features a lethally sexy lawman who takes a beautiful imposter into his protective custody. Look for *Just Past Midnight* by Ms. Stevens from Harlequin Books next month at your favorite retail outlet.

Danger and discord sweep through Antelope Flats when B.J. Daniels launches her western series, McCALLS' MONTANA. Will the town ever be the same after a fiery showdown between a man on a mission and *The Cowgirl in Question*? Next up, the second book in ECLIPSE, our new gothic-inspired promotion. *Midnight Island Sanctuary* by Susan Peterson—a spine-tingling "gaslight" mystery set in a remote coastal town—will pull you into a chilling riptide.

To wrap up this month's thrilling lineup, Amy J. Fetzer returns to Harlequin Intrigue to unravel a sinister black-market baby ring mystery in *Undercover Marriage*. And, finally, don't miss *The Stolen Bride* by Jacqueline Diamond—an edge-of-your-seat reunion romance about an amnesiac bride-in-jeopardy who is about to get a crash course in true love.

Enjoy!

Denise O'Sullivan
Senior Editor
Harlequin Intrigue

MIDNIGHT ISLAND SANCTUARY

SUSAN PETERSON

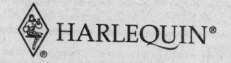

HARLEQUIN®

TORONTO • NEW YORK • LONDON
AMSTERDAM • PARIS • SYDNEY • HAMBURG
STOCKHOLM • ATHENS • TOKYO • MILAN • MADRID
PRAGUE • WARSAW • BUDAPEST • AUCKLAND

ISBN 0-373-22798-1

MIDNIGHT ISLAND SANCTUARY

ABOUT THE AUTHOR

A devoted *Star Trek* fan, Susan Peterson wrote her first science-fiction novel at the age of thirteen. But unlike other fan writers, in Susan's novel she made sure that Mr. Spock fell in love. Unfortunately, what she didn't take into consideration was the fact that falling in love and pursuing a life of total logic didn't exactly go hand in hand. In any case, it was then she realized that she was a hopeless romantic, a person who needed the happily-ever-after ending. But it wasn't until later in life, after pursuing careers in intensive-care nursing and school psychology, that Susan finally found the time to pursue a career in writing. An ardent fan of psychological thrillers, Susan combined her love of romance and suspense into several manuscripts targeted to the Harlequin Intrigue line. Getting the go-ahead to write for this line was a dream come true for her.

Susan lives in a small town in northern New York with her son, Kevin, her nutball dog, Ozzie, Phoenix the cat and Lex the six-toed menace (a new kitten). Susan loves to hear from readers. E-mail her at SusanPetersonHI@aol.com or visit her Web site at www.susanpeterson.net.

Books by Susan Peterson

HARLEQUIN INTRIGUE
751—CONCEALED WEAPON*
776—EMERGENCY CONTACT†
798—MIDNIGHT ISLAND SANCTUARY

*Bachelors at Large
†Dead Bolt

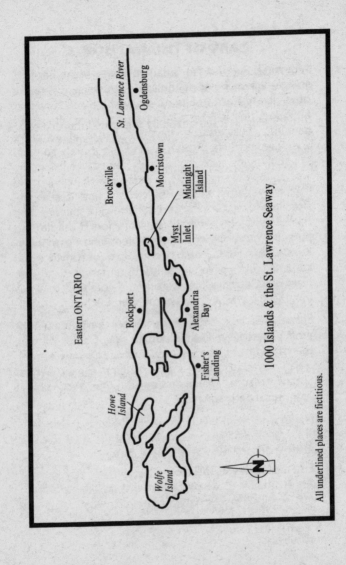

Eastern ONTARIO

St. Lawrence River

Ogdensburg

Brockville

Morristown

Midnight
Island

Myst
Inlet

Rockport

Alexandria
Bay

Fisher's
Landing

Howe
Island

Wolfe
Island

N

1000 Islands & the St. Lawrence Seaway

All underlined places are fictitious.

CAST OF CHARACTERS

Jake Mackenzie—The sole heir to the Mackenzie shipping fortune and the only suspect in the strange disappearance of his wife two years ago.

Cora Shelly—Traumatized by the brutal murder of her roommate and her own personal assault, Cora hides herself on Midnight Island, waiting to be called to testify against the sadistic killer.

Amanda Mackenzie—The second wife of shipping magnate William Mackenzie, the coldly remote and icy Amanda hires Cora as the household's new cook.

Maggie Mackenzie—Emotionally fragile stepsister to Jake Mackenzie, Maggie has a secret that she's dying to tell.

William Mackenzie—Jake's ailing father.

Alice Benson—The head housekeeper of Midnight Castle, Alice tells Cora of the existence of the island's ghostly apparition, The Mournful Lady.

Dr. Sheffield—A guest and friend of Amanda Mackenzie, Dr. Sheffield offers Cora his professional assistance when she begins to have strange and oddly disturbing nightmares.

Vivian Sheffield—The beautiful and seductive wife of Dr. Sheffield, Vivian seems vastly amused by the strange occurrences at Midnight Castle.

Erik Dubane—A sadistic psychopath who promised Cora in court that he would return to kill her and anyone close to her. Now he's on the loose....

For Janet and Margie
Can we grab a cup of coffee and talk about
what we want to do with the rest of our lives?
I miss you guys so much.

To Chris Wenger,
who provided me with all the great information
on the St. Lawrence River and the surrounding area.

Prologue

"How's that feel, Cora? All comfy now?"

Cora Sheldon opened her eyes and stared up into Erik Dubane's sapphire-blue ones. His strikingly classic features were composed into a deceivingly bland expression of concern, and his fingers, smooth and soft as a pampered woman's, stroked the side of her cheek. As she took a shuddering breath, he gently brushed several strands of her damp, clinging hair behind her ear.

Cora squeezed her eyes shut again and wished she could shut out the world. Erik wanted to know if she was comfortable. One minute he was slashing a knife across her throat and the next he wanted to know if she was comfortable.

Somehow she doubted his sincerity. His sanity.

"Answer me, dammit!" he demanded. "Are you comfortable?"

Cora nodded, the grating edge of his voice warning her that he was teetering on the edge. Somehow she needed to keep him calm. She needed to stall for time.

"I…I'm bleeding, Erik," she whimpered. "Y-you hurt my throat." She bit her lower lip, catching the inside edge between her teeth. Damn. She'd been reduced to pitiful whimpers.

She clenched her fists, her heart beating frantically in her chest. She didn't want to cringe. Didn't want to whine. She just wanted to get away from him. "Please don't hurt me any-more."

Erik grinned, flashing perfect teeth. Teeth so white and straight that she knew he'd had braces as a kid, "I won't hurt you, sweet Cora. I've been saving you for last."

He leaned in close, his breath hot and wild. Powerful enough to blast her into nothingness. She squeezed her eyes shut so tight her cheeks ached. Maybe if she didn't look, he'd disappear.

"It isn't that deep a cut, Cora-Bora," he whispered in her ear, his lips moving silkily against the outer edge. "Little bor-ing Cora. Always mousing around. Always curious. Well, you got a real eyeful tonight, didn't you, Cora?"

When she didn't answer, he grabbed a hunk of her hair and jerked her head up and down like a demented puppet, mock-ing her. "I'm a boring slut who needs to be taught a lesson. Teach me a lesson, Erik."

"Please—" she begged.

He traced the edge of the knife down the side of her cheek. "Please what? Please, Erik, make things more interesting? Please give me something to put me in the mood? Is that what you were going to say, Cora-Bora?"

A single tear slid out from between Cora's lashes and burned a hot trail down her cheek. She opened her eyes again and stared up at him. She knew Jennifer was dead. There was no way she could have lived after losing all that blood. So much blood that it saturated her bed's mattress.

Another tiny whimper slipped from between Cora's lips, and she bit down, hating the sound. It made her sound weak. Pitiful.

But somehow she needed to find a way to convince Erik to let her go. If he didn't, she knew she was going to die right here on the seventh floor with Jennifer, and no would ever hear her screams.

The windows were closed and locked, the drapes drawn, and the person who occupied the next door apartment was none other than Erik. She could hear his Doberman, Empress, barking wildly and scratching the door on the other side of the apartment wall. Please, God, let the downstairs neighbors call in a complaint.

"Oh, Cora," he crooned cheerfully in her ear. "Wake up, little Cora."

"P-please don't hurt me anymore," she begged again, forcing the words out from between stiff lips. "Please let me go and I won't tell anyone. I promise."

"Of course you won't tell anyone. We're going to have too much fun for you to tattle." He sat back on his heels. "Now, do you promise not to fight?" His voice was soft and coaxing, as if he were speaking to a small child. "Are you ready to do what I say?"

Cora felt rather than saw the sharp point of the knife trace the skin along the top of her shirt. It dipped down into the valley between her breasts and she whimpered again.

He placed a finger over her lips. "Shh. We mustn't get too noisy, too soon." He pressed his lips to hers. They tasted wet and hard, his perfect teeth grinding against hers.

He drew back. "Are you ready now?"

Just do what he says. Don't make him angry.

She nodded. "Wh-whatever you want. Just don't kill me."

He snorted in disgust and released her. Her head hit the hardwood floor with a dull thud. An explosion of white sparkles burst in front of her eyes.

"You need to grow a backbone, little Cora." He stood up. "But then, maybe it's a little too late for that, huh?"

He nudged her side with the tip of his shoe. "I'm going to run you a nice hot bath. Maybe that will be just the thing to perk you up a bit."

He reached down and grabbed a hunk of her hair again, dragging her across the floor toward the bathroom. Cora bit her bottom lip, refusing to cry out in pain as strands of her hair ripped from her scalp.

He dropped her right outside the bathroom door and poked his head into the room. "A little too small for the two of us. You'll just have to wait right here until I'm ready for you, little Cora." He leaned down again, his breath sweeping the side of her cheek. She turned her head away, but he seemed oblivious. "We're going to have so much fun, you and I. You'll be screaming with ecstasy for more, just like your roommate."

Cora gagged and watched as he stepped into the bathroom. He was crazy. And she was trapped.

She tried to loosen the belt he'd used to lash her wrists together earlier, digging her nails into the palms of her hands and pulling. Think, girl, think! How are you going to get out of this alive?

She rolled up onto her side, gritting her teeth as a surge of such incredible agony threatened to pull her under and pin her to the floor. She looked around, trying to figure a way out.

She wasn't sure, but she might have passed out for a time after he'd cut her. He'd jumped her in the hall when she'd run from Jennifer's bedroom, tackling her and throwing her to the floor. He hadn't expected her to come home when she had, and she wouldn't have been there if she hadn't gotten a head-ache and left the restaurant early.

She lifted her head. The living room seemed miles away down the hall, but somehow she was able to pull herself to her knees, the carpeting stinging and rubbing her legs raw through her torn nylons.

From the bathroom, she heard the sound of water running. Wisps of steam escaped into the hall and gently caressed her face. She struggled harder until the belt loosened, slipping from her wrists. She crawled along the floor, breathing shallowly. He mustn't hear her.

Behind her, she heard Eric whistling. Something familiar. Something she'd heard before—when she was a child. But she couldn't place words with the tune. Her brain seemed frozen in a blast of white-hot fear.

She shook herself. No time for this. He'd be coming to get her any minute. Once he had her locked inside the tiny, windowless bathroom, Cora knew she'd never get away.

Pulling her legs up under her, she stood. Her whole body trembled and the room tilted, almost sending her face-first to the floor again.

She leaned against the wall, steadying herself. To the left, she noticed a slash of red on the eggshell-white wall. *That'll need repainting,* she thought. A giggle, something short and hysterical bubbled up into the back of her throat. Who was she kidding? If she ever got out of this apartment alive, she'd never come back.

"Going somewhere, my sweet?"

Terror ripped at her throat. She glanced over her shoulder. He stood in the doorway, one shoulder leaning casually against the frame, a smirk of such twisted evilness that she almost collapsed to the floor like the gazelle caught in the eye of the tiger.

But she didn't. She took off for the front door, her feet moving with a strength and determination she thought she'd lost.

He tackled her, his hands clamping onto her ankles. She

fell forward, hitting the living room floor hard. He laughed, the fact that she was fighting back amusing him immensely.

"Keep it up. It only makes it sweeter," he said. His hand moved up her leg as he started to crawl on top of her.

Sobs built in the back of her throat, jerking and choking her, threatening to drown her. She drew up her right leg and smashed it backward, aiming for his face. She connected and he screamed in surprise.

His hands loosened on her legs and he rolled off her. Cora scrambled to her feet, taking only a moment to look back. He was rolling on his back, both hands pressed to his face.

"You broke my nose, you stupid bitch."

Cora ran for the door, grabbing the knob and twisting.

She almost sobbed in relief when it turned. It was unlocked.

She yanked the door open and launched herself into the hall, bouncing off the opposite wall. She steadied herself and glanced down the hall. Her hair hung limp in her eyes.

She shook her head and squinted. The hall seemed to tilt at a crazy angle. She used her sleeve to wipe hair and blood out of her eyes. It was like peering down a long, dark tunnel.

She could see the elevator door. Stumbling on the thick carpet, she ran, using the wall to guide her.

Her breath rasped in her ears. When she reached the end of the hall, she smacked her palm on the elevator button. A glance at the panel overhead told her the elevator was on the third floor.

She hit the button again.

"Ooooo, Cora," his singsongy voice filtered down the darkened hall.

She slammed her hand on the button over and over. "Oh, God, please hurry up."

She glanced over her shoulder. He was trotting toward her,

the blade in his hand twinkling in the gloom, blood dripping from his nose. The amusement was gone from his face. Pure evilness. Pure hatred lined every inch of his face. If he caught her, there would be no mercy.

The bell tinged and the elevator doors slid open. Sobbing, she fell inside, one hand slapping the buttons on the panel, not caring which floor it took her to as long as it was down.

The doors slid shut, and she slumped against the back wall of the elevator. She was sobbing outright now, tears and saliva mixing with her blood. The elevator lurched and started down. He pounded on the doors, yelling something. She pressed her hands over her ears.

The doors opened at the lobby, and she stumbled through, tripping. She fell, her knees hitting the linoleum, and when she tried to get up, she collapsed on the floor, too weak to try again.

Behind her, the elevator door opened and closed on her legs, the bell pinging each time it tried to close.

She felt the tunnel of darkness closing in on her, and her vision narrowed to a pinpoint. From a long way off, she heard the long plaintive wail of police sirens and people shouting.

And as she slipped into unconsciousness, she thought, *Please, God, let them be coming for me.*

Chapter One

Four Months Later

A harsh wind skimmed across the waves of the St. Lawrence River and brushed the bow of the small motorboat. Cora Shelly lifted her face to meet the gust, squinting a bit as it pelted her face with a sharp sting. The strong smell of approaching winter, fish and diesel fuel filled her nostrils.

Heavy clouds, thick and dark with the threat of rain, hung low over the gray choppy water. Orange channel markers bobbed wildly on the crest of the waves, and Cora wondered how they stayed anchored in place.

The hull of the boat thudded against each wave and pitched as wildly as the markers. She could only hope she didn't lose her lunch before they reached land.

She ducked her head and glanced toward the back of the boat. Her driver sat hunched inside his mackinaw, his lined, heavily whiskered face averted from her as if to discourage any conversation. Earlier he'd introduced himself as Adam Gracy, her new employer's groundskeeper. She wondered if he was avoiding eye contact because he thought she might demand he take her back to the dock in Myst Inlet.

But as hair-raising as the boat ride was, Cora knew she wasn't about to demand any such thing. There was no going back. She was committed to following through with her promise. A promise sealed with her signature on a contract, committing her to one year of service on Midnight Island.

Besides, the contract's bonus after six months didn't hurt. She would use the money to escape, once her job of testifying at the trial was done. She'd go somewhere warm, sunny and far away from Erik Dubane.

It was a bit disconcerting to know that her new employer had so much trouble keeping hired help that she was willing to pay a healthy bonus if an employee stayed for six months. But Cora wasn't about to complain; she needed the money.

A wave hit the small craft broadside, sending it rocking. She grabbed the edge of her narrow bench seat and hung on, her fingers aching from the cold sting of the late-October wind. It was hard to believe that when she'd left L.A. earlier that morning the temperature had hovered around a balmy seventy-eight degrees. The temperature here on the upstate New York river had dipped below forty.

A fine spray kicked up beneath the bow of the boat, and the wind scattered heavy droplets of water over her. She pulled the collar of her thin wool coat closer around her neck and upper chest, her fingers brushing across the thin scar slicing along the base of her throat.

She snatched her hand away. Now was not the time to contemplate the past. Her concern was getting settled into her new job. The trial would come later.

"How much farther?" she called toward the back of the boat.

Gracy didn't bother yelling into the wind. He simply lifted a gnarled hand and pointed.

Cora faced forward again, getting her first real glimpse of Midnight Island, her home for the next year. She shivered and tried to tell herself the cause was the air temperature and not the forbidding, rock-strewn coast that outlined the tiny island. Trees and scruffy vegetation covered the bulk of the island, seeming to screen it from prying eyes. The screen had already turned to an autumn blaze of deep oranges and reds. But once the winter wind completely blew the last remaining leaves away, Cora was sure, the island would reveal bare branches, tangled scrubs and thorny bushes. It wasn't a welcoming place.

Less than a quarter mile long, the tiny land mass seemed to jut up out of the river with a defiant flare, forcing the huge tanker lumbering down the river and headed for the Great Lakes to give it wide berth. As their own boat drew closer, gulls dove and squawked overhead, angry that their food gathering was so rudely interrupted.

But it was the stone castle, a dark, looming, mammoth structure standing in the center of the island that captured Cora's attention. A granite and sandstone fortress with turrets and towers harking back to an ancient time.

Cora shivered again, her toes curling against the thin soles of her flats. She shoved her hands into her pockets in a futile attempt to warm them. The place looked more like a prison than a home.

At the thought of a prison, Cora dropped her head and clutched her hands into tight fists. A prison. How appropriate. She was actually burying herself alive in a castle prison all because she was being forced to help put Erik away, scheduled to sit in a cold, impersonal courtroom and bare her soul when he came to trial in less than eight months. No one doubted that she'd sit dutifully in an L.A. county courthouse and tell twelve stone-faced people sitting in a jury box what Dubane had done to her roommate, Jennifer, and herself. Cora was known for doing things dutifully.

She sighed and shifted on the hard bench. Perhaps this was her reward—to be trapped on an island, working for some crazed rich woman whose need for privacy bordered on paranoia. But who was she to complain? Her own need for privacy probably rivaled her employer's, especially since no one knew she'd come to Midnight Island—not even the D.A.'s office. Cora didn't plan on taking any chances. Erik Dubane was too clever for her to take any chances. She'd learned that firsthand, the hard way.

In the back of the boat, Gracy turned the tiller, and the boat headed for a tiny cove. A huge dock jutted out from the eastern side of the island, and a stone boathouse stretched the length of a rocky beachhead. The boathouse was massive, sporting ten or so doors. The cove was protected from the worst of the wind by a cluster of rocks.

As soon as the boat turned into the cove, the waves seemed to calm and the wind ceased whipping Cora's curls about her face. She shoved her hair back out of the way with one hand and secured it with the cheap headband she'd picked up in an airport pharmacy.

Gracy eased the craft up to the dock, threw a rope over one of the pilings and then scrambled out to tie it securely. She got up stiffly, feeling as though her entire body had been frozen to the seat.

"'Ere, give me yer hand, missy," Gracy ordered.

Cora reached out, her hand swallowed up in the man's gnarled, callused hand. He pulled her out of the boat as if she weighed fewer than ten pounds.

"Just follow the path up to the house, miss. I'll be along shortly with your luggage." He bent to grab her worn blue suitcase. "Mrs. Benson will meet you and show you to your quarters."

Cora stared at the crushed-stone path leading to a small forest of vegetation with a thick canopy overhead. Darkness was already settling over the island, the black clouds overhead blocking any light from the setting sun. The breeze rustled crisp fall leaves and the resulting whisper sounded dry and sharp to her ears.

"I…I really don't mind waiting for you, Mr. Gracy." She reached for her cosmetic case, ready to demonstrate her willingness to be useful. Anything to keep her from having to travel up the path alone in the gathering darkness.

Gracy scowled. Apparently, he didn't appreciate women who refused to listen the first time. "I got things to do down here, miss. A storm's coming, and I need to make sure the boat is tied down tight. You go along. The house ain't far." He grinned, showing a lot of gum and more than a few missing teeth. "Ye ain't afraid, are ya, miss?"

Something told Cora he'd be only too pleased to hear her admit to being afraid.

"No. I'm not afraid," she lied. "I simply thought you might need some help carrying things up."

He laughed, a rough and grating sound without a touch of warmth. "Get on with ye, missy. I got work to do."

Cora shoved her hands in her pockets and started off down the path, resisting the urge to whistle something comforting.

Once she entered the tunnel-like opening in the thicket leading to the house, the light breeze died. After taking a few hesitant steps, Cora glanced back toward the dock, but the heavy foliage had already closed behind her, blocking her view of the waterfront. She turned and walked briskly up the small incline, determined to reach the house before full darkness fell.

Branches grabbed at her coat and brushed her cheek. She hunched deeper into her coat. Somewhere, a night bird cried.

Cora tried to ignore the snap of branches and the rustle of leaves deep within the darkness bordering the pathway. Small animals, no doubt. Nothing to worry about. Certainly nothing big enough to take a bite out of her.

She rounded a bend and stopped short. The castle loomed in front of her, several yards up a steep hill. A dog's frantic barking led Cora's gaze to the left, where a terrace extended from the southern end of the castle. Bright light flooded the area, bathing it in brilliant white. A man stood just outside the rim of light, a dark, brooding figure flanked on either side by two dogs. The animals were huge, two muscular beasts with enormous heads and even bigger bodies. Rottweillers. Cora swallowed hard. Dogs. The contract hadn't said anything about dogs.

One dog barked, but not at her. All three seemed unaware of her presence, their heads raised skyward. The wind whipping off the water was more brisk on top of the hill, and the man's heavy overcoat blew open to the elements. His body was long and powerful. He was clothed all in black with the exception of a pristine white T-shirt. His hair was dark, and he wore it long and untrimmed.

Cora stepped off the path trying to get a glimpse of his face. Something told her it would be worth the effort. But the shadows from the castle walls kept him safely hidden.

"Quiet, Caesar," he commanded, his tone crisp and deep. The animal immediately stopped barking, but every bone in his body seemed to vibrate with unreleased energy.

Cora cupped her hands over her mouth, but before she could shout a greeting, a loud thumping sound filled the air. Startled, she pressed her hands against her ears as the racket reached a crescendo, crushing down on her with an ear-splitting drumming noise. She fell back a step, her heart pounding.

The man and dogs seemed oblivious. They stood frozen. Waiting.

Suddenly a brilliant light cut through the gathering dark, and a violent wind swirled across the landscape. A helicopter rose up over the far wall of the castle, its sleek body struggling and bouncing a bit in the crosswinds. A few seconds later the copter settled down a short distance from the man.

The passenger door of the copter swung open, and the man ran to get in. At the door he paused and turned in Cora's direction. For a moment his eyes seemed to stare directly into hers, his lean face intense, his dark brows drawn into a fierce frown of disapproval. Unsure, Cora raised a tentative hand in greeting.

There was no answering wave. No reaction. The man simply turned and climbed aboard the helicopter. The engines revved up to a high whine and the craft lifted off.

The moment the copter disappeared over the wall the two dogs swiveled their heads in her direction. Their dark eyes glittered, and Cora swallowed hard against the fear that rose in her throat. They had spotted her and there was no one nearby to hold them back. Dear God, now what?

"Nice doggies," she whispered. "Nice little doggies. Please stay right where you are." She took two steps backward, and the dogs' heads turned to watch her. The path to the castle was steep, but if she went back to the dock, she'd be trapped by the river. Safer to head for the castle.

She turned and headed for the back entrance at a fast walk. About ten yards from the stone porch, the two dogs rose up off their muscular haunches and stood poised, rigid with anticipation. Cora froze. They glared down at her, daring her to run.

Her heart pounding, Cora gave them what they wanted—

she ran. Immediately, two dark shapes streaked toward her, their teeth bared, a terrible snarling sound erupting from their throats.

She was only a few feet from the porch when she slipped on the wet stone and went down. Her hand skidded and she cried out in pain. The dogs howled in triumph. Scrambling to her feet, Cora took off again, sure the dogs would be on her at any moment. She could almost feel their hot breath on her heels.

She reached the steps, but one of the dogs hit her from behind. She fell again, her knee hitting the stone with a bone-jarring thud. The snarling in her ear was unbearable, and just when she was sure their sharp teeth would close around her neck, the back door opened and someone stepped out.

"Caesar! Cleo! Down! Get down, you nasty beasties!" a woman shouted. Her command seemed to have the desired effect, because the dogs' barking abruptly ceased. Both sat, eyeing Cora from inches away.

She got shakily to her feet and rested a hand on the cool metal railing, trying to catch her breath. The palm of her right hand throbbed, and when she lifted it up, she was surprised to see blood dripping onto her pants and making tiny splatters of red on the stone steps. She fumbled in her pocket for her handkerchief, wrapping it around her hand.

"Th-thank you," she managed, looking up at the woman standing on the porch.

Sturdy and as strong-looking as the stone she stood on, the woman wiped her hands on a thick dish towel. Throwing it over one broad shoulder, she lumbered down the steps to Cora. "You poor dear. Those terrible beasties must have scared the devil out of you."

Her accent was slight, something that Cora wasn't able quite to place. The woman immediately wrapped an arm around her and nudged her toward the open door.

Cora darted a quick glance in the direction of the dogs. Both sat obediently at the bottom step, their malevolent eyes watching her every move, daring her to step out of line.

"Mr. Gracy called from the boathouse to tell me you were on your way up. When I heard the beasties yipping, I hurried right out."

Cora allowed the woman to support her up the steps, her knees the consistency of jelly. "Are they always so vicious?"

The woman paused and laughed, her solid body jiggling with whatever humor she seemed to find in Cora's question. "Oh, honey, those beasties just like to sound vicious. They're really pussycats. Why, they're as sweet-natured and loving as dogs can be."

"Somehow I'm finding that a little hard to believe."

Her rescuer patted her arm. "Oh, you'll get used to them in due time. And they'll adjust to you too. By the way, I'm Alice Benson. I'm the head housekeeper here at Midnight Castle." She shouldered open the door and guided Cora into a brightly lit kitchen.

Cora was relieved that the dogs stayed outside, their eyes staring bullet holes in her back as she stepped inside. Maybe if she was lucky she'd find that they weren't allowed in the castle. The only good thing about the dogs was their distrustful nature. They didn't like intruders, and they would be sure to give plenty of warning if anyone set foot on the island.

Cora appreciated that she'd get a warning if anyone came to the island, and getting a warning would be a good thing if it came to the likes of Erik Dubane.

Chapter Two

At the doorway to the kitchen, Cora stopped short, slightly overwhelmed by the sudden rush of warmth and bright lights. She glanced around, more than a little awed at the massive size of the room. It was magnificent. Opulent even. A kitchen that far exceeded any professional kitchen she had ever worked in.

Granted, three years as a professional chef wasn't a huge amount of time on any job, but Cora was pretty certain that even the most jaded chef would be impressed with the facilities in this kitchen.

Along the back wall stood two polished-steel restaurant-style refrigerators. In between them stood a huge metal door. Cora was certain it led to a walk-in freezer. A double glass door refrigerator, two electric ranges and a gas stove stood along the right-hand wall. All the appliances looked new enough to have been off-loaded from a delivery truck less than an hour ago.

In the center of the kitchen stood an oversize butcher's block with an overhead rack holding every pot and pan known to modern man. To the left was a large plank table with enough space to seat fifteen to twenty people. Since it was situated in the kitchen, Cora figured the hired help ate here.

A gigantic stone fireplace lined the outside wall. From the

looks of it, Cora was certain she could stand up inside and still have room to stretch. A cheerful fire burned behind a black iron screen.

"This is quite a setup. It's better than most of the restaurants I've worked in." Cora did a complete circle, taking in everything. "Of course, that's not saying much. My experience is pretty limited."

The fact that she hadn't lived up to her instructor's expectations at the Culinary Institute still stung a little, but Cora pushed the thought aside. Working as an assistant chef at Gamburno's, a small L.A. restaurant, wasn't Da Vinci's five-star ristorante but she had always believed she'd move up, come into her own.

But life had a tendency to throw a person a few curves. Dreams of moving up and getting a job with one of the more prestigious restaurants had disappeared one night four months ago. Now all of Cora's energies went into simple survival.

She reached up and touched the edge of the huge copper sauté pan hanging overhead. It swung slowly on its hook, the cooper catching the light and splashing a flash of brilliance on the walls of the kitchen.

"Heavens, dear, you're bleeding," Mrs. Benson said, reaching up to take her hand. "Come right over here and let me wash that off." Her thick eyebrows drew together in concern. "One of those beasts didn't bite you, did they?"

"I cut it when I fell." Cora pointed to the smear of dirt on her olive green dockers. "It's not deep—just a scratch."

"Nonetheless, we need to get that cleaned and bandaged. What a terrible greeting for you on your first day on Midnight Island." Mrs. Benson bent down and pulled open a drawer. She rummaged around for a few minutes until she finally straightened up, waving a metal box with a red cross painted on the top.

"I knew it was here somewhere." She set it on the counter and then turned on the tap water. She motioned Cora over to the sink.

Cora stuck her hand under the warm water. "I noticed a helicopter leaving when I arrived. A man got aboard. The dogs were waiting with him—they seemed to know him."

Mrs. Benson squirted a generous amount of antibacterial soap into the palm of Cora's hand. "Oh, that was Mr. Mackenzie. He was leaving for a dinner meeting in Albany."

"Does he live here?"

"Oh, my, yes, dearie. Mr. Mackenzie, Sr., owns Midnight Island."

Cora paused in the process of washing off the soap suds. "I thought the owner was a Mrs. Amanda Mackenzie. Is she his wife?"

"Stepmother, dear. Mr. Mackenzie's father, the owner of the castle, is quite ill. He doesn't get out of his room very much." A certain degree of sadness entered the housekeeper's eyes. "Jake Mackenzie is his son. He runs the family business." She handed Cora several sheets of paper towel. "Now dry off, and I'll put a touch of ointment on the cut and a nice dry bandage. You'll be right as rain in no time."

"Mr. Mackenzie didn't seem too pleased to see me on the island," Cora said, remembering the cold, unwelcoming gaze that had cut through the darkness separating them earlier.

She wondered if he hadn't known that the dogs would come after her as soon as he lifted off. Maybe even given them some kind of signal to sic them on her.

"Mr. Mackenzie is a very private man, miss. He tends to be a bit suspicious of strangers. Especially since the disappearance of his wife two years ago." Her face softened for a moment. "A trauma like that tends to make a man cautious."

"What happened to his wife? Was she ever found?"

"I'm afraid not. The police are still investigating, but I think it's been too long. They don't even have any leads."

"How sad."

Mrs. Benson placed a sterile gauze square on Cora's hand and then paused a moment, a slight frown wrinkling her forehead. "Come to think of it, Mrs. Mackenzie, Sr., was the one to make all the arrangements for your hiring. Which is not the usual practice around here. Usually Jake takes care of all that. Perhaps she forgot to mention you were scheduled to arrive today." She used a few strips of tape to secure the gauze in place. "There! All better. Now perhaps you'd like a cup of tea?" She patted Cora's shoulder, and for a minute Cora thought the kindly housekeeper was going to kiss her on the cheek as extra added assurance that her boo-boo was all better. The thought made her smile.

"Thank you. That would be wonderful."

Cora moved to sit on one of the stools pushed under the cutting block, racking her brain for ways to pump for more information. She wouldn't feel safe unless she knew everyone who lived or visited the island. "What kind of business is Mr. Mackenzie in?"

"A business that isn't for idle gossip among the hired help," a crisp voice interrupted.

Mrs. Benson dropped the large copper teakettle she was filling in the sink and whirled around. A stricken expression of guilt flickered across her wrinkled face.

Startled, Cora turned, surprised to see a petite woman in her early fifties standing in the doorway. She was diminutive in size but decidedly not diminutive in her impact on the room. The only word to describe her was elegant. Her pale, perfectly shaded blond hair—obviously a superb professional dye job—was done in a sophisticated upsweep, the soft tendrils artfully woven through richly etched silver combs.

The delicately featured face had undergone at least one, perhaps two, face lifts. Cora had plenty of experience identifying *the look.* It was a tight, frozen, mannequin expression that the wealthy society women, who flocked to the L.A. restaurants, wore. Women who had no intention of giving in gracefully to the relentless onslaught of old age. And from the looks of things, this woman wasn't going to go down without an all-out, no-holds-barred battle.

"Mrs. Mackenzie, I didn't hear you come in." Mrs. Benson's hands fussed in the folds of her apron. "This is Miss Shelly, the new cook. She…she just arrived."

Cora quickly stood up and offered her hand. "I'm pleased to meet you, Mrs. Mackenzie."

Her new employer didn't bother taking her hand, but simply gave her a quick once-over. The frosty flick of her gaze told Cora that Mrs. Mackenzie wasn't too pleased with what she saw, and for a moment Cora wondered if she was going to find herself on the boat headed back to the mainland before even starting her new job.

"You're younger than I thought. I was expecting someone with a bit more maturity."

Cora was stumped. How was she suppose to respond to a statement like that? Sorry, I'll run out and age a few years and then come back?

She bit back the smart remark and tried offering a polite smile. "I'm sorry. But I'm sure you'll be pleased with my work. As soon as I heard about the job, I knew I was interested."

"Really?" One stylishly plucked brow rose in disbelief. "I wouldn't expect most young women to view living on a remote island as something desirable. It's been my experience that young women of today are more interested in city living. Bright lights. Wild parties. Men." She said *men* as if it were an unpleasant word. One not uttered in polite company.

Cora shrugged. "Perhaps I'm different from other women my age. I don't mind solitude. In fact, I enjoy it."

"Really? Well, I guess we'll see if that's true, won't we?" Her expression turned slightly sour and she waved a hand in Cora's direction. "Do you always dress so casually?"

Cora glanced down at her dirt-stained pants. "I'm afraid I fell running from the dogs. I was a bit frightened."

"Well, I can only hope that you'll be more careful in the future. We might live on a remote island, but I expect my employees to conduct themselves with a certain amount of decorum. Which—" she turned her sharp eyes on Mrs. Benson "—reminds me. Alice should have explained to you that I do not tolerate gossip of any kind. I expect employees to respect my privacy and that of my stepson's."

"Certainly, ma'am," Cora said. "I apologize if I was out of line. I wouldn't want it any other way myself." Truth was Cora didn't want anyone prying into her life, either. The more private things were around here, the better she was going to like it.

"Excellent." Mrs. Mackenzie smiled, but Cora didn't miss the slightly patronizing twist to it. "With that simple rule in mind, I'm sure we'll all get along famously."

Mrs. Benson stepped forward. "I was suggesting a cup of tea before I showed Miss Shelly to her room, ma'am."

"I'll show Miss Shelly to her room, Alice." Her cool tone lacked even a slight smidgen of warmth. This was a lady who liked to keep things on a strictly formal basis. "Perhaps you wouldn't mind taking some brandy up to Mr. Sheffield's room. His wife is feeling a bit chilled this evening."

"Of course, ma'am. Right away." Mrs. Benson scurried for the door.

"And, Alice—"

"Yes, ma'am."

"In the future please see that any and all visitors to the island are brought to my attention promptly upon their arrival. Is that clear?"

"Perfectly, ma'am."

"Excellent."

The housekeeper ducked her head, her ruddy cheeks a darker shade of red as she hurried off.

Mrs. Mackenzie motioned for Cora to accompany her. "The four servants' rooms downstairs are already taken, and we've closed off the additional rooms in the basement. So you'll have to settle for a small room upstairs. I'm sure you won't mind."

"That's fine. I'm not in the least bit picky." She smiled. "The kitchen is my favorite room of the house, anyway. I expect I'll be spending most of my time right there."

"Which brings me to the issue of our dining preferences." As she led the way, Mrs. Mackenzie flicked a light switch, bathing the monstrous entry hall with light. Blue floral brocade chairs with intricately carved wood frames lined the hall. The light from above bounced and reflected off the gold-framed paintings of stern, elegantly dressed people from a bygone time. The period clothing indicated that they were probably ancestral portraits.

Cora tried to keep her awe in check, but she wasn't very successful. She stopped, her gaze moving upward to stare at the array of cut-crystal medallions suspended from the multitiered gold chandelier.

"Miss Shelly?" The impatience in her new employer's voice was sharp.

Embarrassed, Cora pulled her attention away from the glittering display. "I'm sorry. It's just that everything is so beautiful."

"Yes, you're quite right. It is beautiful." The corners of Mrs. Mackenzie's mouth tightened again. "If we could get back to my dining expectations—"

"Of course, ma'am."

"I expect breakfast to be served promptly at 8:00 a.m. A full complement of choices should always be available, with a main dish. Lunch is at noon. During the colder months, I expect soup on the menu every day, accompanied by something light and low in fat." She turned and gave Cora a sharp glance. "Low fat does not, however, mean tasteless." Her frown deepened. "Nor do I like anything too spicy. My husband does not tolerate spicy food well. It's for peasants and trailer trash."

Cora ignored the twist of resentment that settled in her belly, thinking of her own childhood spent in a trailer park with her mom. Don't say anything, just listen. You need the job.

"I think you'll be pleased, ma'am. I specialize in light, nutritious foods. May I ask how many people I'll be cooking for?"

"Always plan on at least eight." She clicked off the people on her fingers. "Me, my husband, my daughter, Megan, my stepson…the housekeeper, Mrs. Benson, Mr. Gracy and my husband's nurse. And of course yourself. The staff eats after the dining room has been cleared from our meal. My husband is quite ill so he often eats in his room. You'll be expected to take the tray upstairs and clear it away again after the meal."

She stopped next to a narrow door. "This is the elevator. I had it put in for my husband once he was forced to use a wheelchair." She hit the button on the outside, and the door slid open. She stepped aside so Cora could see the claustrophobic-size cubicle inside. "You're encouraged to use this when bringing my husband's food trays up to him. He rarely, if ever, eats with the family."

Cora nodded.

Her employer allowed the door to slide shut again and then motioned Cora toward the wide marble staircase. They started up.

"I frequently have guests stay for extended visits. Less so during the winter months, but Mrs. Benson will always keep you informed if there are more people to cook for than the usual eight. At the moment my good friend Dr. Sheffield and his wife are staying with us."

The staircase swept upward in a graceful curve of priceless white marble. A thick emerald-green rug with a white border covered the steps. Here, too, the walls were lined with rows of stern-faced ancestors and elegantly gilded mirrors.

Up the stairs, down several halls and past an array of heavy oak doors, they came to a narrow hall with only three doors. A single shaded lamp sitting on an antique sideboard in the middle of the hall provided the only illumination. There was no natural lighting. No windows. Shadows crowded every corner. A thick rug muffled their footsteps.

Cora wasn't sure she'd ever find her way back to the main entry hall, and she thought about leaving a trail of cracker crumbs to find her way back.

She waited as Mrs. Mackenzie withdrew a ring of keys from her pocket and unlocked the last door.

"This is your room. You have a private bath through there." She pointed to a white door on the opposite side of the room. She then turned and pointed to a doorway at the end of the hall. "Through there are stairs leading to the kitchen. I'd prefer that you use those stairs when moving about the house. The main stairs are for the family and guests."

Cora nodded and stepped into the room. Someone, probably Adam Gracy, had deposited her suitcases on the end of a canopied bed. A bedside table with a Tiffany lamp, two chairs and a small dresser were the room's only other furnishings. The nicest feature was a cozy fireplace with a crackling fire licking at a scrolled iron grate.

Mrs. Mackenzie stood in the doorway. Most likely she considered stepping into an employee's room distasteful, right up there with living in a trailer. Cora shook off the resentment.

"I'm sure this will meet your needs." Her tone indicated that she thought it more than likely *exceeded* her needs, but Cora didn't care. The room was perfect.

"This is fine. I know I'll be quite comfortable."

"Excellent. I suggest you relax this evening. You can start your duties with breakfast tomorrow. Good night, Miss Shelly." She paused a moment and then added, "You're the only person on this hall so I'm sure you'll find things quiet and private."

Before Cora had a chance to thank her, she was gone. Startled, she walked to the door and stuck her head out, checking the hall in both directions. Empty. The woman must have flown down the hall. She shrugged and closed the door.

Halfway to the closet, she paused and glanced back at the door. Walking to it, she shot the bolt. Then she grabbed one of the chairs and shoved the upper rung under the doorknob.

The simple gesture brought her intense relief. Since the attack, Cora was in a continual state of fear during the night hours. She often found herself cruising the apartment at all hours, checking and rechecking the locks. Apparently things wouldn't be any different here on Midnight Island.

A short time later, her bags unpacked, Cora took a quick shower and changed into pajamas. It was earlier than she was used to going to bed, but she was exhausted.

As she pulled the down comforter back, she paused again. Changing directions, she walked over to the dresser and flipped open a small velvet case. Inside lay the pricey set of knives Jennifer had given her upon graduation from the Institute. She held the paring knife up and stared at her reflection in the flat of the blade.

Tightening her grip, she walked back to the bed and shoved it under the pillow. She clutched her arms across her chest and sat on the edge of the bed. It didn't matter that Erik Dubane was two thousand miles away, sitting in a jail cell. Since his attack, she hadn't felt safe, not even with the door barricaded and the knife under her pillow.

How was she supposed to keep from becoming a victim again? By never trusting anyone again, she whispered to herself as she slipped into bed and closed her eyes.

CORA WOKE WITH A START. She sat up and glanced around, groggy and slightly confused. Where was she? Nothing looked familiar.

The room was dark except for a sliver of light falling around the base of a small Tiffany lamp. It was the lamp that clued her in. She'd left it on when she'd climbed into bed. She was in Midnight Castle.

It was so cold in the room the tip of her nose ached. A

glance at the fire told her the reason. Even the embers had died hours ago. She wondered if any actual heat was coming out of the heating vent on the opposite side of the room.

The clock read 2:00 a.m. Stretching, Cora realized what had awakened her. Rain, mixed with sleet, lashed the windows, making a tinkling sound as it hit the glass.

She shivered and snuggled deeper beneath the down comforter, trying desperately to empty her mind and get back to sleep. No doubt once her day started, she'd be busy until nightfall. But then, as she began to drift off the sound of the doorknob turning pierced her awareness.

She sat bolt upright, the hair on the back of her neck rising to attention. She strained to see through the shadows hugging the edges of the room. Total darkness.

She held her breath and waited. Sure enough, it happened again. The doorknob moved to the right, and then a few seconds later, it moved to the left.

Please, God, let me have remembered to have locked the door.

The knob moved again. She pulled her knees up close to her chest, her heart beating frantically in her chest. Someone was definitely trying to get in.

Sliding out of bed, she ran to the door and pressed her ear to the polished wood. The muffled sound of someone's feet moving on the rug outside the door filtered back to her.

The knob moved again as if the person didn't quit believe she'd had the foresight to actually lock the door before retiring.

"Who's there?" she demanded.

The knob stopped. Silence.

She shivered, her ear aching from pressing it too hard against the door. "Who's there? What do you want?"

A few minutes later the footsteps padded softly away.

Running to the bed, Cora grabbed her bathrobe and pulled it on. A quick glance told her that her slippers had disappeared. No time to look for them.

She grabbed the knife from under her pillow and ran for the door. Her fingers fumbled with the lock.

She burst out into the dark hall and glanced both ways. Empty. A silence hung as heavy as the dark mahogany sideboard lining one side of the hall.

Damn. She was too late.

She held her breath, listening. A chilling draft drifted up the back stairs and spilled into the hall. Cora struggled to ignore the aching cold seeping up through the soles of her bare feet.

Wood creaked. Someone was on the stairs.

Cora raced to the head of the stairs. Another muffled creak. Whoever had fiddled with her door had decided to take the back way down to the kitchen. She tightened her grip on the knife and flicked the light switch. Nothing.

She grabbed the railing and started down the narrow, circular stairs, keeping her back pressed tight against the wall. As she neared the kitchen, sweat broke out on the back of her neck, chilling her more.

The stairwell was empty. Whoever had been on the stairs was gone.

At the bottom of the stairs, the door to the kitchen was open, and a faint glow filled the room. Movement of the light on the opposite wall told her that someone had kept the fire in the fireplace stoked.

As Cora's toes touched the bottom step, a low, throaty growl froze her in place.

Her heart skipped a beat. Was it possible that what she'd

heard on the stairs was a dog? Her hopes that they'd be relegated to the outside appeared to be wrong. The growl could only mean they were allowed free run of the house.

The animal moved to stare up at her, his jaws gaping open and displaying an unbelievably sharp array of teeth.

"Nice, doggie," Cora said, her voice trembling. She glanced over her shoulder. Her room was well beyond her reach at this point. If she ran, the dog would be on her in two seconds flat.

"He's taking advantage of your fear," a deep, velvety-smooth voice said from somewhere within the dimly lit kitchen.

Startled, Cora leaned forward and peered into the room. The speaker sat at the other end of the plank table. A tall imposing figure slouched lazily in a high-backed chair. A plate of food sat in front of him.

The overlong black hair and intensely hostile expression on the man's face told Cora he was very same person who had stared daggers in her direction earlier in the evening. Jacob Mackenzie had obviously made it home from his meeting in Albany, and from the expression on his face, she figured he wasn't too happy to find her inside his house.

"Would you mind calling your dog off?" she asked.

"Walk around him," he replied. "If you're going to live here for any length of time, you're going to need to show him that you're not afraid."

"But I *am* afraid."

He sighed, the kind of sigh that told Cora he had no understanding or tolerance of people who were skittish around dogs. His dark eyes, an intense brown that was almost black, glittered in the soft light of the fire. "He's trying to intimidate you. It's a canine form of domination."

"Well, he's succeeding," Cora snapped. "I'm feeling very intimidated and more than a little dominated." She refrained from adding that it wasn't just the dog who was intimidating her. His master was doing a pretty good job of it, too.

"He's harmless." Mackenzie continued to eat, spearing a piece of meat and popping it in his mouth. He chewed slowly, his expressive eyes regarding her with cynical amusement. "He probably doesn't like the fact that you're carrying around a—" he squinted a bit "—is that really a paring knife?"

She nodded mutely.

"What were you planning to stab—an ornery onion or an out-of-control tomato perhaps?"

Cora flushed and shoved the knife in her pocket. "Just call your dog off."

He set his fork down, a tight smile pulling at one corner of his perfectly chiseled mouth. "No need to get testy. A simple request will do."

"I thought I'd already done that."

He snapped his fingers. "Come, Caesar."

The dog immediately got up and moved to the other end of the table. He sat next to his master. For the first time, Cora noticed that Caesar's twin, Cleo, sat on the man's other side. Both dogs glared at her, their brown eyes following her every move.

Mackenzie picked up his fork and continued to eat. He acted as though she was no longer there, focusing totally on his meal. The clean line of his jaw moved effortlessly, and as he tipped his head forward to take another bite, several strands of the jet-black hair fell forward, brushing his cheek.

With the glow of the fire, the stone walls and the dogs seated next to him, he almost looked like a lord of some manor house a hundred years ago. All he needed was a leg of mutton to gnaw on, a cape of velvet draped over his shoulders and a broadsword hanging from one lean hip.

Cora straightened up. She didn't plan on starting the job by being intimidated by anyone, least of all this arrogant man. His dogs maybe, but not him. She stepped into the kitchen.

"Thank you for calling him off."

He didn't bother to look up. "Was there something else?" It was clearly a dismissal.

"I wanted to know why you were fiddling with my bedroom door a few moments ago."

He sat back, the dark eyes appraising her with open amusement. He took a moment to swipe his napkin across his lips and then threw it carelessly on the table. "What are you talking about?"

"Someone tried to get into my bedroom a few minutes ago. I followed whoever it was down here to the kitchen. You're the only one in the kitchen, so I'm assuming you were the one who tried to get in."

He laughed, the sound low and rough. "Well, you assumed wrong. I got home thirty minutes ago and have been down here getting something to eat the entire time." He waved at the plate in front of him. "And seeing as you're the new chef around here, I might add that this undoubtedly tastes worse than Caesar's dog chow. I can only hope your future creations are better."

A blast of heat scorched Cora's cheeks. "For your information, that isn't my creation. Your *mother* suggested that I wait until morning to start cooking."

"Stepmother," he said curtly.

"I'm sorry. Your stepmother." He was back to ignoring her, and since her pride was pricked, Cora couldn't help adding, "Besides, when you eat something I've made you'll know it. Mainly because it'll be so good you'll think you've died of ecstasy."

As soon as the words were out of her mouth, Cora wanted to bite them back. Wrong choice of words in the presence of a man like this.

Sure enough, the word was barely out of her mouth before the lazy grin reappeared. He was back to looking at her, his gaze even more assessing. "Really? Just one taste and I'll be in the throngs of total ecstasy?"

She swallowed hard. Oh no, had those words really come out of her mouth? Why did she have to let her damn pride get in the way? It only made things worse.

He sat back. "You can be assured that I'll be looking forward to breakfast and a taste of some of that personal ecstasy you say you serve so well."

The innuendo hung between them for a long, heated moment, stretching out on a gold thread of expectation, but finally he broke the moment by lifting his glass and taking a sip of wine. His dark eyes, however, watched her over the rim of the glass. Cora knew her cheeks were the same deep rich red of the expensive Merlot he sipped.

"This is a very old structure, Ms. Shelly. There are a lot of creaks and groans as the stones and wood of the castle shift and settle with the wind off the river. You'd best get used to it."

"What I heard wasn't from wood or stone shifting or creaking. I heard and then saw the doorknob of my room moving. Whoever was trying to get in my room didn't stop until they realized the door was locked."

"You lock your bedroom door? And you carry a knife around." His gaze was so intense, so fiercely penetrating that Cora fought against its impact. Strangely enough, she didn't find the darkness of his look frightening. Instead, she felt a strong unexpected pull. An attraction that seemed to come out of nowhere.

A flash of attraction shot through her, surprising her. She tried pushing it down, drowning it with force of will, but it hung there between them.

She straightened her spine. "I always lock my bedroom door." She didn't dwell on the knife issue. That would cause too many questions she'd prefer not to discuss.

"Really? How interesting. Do you do this because you expect a small invasion?"

Cora gnawed her inner cheek with frustration. Stay calm, she thought. He has no concept of the terror she'd lived through. Or the fears that she'd had to deal with, and it wasn't worth her while to try to explain things to him. She'd learned quickly that people just didn't understand.

Besides, something told her trying to explain things to this man would be a waste of her time. Jacob Mackenzie had the look of a man who would have no comprehension of total fear. It wasn't something in his vocabulary.

"This is a very new place for me, Mr. Mackenzie. Like you, I appreciate my privacy. I intend to make sure I have it."

He was quiet for a moment as if considering her response. But then he nodded, his hair moving like fine silk against his lean cheeks. "You're right. Everyone is entitled to privacy. I'll check with the other employees tomorrow to see if anyone stopped by your room during the night. And the name is Jake."

"I appreciate your understanding."

Caesar shifted position, and Cora jumped. She didn't miss the flicker of irritation that crossed her employer's face.

"You're going to need to get used to the dogs. If you don't like them, you at least need to learn to tolerate them."

"I was rather hoping that they were confined to the outside."

He laughed. "No, they have free run of the house and grounds."

Cora clasped her hands behind her back. "F-free run?"

He nodded and stood, unfolding a finely muscled body like some kind of restless animal. His height was startling—well over six-three with broad shoulders and an overall sleekness that spoke of a natural athlete, a person totally comfortable in his skin.

As she'd seen earlier, he was clothed all in black, with the exception of a white T-shirt beneath an expensive, dark wool jacket. The jacket probably cost more than a year's wages for her. The effect was one of rich, casual elegance, something she was familiar with only at a distance.

When he stood, both dogs stood, too, their heads turned up to watch him with eager anticipation. She swallowed hard, her eyes unable to leave the sight of their jaws dropping open as if anticipating a command to snap her in two.

Jake crooked a finger in her direction. "Come here."

She didn't move, her heart racing. "What?"

"Come over here." He pointed to a spot in front of him, and she felt a twist of anger at his arrogance. What did he think she was, one of his dogs?

"You need to get over this ridiculous fear of the dogs."

Cora backed up a step, her anger replaced by immediate trepidation. "No. I'm not coming any closer. We can peacefully coexist, but we'll do it from a distance."

Jake sighed. "All right. If you won't come here, we'll come over there."

Cora squeaked a protest, but before she could move, he crossed the kitchen to stand in front of her. She cringed as the dogs followed, faithfully glued to his side.

"Give me your hand," he demanded.

"No." Cora knew she was being petulant, but she didn't care. All she could focus on was Cleo's gaping jaws less than a millimeter away. She stuck both hands behind her back.

"Don't be such a wimp."

The wimp remark hit a tender spot. She *was* a wimp but she hated admitting it to anyone. She bit her lower lip and forced herself to extend her hand. She squeezed her eyes shut in anticipation of the dog's razor sharp teeth clamping onto her hand. Every muscle in her body tightened to the aching point.

But instead of sharp teeth, she felt Jake's hand slide over hers. His palm was warm and rough with calluses, as if he were a manual laborer and not some desk-bound businessman who rode around in private helicopters and corporate jets.

An unexpected shiver ran up the length of her spine as if someone had taken a feather and gently ran the tip from her lower back to the nape of her neck. For a brief moment, she felt light-headed and she fought the sensation, telling herself it wasn't his touch but a strange reaction to the nearness of the dog. But a tiny voice in her head told her differently.

As Jake covered Cora's hand with his own, he marveled at the softness of her skin. It was a small hand, compact with carefully clipped nails. No polish. No rings.

A part of him felt drawn to simply hold it for several seconds, but one glance at her face told him that her anticipation of touching the dog was eating a nervous hole right through the bottom of her stomach.

He guided her hand over to Caesar's nose, allowing him to sniff her scent. As he allowed Caesar to get his fill, Jake found himself indulging in her sweet scent, too. Nothing expensive or sophisticated. Instead, something light and citrusy, like cut grapefruit sliced on a warm summer morning—stingingly fresh and enticingly tantalizing.

"Always let a strange dog catch your scent first," he said, moving her hand down to stroke Caesar's thick neck. He forced her fingers to the sleek, velvety hair. "Move slowly. Never touch a strange dog on the top of his head. He'll take such a move as aggressive. Always touch a dog's neck or chest first. It's less threatening."

She jerked her head, nodding too rapidly, and he wondered if she had even heard what he was saying. Her nostrils flared, and her breath came in short little pants.

He paused a minute, studying her expression. Total and absolute fear. Her teeth worried the ripe lushness of her bottom lip, and he thought she might tear it open at any moment.

Her hand trembled in his, and she held her slight fame as taut as a newly drawn bow. The fear gave her delicate features a strangely appealing, sweetly vulnerable look. The vulnerability was enhanced by the wild, childlike curls haloing her head.

He wondered what terrible thing had happened to her that she was so petrified of dogs. But he also bitterly reminded himself that he made it a strict policy to steer clear of anything sweet. Sweet and vulnerable brought trouble.

Caesar's regal head stood about level with her slender waist, so he guessed she might top out at five feet. He moved her hand slowly up to Caesar's ear, allowing her to stroke the soft fold. The dog tipped his head and leaned into her hand, his eyes getting that slightly glazed look he got when sliding into total contentment.

A shuddering breath slipped from between her lush lips, lips that were nowhere near childlike. Almost too womanly, he thought ruefully. She intrigued him, an interesting combination of fear and trust. Trust because she was willing to turn total control of her safety over to him.

With her other hand, she reached out and touched Jake's shoulder, steadying herself, and a sharp tug of desire ripped through him, catching him by surprise. He prided himself on his ability to control such juvenile feeling.

Irritated, he brushed the feeling aside. She was barely more than a girl. Twenty-one. Twenty-two at the upper end. Too young for his jaded age of thirty-three.

A pang of guilt hit him. She wasn't much older than Natalie had been when she'd come to live at Midnight Castle as his wife.

Fool! Hadn't he learned anything from that little fiasco? He didn't need another mess to complicate his life. Work and more work was his focus now. There was no room for fragile women who were frightened of dogs and their own shadow.

"His ear is soft," Cora said, her voice hesitant, almost whispery.

"Fancy that—soft fur on a dog," he said sarcastically, desperate now to push her away with words.

She glanced up at him, a slightly confused but guarded expression on her elfin face. His gruffness had surprised her, but she didn't pull away. He stared into the chocolate brown of her wide, innocent eyes and marveled at how they complemented and enhanced the cinnamon richness of her wild curls. Curls that caressed her small cheeks with a softness that begged to be touched. Damn but she was sweet enough to gobble up in one bite. No wonder Caesar was responding to her.

At that moment Caesar shook his massive head and his neck chain rattled, breaking the spell. Cora stumbled sideways trying to avoid the huge animal as he moved closer. He nosed her with the tip of his muzzle, and her hand came up to grab the front of Jake's shirt.

The heat of her fingers seared his skin, and he was flooded with her scent again. A strange and unexpected tightness settled into his groin. He gritted his teeth. What the hell was going on?

He shifted position, angling himself away from her. Oh, yeah, he knew what was going on. It had been too long since he'd slept with a woman, that's what was happening.

She looked up again, suddenly conscious that she was hanging on to his shirt. "Sorry." She dropped her hand.

"What happened to make you so afraid of dogs?" he asked, determined to get their conversation flowing in another direction, anything to keep his mind off the desire coursing through him.

He grabbed Caesar's collar to keep him from knocking her against him again. Jake didn't think he could handle the feel of her against him again.

"My neighbor had a vicious dog. He bit me once in the hallway outside my apartment." She rubbed a spot on her forearm, as if remembering the bite.

Jake took her arm and gently pushed up the sleeve. Two healed, jagged-edged puncture marks testified to the reality of the bite. He used his thumb to trace the outline of the scars. "Nasty-looking bite. Did you sue the neighbor?"

Fear seemed to seep into her eyes. "I called the police. B-but my neighbor—he wasn't too happy about that." Her voice broke and she glanced away as if the memory of the bite was more than she could handle.

He cupped her chin and directed her gaze back to him. "Not all dogs and neighbors are bad, you know."

She nodded and forced a smile. But the talk of the bite had

changed the atmosphere between them. The current of electricity had vanished. It was if she had flicked the switch, shutting it off in a moment of panic.

She stepped back, crossing her arms. "I'd better get back to my room. I have a long day tomorrow."

She tentatively patted Caesar's massive neck with the tips of her fingers one last time before walking over to the stairs. Jake knew that she was trying to respond to his wimp remark earlier. She didn't like anyone thinking she was afraid, but her fear wasn't gone. It still lingered in her eyes.

"Good night, Mr. Mackenzie. It was a pleasure to meet you."

Perplexed by the sudden coolness in her attitude, Jake nodded. "The pleasure was all mine, Ms. Shelly. Be careful, don't stumble over any ghosts on the way back upstairs."

She frowned, apparently not very pleased with his continued levity regarding her earlier predicament. But she didn't stick around to argue the point. She simply slipped through the doorway and disappeared up the stairs.

Jake sat back down and pushed his plate aside. If he planned on eating some of Ms. Shelly's ecstasy-inducing breakfast tomorrow morning, he figured it didn't make much sense to eat now. Besides, Cora Shelly intrigued him too much for him to allow her to slip away unnoticed. He planned on peeling back a bit of that protective layer to see what lay beneath.

Chapter Three

At seven forty-five the next morning, Cora stopped rushing around and stood at one end of the huge mahogany dining room table. She wiped her hands on her apron and took a deep breath.

Unable to fall back to sleep last night, she'd finally given up, climbed out of bed, showered and headed for the kitchen. She spent several hours baking, believing that it made more sense to make a good impression this morning than it did to lie around in bed trying to sleep. She'd learned over the past several months that being hypervigilant had it downfalls, especially when it came to getting a good night's sleep.

She stood back and surveyed her morning's work. The massive sideboard held an impressive array of chafing dishes and warming trays. She had laid out several mushroom-and-sausage quiches with light buttery crusts and bubbling cheese, a tray of crisp bacon, lightly battered French toast, a platter of homemade blueberry muffins and gooey, thickly iced cinnamon sticky buns.

An assortment of cereals, a fruit tray and bagels with tubs of cream cheese rounded out the breakfast spread for her first morning at Midnight Castle. Someone had laid a generous pile of kindling in the fireplace with pieces of crumpled newspaper under a good-size log. Cora had taken one of the long fireplace matches and lit it earlier. The welcoming fire crackled and burned, an attempt to lighten the darkly paneled room and take the chill off the damp morning.

There was no denying the twinge of nervousness twisting in her belly. She wanted, no she *needed*, to make a good impression. This job was important, and something told her that Mrs. Mackenzie wasn't a person who was easily impressed. No doubt she fired anyone who didn't live up to her expectations, and second chances were rare, if nonexistent.

She walked over to the sideboard and carefully regulated the burner under one of the warming trays. It wouldn't do to have the French toast charred before anyone got to taste it. She readjusted the spoon in the tiny bowl of confectioner's sugar and then moved the warmed Vermont maple syrup closer. Cora knew she was fussing, but she chalked it up to nervousness.

As she straightened up, a flash of movement outside the patio doors that led to the garden caught her eye. Curious, she stepped closer, nudging the sheer gauze curtain aside a crack. The patio and yard were empty. To one side of the patio, a canvas sheet was pulled back to display a healthy stack of cordwood.

Crystalized snow covered everything. Apparently more than a inch of sleet and snow had fallen during the night. No wonder she'd been so cold. Winter came early to this part of the country. She couldn't remember the last time she'd seen snow.

As she turned away, two black streaks raced across the lawn, and Caesar and Cleo bounded onto the patio. A few seconds later Jake Mackenzie followed. Apparently the cold had little effect on him as he wore no jacket and his head was bare.

His thick, blue-black hair whipped free in a stiff wind. A slight reddish tinge touched his face, directly below the sharp blade of his cheekbones.

He wore a flannel shirt with the sleeves rolled up, showcasing the corded muscles of his forearms and the brush of dark hair shading his tanned skin. Cora figured that his business must take him to warmer climates. No summer tan could last that long this time of the year.

His jeans, worn and faded, hung over unlaced work boots, and the snug fit in all the right places made the pulse in her neck race just a little. He looked very different from the elegant but casually dressed executive whom she had confronted in the kitchen last night. But this look wasn't any less pleasing to her eye.

He pushed a wheelbarrow filled with freshly split wood onto the patio and parked it next to the woodpile. She watched as he pulled a red ball out of his pocket, showed it to the dogs and then whipped it out onto the middle of the lawn.

With a smile, he watched the beasts scramble off the patio, all sleek muscle and sharp toenails, as they scrambled to reach the ball first. Cleo, perhaps a shade lighter and swifter than her brother, reached the ball first. Her teeth flashed white, and the ball came up clenched in her jaws. She dodged Caesar and ran full tilt for the side yard, her brother close on her heels.

After a few seconds Jake turned and started stacking the wood on top of the pile. Even beneath the cloth of his clothes, she could see the effortless stretch and pull of his shoulder muscles. Her eyes dropped a little lower and settled on the taut muscles of his butt. Even nicer.

Her fingers tightened on the curtain. She wanted to look away, to ignore the powerful display of maleness, but she couldn't. She was drawn to him. Drawn to his easy grace and startling beauty like an insignificant field mouse is drawn to the darkest panther.

As she leaned closer, her breath condensed on the cold glass, and she reached up to wipe it clean. Jake seemed to catch the movement out of the corner of his eye, and he looked up.

Their eyes met and he smiled. It was a familiar smile, a teasing, cynical smile as if he was well aware how long she had been standing there looking at him.

Startled, Cora stepped back and let the curtain drop into place. Heat infused her cheeks and she gnawed her lower lip. Why hadn't she just waved a greeting? Now he thought she was spying on him like some kind of awkward schoolgirl. Her hands tightened into fists. Why was she so uncomfortable in his presence? So clumsy and inept? Turning away, she headed for the kitchen.

TWENTY MINUTES LATER Jake opened the patio doors and entered the dining room. Amanda was already seated at the table, her appointment book open to the left of her plate. She was sipping coffee while making notations in the book.

She glanced up at him, an immediate frown springing to her face. "I really wish you wouldn't come to meals looking like the hired help, Jacob. We have guests."

Jake snatched a piece of bacon off the sideboard and took a bite. "I'm sure the Sheffields have seen a man in work clothes before. Besides, I'm hungry and I still have a few more chores to do before I leave for New York."

"At least you could have left the dogs outside."

Jake pointed to the rug by the fire. "Go lie down."

Both dogs obediently padded over to the rug and plopped

down. He grabbed a plate off the warming tray and slid two hefty slices of quiche onto his plate. With the other hand, he scooped up some bacon. "They'll be fine. As to the clothing, it seems somewhat of a waste of time for me to shower for breakfast and then have to do it again before I leave." He stuck a sliced sesame seed bagel in the toaster and sat down.

"Well, I still don't appreciate it." Amanda grasped the handle of a tiny antique silver bell and rang it briskly.

The kitchen door swung open, and Jake watched Cora cautiously enter the room. She wore white pants and a chef's shirt, every button carefully and properly buttoned up to the top of her slender neck. Somehow it seemed to make her seem even more vulnerable. Her large eyes immediately sought out the two dogs lying with their heads on their paws. He was fairly certain she suppressed a shudder.

From the front hall, Mrs. Benson appeared. Jake marveled at his stepmother's level of control over the servants in the house. All of them seemed to intuitively grasp the fact that they needed to be at her beck and call at any point during the day. It seemed little Cora had caught onto that fact quickly, too.

Her ability to adjust boded well for her. The last four cooks had been on the receiving end of Amanda's wrath for not grasping that important point. None had lasted more than two months on Midnight Island.

Of course, the fact that one of the four had been a tabloid spy, looking to gather a bit of gossip on the family, hadn't helped matters. That incident and Natalie's disappearance only served to make him cautious when it came to hiring new staff. Which duly explained his reservations toward Cora Shelly. What was such a young, obviously skilled chef doing burying herself on some remote island? There was a story behind all that and he intended to find out what it was. Jake didn't like secrets of any kind.

"Was there something you required, Mrs. Mackenzie?" Cora asked, pointedly avoiding a glance in his direction.

Jake worked to keep his amusement from showing. He knew she was aware that he had caught her peeking out the window at him. Now she was embarrassed and had decided to ignore him. He shook his head and lifted his cup. Youth. Had he ever been that young that he'd gotten his insides in a knot about what people thought of him? Not in a long time.

He took a healthy gulp of the hot liquid and savored the rich flavor. Apparently, Ms. Shelly knew how to brew a decent cup of coffee. In Jake's mind, an excellently brewed cup of coffee was the ultimate sign of a competent cook. Perhaps there was more to the shy Ms. Shelly than he'd originally thought.

Amanda pointed at her cup. "Fresh coffee, please. Mrs. Benson stay a moment, I have a few chores I'd like you to take care of this morning," Amanda ordered. "But first—" she glanced at Jake "—this is Cora Shelly. She's taken over the kitchen duties from Mr. Trevor. Cora this is—"

"Ms. Shelly and I met last night," Jake said.

One of Amanda's artfully drawn eyebrows arched upward. "Really? How interesting. I was under the impression that you had decided to stay overnight in Albany following your meeting."

He shrugged. "I got done early and decided to come back."

"What time did you get in?"

"Around 2:00 a.m."

As expected, Amanda's sharp gaze shot in Cora's direction. "You didn't mention you were a night owl, Cora."

Cora gingerly picked up the coffee carafe and moved to

the table. "I guess I had first-night jitters in a new house." She poured a cup for Amanda and then glanced at him. "Would you care for more coffee, Mr. Mackenzie?"

"Jake," he murmured as he noted the slight tightening at one corner of her mouth. She definitely wanted him at a distance.

He captured her gaze with his own, using the intensity of it to keep her teetering on the edge of nervousness. People tended to reveal information about themselves when slightly edgy. "Cora thinks that someone tried to break into her room last night."

Her gaze immediately slid away from his, her dark lashes brushing the curve of her pinkened cheeks.

Amanda's teacup rattled sharply as she set it in the saucer. "Who?" she asked stiffly, turning to Cora.

"I'm not sure, ma'am. I just woke up to someone trying to open the door."

The toaster popped up and Cora grabbed his bagel as if it was a tiny life ring. It was obvious that she didn't like the direction the conversation was taking, and her feeling of betrayal that he'd announced her fears in the middle of the dining room was also evident.

"Slab a little of that blueberry jam on it, would you, Cora?" he said.

She nodded and he watched as she meticulously spread a thick blanket of the dark, pebbly jam over the bagel. Her gaze never lifted from the plate. She fascinated him. Last night she'd been a frightened rabbit, yet she'd chased what she thought was an intruder down the stairs to the kitchen with a small paring knife as her protector.

And now, in the light of day, she was embarrassed, all her shutters drawn tight. She was almost withdrawn. A mystery waiting to be unraveled. Perhaps he needed to stay on the island more often.

"No one would try to break into your room," Amanda scoffed. "You were obviously dreaming. Or perhaps Dr. or Mrs. Sheffield got up during the night, became confused and tried your door by accident."

"What am I being accused of doing?" a new voice chimed in.

Jake's amused observation of the new cook vanished with the appearance of his stepmother's close friend, psychiatrist Daniel Sheffield. Personally, he thought *quack* might be a better description of the man.

Sheffield and his wife had already been on the island for two weeks, and Jack knew they planned on being there for several more weeks, at the very least. In Jake's opinion, the man used the island as his private vacation retreat, and he couldn't deny that that irritated him, mainly because of his strong dislike of the man.

Jake had never understood his stepmother's fascination with the man, and his visit was one of the reasons Jake planned on making himself scarce over the next couple of weeks. But then, he had to admit that Megan, his stepsister, wasn't getting any better, and having a psychiatrist of Sheffield's reputation agree to come to the island to treat her seemed like a better option than carting her over to the mainland for treatment. He knew only too well his stepmother's feelings on hospitalization. She had a paranoid fear of it.

"Good morning, Daniel," his stepmother said. "Our new cook seems to think that someone tried to break into her room last night. Did you or Vivian get up and wander around at some point during the night?"

Sheffield drifted over to the sideboard and perused the offerings before answering, "Not that I'm aware of. After we enjoyed that rather excellent brandy you sent up, we both went to sleep. In fact, Vivian's still asleep." He took a plate and heaped a substantial portion of everything on the sideboard and then took a seat across from Jake.

Amanda waved a dismissive hand. "Just as I thought. You must have been dreaming, Cora. No one tried to get into your room last night." She smiled indulgently in Sheffield's direction. "Of course, that might indicate you're in need of Dr. Sheffield's assistance. You specialize in dream analysis, don't you, Daniel?"

"Yes, but at the cost of $250 a session, I don't think your little Cora will be able to afford me."

"At those prices, I'd say screw the shrink's couch," Jake said. "I'll loan you my Magic 8 Ball. It's a whole lot cheaper, infinitely more accurate and decidedly less long-winded."

"Jacob! Dr. Sheffield is our guest," Amanda admonished.

Mrs. Benson moved closer to the table, her hands twisting in her apron. "Perhaps Cora heard The Mournful Lady last night."

Sheffield lifted his head, his fork halfway to his mouth and dripping syrup. "The Mournful Lady? Who or what is The Mournful Lady?"

Jake sighed heavily and sat back. Great, here we go. Superstitious nonsense about ghosts and apparitions ran rampant through the staff. Nothing like the mention of it to get his stepmother's dander up. Mrs. Benson should have known better than to bring up such a sore subject.

"It's nothing, Daniel." Amanda shot a disapproving look at the housekeeper. "Silly superstitious rambling from a staff member who obviously has too much time on her hands."

Sheffield laughed, his huge belly straining the buttons of

his vest and rubbing the edge of the table. "No, don't shush the poor woman. I'd love to hear this." He smiled in Mrs. Benson's direction. "Go ahead, Mrs. Benson, tell me more about this Mournful Lady."

Mrs. Benson darted a nervous glance in Amanda's direction. "Well, a few of us have seen the figure of a lady wandering around upstairs. And sometimes, at night, we hear her crying."

Jake shifted his attention to Cora. She stood with a knife smeared with jam suspended over his bagel. Her gaze was transfixed, her lips slightly parted as if she was about to say something. He shifted uncomfortably. Damn, but her otherworldly, dreamy look pulled at him, making her seem almost ethereal.

Sheffield shot Jake an exaggerated wink. "And do you recognize this lady, Mrs. Benson? Is she someone you know perhaps?"

Mrs. Benson's expression took on a confused look, as if she wasn't quite sure if she was being made fun of or not. "No, sir, I don't recognize her. But her face is never quite clear enough for that. She has very long hair—to the middle of her back. And she cries with such heartrending sobs."

"Crying, you say? How is she dressed?"

"A nightgown, sir. A long white nightgown with lace and satin all over. It's really quite beautiful."

"A nightgown?" Sheffield smiled across the table at Jake. "Have you seen this lady, Jake? She sounds like quite a beauty."

Amanda clicked her tongue in disapproval. "Daniel, you're incorrigible. Please don't encourage this nonsense. Mrs. Benson, I want you to strip down the front parlor, wash the walls and rugs and polish the furniture. That should keep you from dwelling on the subject of ghosts and goblins."

"Yes, ma'am," the housekeeper said stiffly. "Was there anything else?"

"Most definitely not."

The woman nodded and left the room.

"Your bagel, Mr. Mackenzie."

Jake looked up to see Cora standing at his elbow. The transfixed expression was replaced with one that was all business. "Thank you." He took the plate, allowing his fingers to brush hers, liking the look of confusion that clouded her eyes for just a fraction of a second. "Do you believe in ghosts, Cora?"

"No, sir, I don't."

"A pity. A bit of ghost-hunting might make your stay on Midnight Island a tad less tedious and a whole lot more adventurous."

"I like tedious, and I am definitely *not* looking for adventure."

"Really? I don't know many young women who aren't looking for adventure."

"I'm not like most young women."

She turned away, the tilt of her head telling him that she wasn't interested in continuing the conversation. "Mrs. Mackenzie, would it be all right for me to use one of the phones after cleaning up from breakfast? I have an important call to make." At Amanda's impatient frown, she hurried to add, "I have a calling card, ma'am, so nothing will show up on your bill."

"Of course you can use the phone, Cora," Jake said, standing up. "You don't even need to ask. In fact, there's no need to wait until after breakfast. I'll show you where you can make that call with some degree of privacy."

"I hope you don't plan on making it a habit to conduct personal calls during working hours, Cora. We only have one line into the house, and I don't like missing important calls." Amanda shut her appointment book with a sharp snap.

"No, ma'am. There won't be any need for me to make a lot of personal calls."

"You don't have a big family who will be calling and interrupting you at all hours, do you?" Amanda pressed.

"No family will call, Mrs. Mackenzie."

Amanda raised a questioning eyebrow. "No one will call, or are you saying that you have no family?"

"Both, ma'am. No one will call and I have no family."

Jake listened intently to her responses. He could tell from the slight tightening around Cora's mouth that giving out even that tiny morsel of personal information hadn't been easy for her to reveal.

When she'd told him last night that she was a private person, she hadn't lied. This was a woman who guarded her privacy with a vengeance. An individual who erected high walls and ducked down behind them, hiding from everyone.

But in spite of her intense need for privacy, Jake knew that his own family came first, and he intended to find out the answers to his questions.

"I'm sorry," Amanda said automatically, her tone revealing no real sympathy or understanding. In fact, Jake was fairly certain his stepmother actually seemed relieved by this information. As if the thought of the young cook having family would be an inconvenience. "In any case, go with Jake and make your call. Just don't linger. You have work to attend to."

"I wouldn't think of it, Mrs. Mackenzie. Your dietary needs far exceed any need for me to consider any personal concerns."

Jake relished the tiny touch of sarcasm. Who'd have

thought the meek little cook would give Amanda a glimpse of the fire that burned within. Cora Shelly was turning out to be more of an enigma than even he had initially thought. And if there was anything Jake liked better than a challenge, it was a complicated, virtually unsolvable puzzle.

As CORA FOLLOWED JAKE out of the dinning room, a tall redheaded woman almost bumped into them. Dressed in a short leather skirt, boots and skin-tight sweater, the woman ignored Cora but bestowed a flirtatious smile on Jake. He murmured a quiet greeting but continued on out into the hall.

The enthusiastic greeting from Dr. Sheffield behind them told Cora that the redhead was most likely the psychiatrist's late-rising wife. She was glad to have dodged another introduction, even though it meant finding herself alone with Jake Mackenzie.

She needed time to mull things over. Apparently Amanda Mackenzie was going to be even more demanding than she'd originally thought. The woman might be interested in protecting her own privacy, but she obviously didn't have any qualms about sticking her nose into the lives of her employees. That particular revelation made Cora more than a little nervous.

"You can use the library," Jake said, breaking into her private rant. "I use it as my study when I'm here, but you're welcome to go in at any time to use the phone or—" he glanced at her and smiled knowingly "—as a place to hide for a while when you need to get away." He opened one of the double doors and stepped aside.

"I appreciate the offer, but I rarely use the phone. And I'm sure there's one in the kitchen, isn't there?"

He nodded. "But not a lot of privacy." He pointed toward a huge cherry wood desk taking up one end of the room. "The phone is on the desk. I believe there is a phone book in the bottom right-hand drawer of the desk."

"That's all right—I know the number."

He waited.

Cora shifted uneasily. "I'm sorry I left so abruptly last night."

He shrugged, every look and motion creating an air of nonchalance, seeming to demonstrate how unaffected he was by what she was saying. "As I mentioned before, Cora, you seem to startle easily."

Cora stepped around him, trying desperately not to inhale the intoxicatingly fresh scent of pine and honest sweat that seemed to radiate off the thick flannel of his shirt. She was afraid it would make her dizzy, especially since the darkness of his eyes seemed poised to swallow her whole.

She stopped short, studying the wall on both sides of the doorway. "Is there a light switch?"

He leaned around her, his arm lightly brushing the tips of her breasts with the inside flat of his arm. She anchored herself in place, determined not to react in any way. Something told her that if she jumped, he'd laugh at her, and Cora hated the thought that he viewed her as any more skittish than he already thought.

He flicked on a switch, and soft light filled the small alcove around the desk at one end of the room. "Will that be sufficient?"

His voice was as smooth and rich as the wood of the desk, and the closeness of his muscular frame seemed to press in on her. It confused her, shooting a strange, unfamiliar longing through her. A longing she knew she needed to ignore.

She fought to focus her attention on the decor of the room. Anything but Jake Mackenzie. Floor-to-ceiling bookshelves covered every inch of available wall. The books on the top shelves could only be reached with an antique rolling ladder positioned at one end of the room. Cora was sure there were more than a few first editions among Mackenzie's impressive collection.

"It's a beautiful room. I've never seen so many books outside of a public library."

Jake seemed amused by her awe. A slight twinkle danced in his exquisite eyes. "It's my father's collection. He is quite proud of it." He stepped back a step and Cora almost whimpered in relief.

"If you don't need anything else," he said. "I'll leave you to make your call."

She shook her head. *Nothing, except for you to leave and let my hormone level return to normal,* she thought.

The slight quirk at the corner of his perfect lips told her that he'd read her relief and found it amusing.

"Take as long as you need," he said.

The door slid shut on its track.

Cora walked over to the desk, fumbling in her pocket for her calling card, trying unsuccessfully to quell the slight flutter in her stomach—the flutter she'd come to realize appeared whenever she was close to Jake Mackenzie.

She leaned down and turned on the powerful desk lamp, holding the card under it to see the numbers. Snatching up the receiver, she dropped down into the chair and punched the number in. She waited as the lines hummed and the connection was made.

A few seconds later she got through. "Los Angles County District Attorney's Office. How may I direct your call?"

"Yes, I'd like to speak to Assistant D.A. Jeffery Greene?"

"May I ask who's calling?"

"No."

There was a moment of stunned silence on the other end of the phone and then the operator said, "One moment please."

The line hissed and hummed until a deeper, male voice came on. "Jeffery Greene."

"Hello, Jeff. It's Cora."

"Cora! Where the hell are you? Wait, don't answer that—I want to shut my door first."

The receiver rattled against his desk as he laid it down. Cora stiffened, waiting for his return. An uneasy feeling crept up her spine. There was a distinct edge to Jeff's usually calm, laid-back tone.

The phone rattled again and Jeff said, "Okay, I'm alone. Now, where are you?"

Cora ignored his question. "What's going on, Jeff?"

"Nothing's going on. I just need you to tell me where you are."

"I'm at my new job."

Jeff sighed. Cora knew he hated her insistence on secrecy, her outright paranoia when it came to Erik Dubane. But Jeff hadn't lived next door to the charming psycho for months. He hadn't put up with strange break-ins that moved their personal belongings and left disturbing "gifts" for the two of them.

Originally, Erik had played the role of the concerned neighbor, until Jennifer had gotten an inkling that he was the one breaking in and moving things around. No one, not even the cops, had listened to their pleas of being harassed. Not until he'd attacked them, killing Jennifer.

"I'm not playing twenty questions, Cora. Tell me where you are."

"I'm somewhere safe. Now tell me what's wrong. I can tell from your voice that something's up."

There was a long pause on the other end. Cora could imagine Jeff sitting in his tiny, cramped office with stacks of files and briefs piled high on every flat surface available.

He had a habit of running a beefy hand through his blond crew cut. She knew he was debating with himself as to whether he'd give her the bad news or not. She knew without him even saying anything that it was bad news. It was the way her luck was running lately. All bad. It had been the way Jennifer's luck had been running, too—right up until the night she was murdered.

"Erik is gone."

Air shuddered in Cora's throat and her fingers tightened on the phone. She squeezed her eyes shut.

"Cora…are you still there?"

"Wh-what do you mean, he's gone?" She stood up and then sat back down again, unsure her legs would hold her. Her hand went to her throat, her nail slowly tracing the line of her scar. "What happened? Did the judge let him out on bail?"

"No. He's definitely *not* out on bail. He escaped on the way back to lockup. He was in court for another bail hearing."

Cora dropped forward until her forehead rested on the green felt desk blotter. She rocked back and forth, her head hitting the desk with light thuds. Damn them to hell for letting him get away. Hot tears welled up in her eyes.

From a great distance away, she heard Jeff's voice. "Cora…Cora, are you there? Talk to me. Tell me where you are. I'll send a team of officers there to pick you up and bring you here. I'll put you in protective custody. I'll make sure you're safe."

Cora sat up, her spine ramrod straight. "*No.* I'm safer if no one knows where I am."

"You need—"

"I don't *need* anything. You promised me, Jeff. You *promised* that everything would be all right. You said I'd be safe and he'd never get out of prison."

A sob slipped from between her lips, and she clamped a hand over her mouth, holding back the next one. Her shoulders shook as she struggled to regain control.

Finally she tried again, "I should never have trusted you. He's going to find me. I know he's going to find me."

"Deep breath, Cora. No one is going to find you."

"How long has he been gone?"

"Five days."

Another sob slipped out. She tightened her lips. Five days. A lifetime. Time enough for him to track her.

"Listen, the police will find him before he gets anywhere near you. He's probably out of the country by now."

"One would hope," Cora whispered, rocking back and forth.

"Tell me where you are. Tell me so I can send—"

Cora carefully replaced the receiver in its cradle, cutting off Jeff's voice. Her fingers stumbled, and the receiver slipped and clunked on the desktop. She used her other hand to guide her, putting it back in place.

Stunned, she turned to stare out the window. Dark clouds, heavy and roiling with an underbelly of blackness, rolled in. A heavy mist had cloaked the edges of the shore, threatening to cover the entire island.

She pressed a hand to her mouth, the moistness from her palm wetting her lips. Good God, what was she going to do? Coming here had been a last-ditch attempt to be safe. But she should have known better. When they led Erik off in handcuffs, his elegant lips had stretched into a predatory grin he'd made no attempt to hide.

As he passed, he'd blown her a kiss. "I'll be back for you, sweet Cora, and anyone else you care about. Wait for me."

Something told Cora that Erik was on his way.

Chapter Four

Fear surged through Cora's blood. She closed her eyes and rubbed her damp palms across the tops of her thighs, desperate to regain control.

A part of her screamed for her to run. To find safety, but she wasn't sure anymore where that was. She'd thought she was safe moving all the way across the country, and now she learned that was an illusion.

She knew she had to hang on, to keep herself from deteriorating into a state of useless panic. She needed to develop a plan of action. Her closed fist hit the top of her thigh. Think, dammit, think!

She sucked in a shaky breath of air and lifted her head. Over the past few months she'd quickly learned that if she got too panicked, she crashed and tipped over the edge.

First her body would shake and then her mind would start to flash back, retrieving horrible memories of that night four months ago, the night Erik changed her life forever.

The psychologist, the one who had worked with her right after the attack, had warned her that she'd have to deal with these flashbacks for a while, maybe the rest of her life, and Cora was learning the woman was right.

Anxiety or stress of any sort seemed to touch off the memories, moments so frightening that Cora's whole body would tremble and her limbs would melt to the consistency of heated syrup.

But she had to learn to maintain control. She needed to consider her next move. With Erik loose and possibly looking for her, Cora knew that her vulnerability factor had jumped into the danger zone.

The odds of him finding her here on Midnight Island were slim. She'd told no one she was coming, and she'd left no trail for him to follow, even if he left prison and immediately sought her out. She had simply cleaned out the tiny studio apartment she'd been living in since the attack and left, leaving no forwarding address. There hadn't been anyone to leave the information for—not with Jennifer dead and no family to speak of.

The only other person in California who knew about her leaving was Mrs. Mackenzie's lawyer, and Cora had a strong feeling Anthony Bellows III, Esq., an upscale lawyer with a client list that read like something out of *Who's Who,* didn't run in the same circle as Erik Dubane.

She stood up and her knees almost folded from the adrenaline rush. But she stiffened them, forcing them to support her weight. She would not give in. She could handle this. The psychologist had assured her she'd learn to deal with it.

In fact, the woman assured Cora she was strong enough to handle anything thrown her way, and Cora desperately wanted to believe her. If she wasn't strong enough, Erik would have won. He'd have succeeded in his attempt to take over her life.

Rounding the end of the desk, she glanced around, trying to focus her mind on something—anything. She needed to get the shakes under control. Then she needed to concentrate on a plan to deal with this new development.

But if she tried to make a plan now, Cora knew she would

reduce herself to a puddle in the middle of the library floor in a matter of minutes. Better to push thoughts about Erik aside for a few minutes to prevent herself from making a decision she'd regret later. It was a strategy she'd adopted shortly after the attack. So far it had worked well for her.

She focused on the room, shoving thoughts of Erik and his escape out of her mind. She noticed a small oak stand with a bouquet of lilies sitting a few feet away. Above it hung a portrait that seemed to dominate the entire room.

Curious, Cora moved over to the picture and sat in the leather chair across from it. Air whooshed out of the cushion as she sank into the buttery soft leather.

She studied the picture. It was an oil painting of a woman sitting on a bench in a small arbor, her legs spread wide and her hands clutching the fabric of her dress between them, as if a stiff breeze had just blown the dress upward and she had rushed to keep it from totally exposing her. Her head was thrown back, and the wind whipped her jet-black tendrils out behind her. They streamed in the breeze like velvet ribbons, alive and as vibrant as the woman they adorned.

The woman's beauty was astounding. Erotic, even. It seemed to spill out of the painting like a heady perfume. Something wild and unruly seemed to infuse the woman's lush body, making her seem uncontrollable, a totally wanton and sexual being.

Her head was tilted and she had an overt come-hither look in her eyes. The eyes were a striking emerald color and sparked with something defiant. Challenging. The pale gauzy fabric of her dress had slid up over her legs to reveal the shapely curve of her calfs and the startling whiteness of her thighs. She seemed poised on the verge of laughter, as if daring the artist to go even further.

It wasn't anything like the ancestral portraits hanging in the Mackenzie entry hall. It was something much more modern. Much more decadent and earthy.

Cora leaned back, allowing her arms to slide up onto the arms of the oversize chair, and rested her head against the cool leather. She wasn't quite sure how, but she knew without question that the woman staring boldly down at her was Jake Mackenzie's wife—the woman who had disappeared without a trace two years ago.

She glanced down and considered the bouquet of freshly cut flowers sitting directly beneath the portrait. The white lilies were so fresh that tiny drops of dew still clung to the graceful sweep of the petals.

As she watched, a single drop of dew slid off the tip of one delicately veined petal and fell to the tabletop, splashing onto the polished wood of the table like a single tear. Suddenly, a sense of deep sadness washed over her.

Someone, Jake no doubt, had gone to great pains to set up this informal memorial of a much beloved woman. Perhaps the tough and cynical Jake Mackenzie wasn't exactly who he pretended to be. Perhaps his brusqueness hid a heart filled with terrible pain and sadness.

It wasn't hard to picture him with the woman in the portrait. She was definitely his match—bold and sexual. She could almost see Jake sitting in this very chair, his fingers restlessly raking through the dark strands of hair, giving him a rumpled, distressed look as he considered the endless depths of his grief and despair. She swallowed hard against the sadness that welled up in the back of her throat.

But then, just as quickly as the maudlin mood hit her, Cora shook it off. What was wrong with her? This sentimental romantic dribble wasn't like her at all. Just because she'd felt a twinge of attraction for Jake Mackenzie didn't mean she needed to make him into something he wasn't—a Heathcliff wanna-be.

Better to realize that his wife had left him because he was a boorish, self-centered brute who enjoyed flirting with anything in a skirt. No doubt a much more accurate assessment of the man.

She sat up and moved to the edge of the chair, studying the picture more critically and, as she did, a cool breeze caressed the back of her neck. Startled, she glanced at the fire, but it still burned hot, its flame a bluish white in the center and a pile of red coals beneath.

The icy draft spread to her face and hands, making the tips of her fingers ache with the cold. A swarm of goose bumps slid up the length of her arms to her shoulders. She shivered.

Puzzled, she crossed her arms, trying to conserve what body heat remained, but she couldn't seem to recapture the warmth she'd enjoyed a few moments ago. It was if someone had opened a window and allowed the damp, cold air of the river to roll in unabated.

She stood, thinking that if she moved around a little the warmth would return. But then she heard it. A strange, forlorn whimpering. It was like a tiny wail, whistling in on the cold breeze touching her cheek and the tip of her nose. She tightened her arms around her and looked around. The cry seemed to be coming from the direction of the painting.

She bent down and spotted an old heating vent beneath the table. The soft muffled sob seemed to come through the grate. The sound was familiar, like the one a woman made when she cried into her hands, trying to muffle the sound so no one knew she was weeping.

The cry was soft and heartrending. Not too different from

her own sobs after being rescued by the police following Er-ik's rampage. Cries of relief that she'd survived, but cries of great pain, too. Deep emotional pain.

As the sobs rose to an eerie crescendo, she walked closer to the vent. The sound was mournful, rising and falling as if riding on the wind. Was this the ghost Mrs. Benson spoke about?

The hair on the back of Cora's neck rose. She glanced around, unsure of what to do next. The wind outside picked up, lashing rain against the windows, and the lamps flickered, plunging the room into momentary gloominess.

She clenched her hands, praying the electricity didn't go off. The lights flicked back on.

"You hear her, too, don't you?" a voice whispered from be-hind her.

Cora whirled around.

A young woman, her face intense and secretive, stood be-hind the massive desk. She wore an ill-fitting dress and bulky sweater, an outfit that could only be called frumpy. She wasn't tall, standing only a few inches above Cora's own five feet.

Her hair was long and in a single braid down her back. Short straggly strands and broken ends stuck out of the braid at odd angles, giving the braid the appearance of being done by an inept four-year-old.

Cora frowned. Where had she come from? There wasn't any door on that side of the room, but as she watched, the woman turned and closed a panel in the wall. Suddenly the wall lay flat again, no seam visible in the ornately carved wood.

A thrill raced through Cora. Of course, what castle would be complete without a few secret passageways? But as quickly as the thought flashed across her brain, a jolt of fear burrowed its way into the pit of her stomach.

Secret passageway? Anything secret had the potential to be dangerous. Unless she knew exactly where each and every passage led, she lived in peril. At any point, she could be ambushed.

From across the room, the woman silently studied Cora with a pair of washed out blue eyes. "You startled me," Cora said, moving closer to the woman. "You must be Megan. Your stepbrother told me you lived here, too."

The woman's eyes widened, streaks of dark blue seeming to spill into the lighter color of the iris, darkening both eyes with alarm. She raised a finger to her lips. "Don't talk about him. She'll hear us and she won't come."

"Who will hear us? Who won't come?"

"The Lady." She leaned forward again and whispered, "She never comes when my stepbrother is around. She's frightened of him."

"Jake frightens her?" Cora frowned. "Why?"

The woman ignored her and tilted her head as if listening to something far off, and just as abruptly as it started, the crying stopped, cut off in midcry.

"See, she stopped. She's afraid he's heard us and he'll come."

"I...I don't think it was anyone really crying. It must have been the wind off the river." Cora forced a calmness into her voice that she didn't feel.

Impatience flickered across the young woman's face. "Of course it was someone crying. It was the Lady. She cries all the time now."

"What lady?"

"*The Mournful Lady,* of course. Who else would cry so?"

"Wh-who is she?"

A smile, something faint and secretive pulled at the corners of the woman's mouth. "Oh, that's a secret. No one is supposed to know. She never shows her face." She turned slightly to look over her shoulder and tilted her head again, as if listening to someone whisper in her ear. She nodded as if agreeing to something.

A chill shot up Cora's spine. This was getting entirely too creepy.

The woman mumbled something under her breath, the words so soft that they were barely more than a sigh. Her smile evaporated, and she jerked her head in the direction of the library door. "She disappears when he shows up, too."

Startled, Cora glanced toward the door, jumping when she saw Jake framed in the doorway. What was it with these people? Didn't they ever knock? It was if they all walked around on cat feet, sneaking up on people at the oddest moments.

An exasperated scowl had settled across Jake's darkly handsome face, and his eyes snapped with impatience. Obviously, he wasn't happy about something.

"Where have you been, Megan?" He didn't wait for an answer but glanced over his shoulder and gestured to someone in the hall. "She's in here, Mrs. Benson. Please tell Amanda that we've found her."

"Tell that old biddy to go take a flying—"

Jake raised a hand and cut his stepsister off. "Enough. Mrs. Benson has been looking all over for you. She thought you were coming down to breakfast and then suddenly you disappeared."

Megan hunched her shoulders, as if trying to fold them in upon herself. The oversize sweater she wore shifted and twisted slightly on her chubby shoulders. A small frown sprang up between her poorly tweezed brows. "Tell the old bat to leave me alone." Megan's voice was high-pitched and petulant, sounding much like that of a small spoiled child. "She's always trying to tell me what to do—ordering me around. I don't like her."

As Cora shifted uncomfortably, Megan turned in her direction, her gaze connecting with Cora. A crafty grin appeared on her lips and she pointed at Cora. "I want her to be the one who keeps an eye on me. I like her." She reached up to twirl several strands of escaping hair with one finger. "At least she isn't bossy or nosy like Mrs. Benson."

Cora didn't dare glance in Jake's direction, concerned that he wasn't going to be too pleased with his stepsister's sudden and unexplained affinity for her.

"Cora was hired to cook, Megan. She isn't here to look after you." The touch of impatience that flavored his tone told Cora that she'd guessed right. He wasn't enamored with this sudden unexpected bond of friendship. "You know that you're perfectly capable of taking care of yourself. Mrs. Benson was simply checking to make sure you made it downstairs to breakfast."

Megan snorted. "Then why does she follow me around all the time? Why can't she keep her big fat nose out of my room?" Her face darkened. "I might be crazy, but I'm not stupid. She's your damn spy."

"She is not my spy and you're not crazy."

"Well then, she's Amanda's spy. "

"I'm not in the mood to discuss spying right now. Just do me a favor and go eat."

His stepsister shuffled past, mumbling under her breath. But when Cora attempted to follow, Jake blocked her way, sticking a leg out.

Startled, she stopped short. But when she opened her mouth to protest, he held up a hand and waited until his stepsister had disappeared down the hall.

Then he turned back, his leg brushing hers as he angled his body toward her. "Look, I'd appreciate it if you didn't go out of your way to encourage Megan. She can be difficult at times."

Cora tried to ignore the slight flutter in her chest, her undeniable reaction to the closeness of him. It irritated her that she was so affected by him and he seemed so oblivious. "Perhaps you could tell me exactly what it was that I was doing that can be called encouraging?"

He stepped closer, his height and frame seeming to loom over her, making her feel even smaller and more insignificant than usual. His thigh grazed the side of her leg and his hot breath brushed her cheek. He had effectively boxed her in, preventing her from leaving.

"All this ridiculous talk about ghosts encourages her."

"I wasn't encouraging her. I didn't even bring the subject up. She did."

"I disagree. If you're going to ask her questions about the ghosts, you're encouraging her."

Cora struggled to concentrate on what he was saying, but she had a hard time. His closeness, his height, his refusal to let her get by raised her anxiety level and triggered a feeling of panic.

She backed up a few steps. "P-please, I don't like it when people stand too close."

Impatience flashed in his eyes again, but this time she saw him try to quell it, as if he realized he was truly scaring her. "Look, I apologize. I just didn't want you jackrabbiting like you did last night. I wanted to make sure you understood how things are run around here."

"Then just tell me. You don't need to use your size to intimidate me. I'm a very reasonable person."

"I'm sure you are." He paused to shoot a glance down the hall, as if checking to be sure that Megan had moved out of earshot. "I just wanted you to understand that Megan can be difficult. She gets excited and then we have a hard time with her. What I don't need right now is her getting lost in a fantasy world because you can't curb your imagination."

The reprimand rubbed Cora the wrong way, effectively shutting off her anxiety. "For your information, I'm not the one who keeps bringing up the topic of ghosts. Your staff and stepsister seem slightly obsessed with the subject."

"Megan has always been a handful, but she seems to have taken an instant liking to you." The coolly appraising look on his face seemed to indicate that he wasn't quite sure why his stepsister had made such a poor choice. "The less discussion there is about ghosts, the better we're all going to get along. So whoever is bringing up the topic, I'd appreciate *your* help in stopping it. Do we have an understanding?"

She nodded, acutely aware of the warmth that seemed to radiate off his body like heat from a rock lying in the sun too long. A few moments ago she could barely move she was so chilled, and now she felt as though she might burst into flames at any moment. How could any man hold such power over her?

"If you'd excuse me, I'll get back to work." She moved to step around him, but he didn't budge. His boot remained jammed across the doorway, and the darkness of his eyes seemed to melt over and around her, making her wish she was wearing protective clothing and glasses. Anything to hide her from his penetrating gaze.

"I really do frighten you, don't I?"

"Not at all," she lied, tugging nervously at the neck of her shirt and trying not to think about the fact that this man's wife had mysteriously disappeared one day.

He reached up and gently stilled her hand and, before she had a chance to pull away, he pushed down the collar of her shirt. His thumb lightly skimmed the surface of her neck, touching and tracing the line of her scar. Her breath caught in the back of her throat and every nerve in her body immediately stood guard.

"It's quite faint, actually," he said. "Hardly noticeable at all."

His tone was matter-of-fact, as if he was her lover and she had asked him what he thought of a part of her body that worried or concerned her.

But he wasn't her lover and she hadn't invited him to comment or touch her. She stepped back, almost stumbling in her haste. "P-please, don't."

The intensity of his gaze didn't change. "I wouldn't have noticed it if you weren't always touching it or fiddling with your collar."

She opened her mouth to respond, but nothing came out. Damn him for doing this to her. For making her feel so vulnerable.

His gaze remained focused on her neck, and the heat of it seemed almost like a hot caress. "Actually, the scar is a little too straight. A little too perfect." His glance flicked up to her eyes. "There's no way this was caused by the dog attack you told me about last night. How did it happen?"

She turned away and lied, "If you must know, I had surgery."

"Really?" His tone told her he didn't buy the explanation. But to her relief, he didn't seem inclined to pursue the topic. But then his next comment made her wish he had. "Something's wrong. Did you receive some bad news? Something that upset you?"

She turned back around, determined to blast him with her anger, but the warmth of his breath seemed to stroke the curve of her cheek. She shoved her hands in her pants pocket, digging her fingernails into the center of her palm in an attempt to steady herself. She would not allow this man to get to her. To throw her off balance.

"I'm fine." She boldly met his gaze. "I'm not a sophisticated person, Mr. Mackenzie. All I ask is that I be allowed to do my job. No games. No pretenses. Just clean honest labor for a decent day's wage."

He leaned a shoulder against the door frame, his arms folding casually across his broad chest. It was a relaxed pose but it continued to effectively block her from leaving. "My radar tells me that you're not fine. That you're upset about something and hiding it. Hiding something or hiding from someone. Which is it, Cora?"

Her heart beat in her neck, the pounding so violent that she heard it echo in her ears and she was sure he could see her pulse moving beneath the skin of her neck. "What do you mean?"

"Hiding, as in, taking cover, secreting oneself from others. You know, lying low. Keeping out of sight." He smiled but there was no missing the hardening of those dark eyes. He was like those damn beasts of his. He'd latched on to something and he wasn't about to let it go until he had an answer.

"I'm here to work. That's all."

He nodded and the unrelenting glint in his eyes sliced into her like twin razors. He wasn't convinced. "Let me make something perfectly clear to you. I'm a reasonable man with only a few expectations of my employees. One of those expectations is hard work." He straightened up. "But the most important thing is honesty. I despise being lied to. So if I ever find that you've been less than honest with me in regards to why you're here, Ms. Shelly, you can be sure that I won't be happy. Do we understand each other?"

Cora swallowed against the flutter of nervousness in her stomach. "Perfectly."

"Perhaps I've offended you with my frankness?"

Cora could tell from his voice and expression that he didn't give a damn if he had. This was a man who liked getting his own way and anyone stupid enough to go against him was going to get run over. "No offense taken," she said. "I just consider myself forewarned."

"Excellent." He considered her for a moment and then added, "I might be tough on my employees but I also look out for them. If you need anything, let me know. I'll do what I can to help."

"You have a strange way of showing your compassion. One minute you're accusing me of being here under false pretenses and the next you're telling me that I can trust you. Which way is it, Mr. Mackenzie? Tough boss or pussycat?"

He laughed, something soft, deep and deliciously rough. It sent a renegade zing of delight up the center of her back. "Don't ever doubt that I'm a tough boss. Is that a problem?"

"Not in the least."

"Then I guess we'll get along famously," he said.

Cora wasn't so sure about that, but she wisely kept that comment to herself.

He nodded and moved as if to get out of her way. But then he paused, and something told Cora that his next statement was going to throw her. She wasn't sure how she knew, but she did. Mainly because this was a man who enjoyed springing traps when the mouse least expected it. And as much as she would have liked to deny it, Cora felt like a tiny mouse poised to walk into his trap.

"Oh, one other small matter. I would appreciate it if you'd get me a copy of your driver's license and Social Security card. I keep those things on file, and Amanda mentioned that she hadn't gotten copies of them from you yet."

Cora's heart hammered a harsh beat of warning deep in her chest. Of course. Her driver's license and Social Security card. The two things that would allow a skilled investigator to trace her. To find out her true identity.

Four months ago, Cora had known she wanted to disappear. She paid what little money she had for a forged Social Security card and a California driver's license. She knew at the time that they weren't good quality—nothing that would pass careful scrutiny. She just wanted an added level of protection against Erik.

It wasn't a big deal, because she was smart enough to know that she had to seek out jobs that were small and family run. Places that didn't have the resources to carefully check her credentials. She should have known that Amanda Mackenzie not checking out her credentials closely was too good to be true.

Jeff Greene had helped her to find a job outside of the San Francisco area. A chef's job in a small trendy restaurant in San Diego. Cora knew he'd done it to make sure she was out of the media spotlight, to lessen the psychological pressures that weighed on her as she waited to testify. And she also knew that he'd fixed things with the owners. They paid her under the table and didn't ask questions.

But Jeff had been pretty up-front about saying that if anyone wanted to really dig deep enough and hard enough they'd find her. He'd reassured her that Erik wasn't going to get out and get a chance to do that, but he'd already been proven wrong in that point.

"I'm getting the impression that you're not happy with your stepmother's decision to hire me," she countered, trying to stall.

"Not at all. I just happen to like doing a more extensive check on potential employees. We've had problems in the past, and I'd like to be sure I know something about the people who come to Midnight Island."

"What kind of trouble?" she asked, continuing to stall.

Something raw and painful passed across his features. But as quickly as it appeared, it was gone again.

"Nothing significant," he said. "But I'm not the kind of person who makes the same mistake twice."

"I don't have the papers on me."

"You can bring them to me when you have a free moment." He stepped aside, indicating that she was free to leave.

Cora nodded and quickly took her opportunity to escape. Behind her, the library door slid shut.

As she headed down the hall, her stomach twisted with anxiety. She could only hope that whatever weasel he was planning to hire to ferret our every detail of her life wasn't too thorough. But something told her that Jake Mackenzie didn't hire incompetent people.

"He killed her, you know."

Cora whirled around, coming face-to-face with Megan. She stood outside the door of the dining room, a buttered bagel in one hand and a coffee mug in the other. A trail of crumbs ran down the front of her sweater.

A feeling of dread hammered at a spot directly between Cora's eyes. What now? She wasn't sure she could handle any more surprises. "Your stepbrother killed someone?"

Megan took a small bite of the bagel and chewed slowly. Her gaze never left Cora's. Finally she nodded, a secretive smile pulling at the corner of her mouth.

"Wh-who did he kill?" Oh God, did she really want to know this?

"Natalie, of course. He killed Natalie and then hid her body."

Fear drilled a hole in the softest part of Cora's heart. What kind of family had she walked into? She stared at Jake's stepsister, the impact of what the woman had just revealed hitting her like a concrete block dropped from the castle's highest turret.

"How do you know he killed her?"

Megan chomped off another bite and chewed. "Because I saw him do it, that's how."

Before Cora could ask another question, Megan turned and headed up the stairs, her smile metamorphosing into something smug and triumphant.

Cora stood in the great hall totally stupefied. She'd just learned that the maniac who had promised to find her and kill her had escaped from prison. And now she learned that it was a very real possibility that her new employer had killed his wife and dumped her body somewhere on Midnight Island. Her refuge had suddenly taken on the atmosphere of a den of snakes.

Chapter Five

Cold rain and periods of sleet lashed Midnight Island much of the night and all the next day, keeping the residents confined to the castle. By early evening, Jake had a bad case of cabin fever. Although he liked the isolation of Midnight Island, away from city noise and congestion, he wasn't happy when he couldn't get outside and work on the property. It was the reason he came to the island in the first place. He spent enough time in the city sitting behind a desk dealing with the business of running Mackenzie International.

He might be the best there was in the business when it came to dealing with a shipping crisis, but even he knew he needed time to destress and relax. It was something he learned from his father by default. William hadn't learned that lesson until after his first heart attack at sixty.

Jake shifted positions and nudged the telephone receiver closer against his ear. He was having a hard time focusing on the voice at the other end. Martin Fielding tended to get a little long-winded at times.

He gazed out the window at the new crop of clouds headed across the river. Another storm was building, and the previous one had barely left an hour ago. If this kept up, he wouldn't be able to get the helicopter off the island tomorrow afternoon, and he'd be stuck here for another night.

"The name is Shelly, right? *S-H-E-L-L-Y*?" Fielding's question drew Jake's attention back to the phone conversation.

"Yes, Shelly. Cora Shelly. She's about twenty-two." Jake rummaged around on the desk until he found the pad he'd jotted some quick notes on. Amanda hadn't exactly been thrilled that he'd questioned her regarding her hiring practices, but she'd answered what she remembered of Cora Shelly's employment application and promised she'd have her attorney, the one who had done the actual hiring out in San Diego, send him the application and interview notes.

"According to Amanda, the woman was living in San Diego. Amanda doesn't know whether she's from there originally, but San Diego is as good a place as any to start. Apparently she worked in a small restaurant called…Angelo's. I don't have any more than that right now, but as soon as I get more I'll call."

"Why not just ask the cook?"

"I have, and she's giving me the runaround. I'm also getting strong vibes that she's hiding something and I don't want to spook her."

"So fire her and be done with it."

Jake didn't respond right away. Mainly because he knew that was an option. One he wasn't interested in taking for some reason. Anyone else would have been out of there on the next boat if they appeared reluctant to hand over their identification. But Cora Shelly was different. Something about her appealed to him, and he wasn't about to can her—just yet, anyway.

"I'd prefer to do a little investigating first. Amanda hired her and seems interested in keeping her on. Do the background check and get back to me."

A heavy sigh filtered over the phone line. "When are you going to learn to follow my suggestions?"

Jake laughed easily. "I know, I know—we shouldn't be hiring anyone without first going through you. I reminded Amanda of that fact less than an hour ago."

"I should hope so. Because the trouble you had with that painter three years ago was completely preventable. Why else would you be paying me that huge retainer if you weren't interested in listening to my vast wisdom regarding background checks?"

There was no arguing with that kind of logic. The retainer Jake paid to Fieldstone Investigations was hefty but well worth the investment. It meant Fielding and his staff of savvy, experienced investigators were at Jake's disposal at any hour of any day or night.

"I do this for a living, Jake. I live, eat and breathe background checks. In fact, I'm better at it than the FBI and the CIA combined. Hell, half my guys were trained by the FBI or the spooks before coming to work for me. And then I taught them all I know—which is a hell of a lot."

"I know all that, Marty. But for some reason Amanda decided to do the hiring this time." He shifted the receiver to his other ear. "In any case, get started on this one right away. I want to get a feel for what Ms. Shelly is hiding."

"Any chance she's an illegal?"

"No, that's not the issue."

"Could she be running from the authorities or pose a serious threat to you or the family?"

Jake conjured up a visual of Cora—petite and defenseless except for a tumble of cinnamon curls spilling into those huge expressive brown eyes. Oh, and her wicked little paring knife.

He grinned. "Dangerous? No, I don't think that's an issue. A little on the determined side, maybe. But definitely not dangerous."

He glanced toward the door to the front hall. Whatever she was hiding from had her scared. Scared, closemouthed and outright cautious.

"You worried someone might be coming after her?"

"Could be—I'm not sure. She's got a backbone of pure steel, but I'm getting the feeling that she's frightened of something. If someone is out to hurt her, then I want to know who. And I want to know why."

"Sounds like you're taking this more personal than usual. Is there something about this woman you're not telling me?"

Jake paused, surprised at Fielding's perceptive assessment. Was he right? Something told him that that was a distinct possibility, but he shook the feeling off. He was simply looking after his family. "No. I just don't like anyone messing with my employees."

"All right, I'll get on this. Call me as soon as you have more information."

"I will."

Fielding paused a minute, then added, "Any chance that while I'm conducting this investigation, you'd want me to pick up where I left off with my investigation of Amanda and the disappearing act she pulled three months ago? I still have her folder sitting in my files. Haven't touched it since you told me to back off a few weeks ago."

"Not a chance. My father doesn't seem interested in finding out what she was up to. He was quite clear that I was to stop snooping around, and I intend to honor his request. Just throw the file out."

"Okay, if that's what you want. But that little tidbit I dug up on her just suddenly appearing out of nowhere in New York City over twenty years ago is too damn interesting to just let drop. It wasn't too long after that that she wangled her way into Mackenzie International and shortly after that a job as your dad's assistant."

Jake didn't bite. He couldn't bite. Although he wanted Fielding to dig deep enough to find out the truth about Amanda, he knew his father would have his head. In the beginning he had respected his father's decision, even though he'd never warmed up to Amanda. But then, three months ago Amanda just upped and disappeared for three weeks. No warning. No phone calls.

She simply disappeared and then reappeared with no explanation for her absence. And that included no explanation to Jake's father, either. Not that his father voiced any need to know. He was too trusting for that.

His father's capacity for trust always amazed Jake. Especially since he'd lived and worked in the cutthroat corporate world his entire life. And the man had been undeniably successful in that world. But when it came to his father's love life and Amanda, Jake thought of the man as entirely too naive, like a lovesick schoolboy.

Now that he thought about it, he realized he'd been raised the same way. Probably explained his subsequent humiliation at the hands of Natalie.

"Your dad is pretty sick, right?" Fielding said, breaking into his thoughts again.

"Yeah, things have been going downhill pretty fast. The doctor has been frank, telling him that there isn't much more they can do at this point. He's worn-out."

"I'm sorry, Jake. I know you two have always been close."

They had been close. Until Amanda stepped in and tried to drive a wedge between them. Not that he begrudged his father some happiness these past six years. He just wished it was with a woman who wasn't so secretive. After dealing with Natalie and her little games, all he wanted was a woman who was straightforward and honest. Was that too much for a man to ask?

"Amanda's a smart lady," Fielding said. "Isn't it possible that she's positioning herself for more money? A bigger chunk of the estate?"

"She's his wife, Marty. She's entitled to whatever he leaves her. Besides, there's more than enough to go around."

Fielding laughed. "Spoken like a truly misguided rich guy. Misguided but honorable."

"Just do the investigation on our new cook and I'll be eternally grateful."

"Will do."

A few minutes later Fielding hung up.

"Working late as usual, I see."

Startled, Jake glanced up to see Vivian Sheffield standing poised in the doorway. Posed might actually have been a better description.

She stood with one hip cocked and one arm stretched upward along the door frame. Her robe gaped open at the top, giving him a clear view of the generous swell of her breasts.

As she caught the direction of his gaze, her seductive smile widened, curling up one corner of her lush lips. Her thick red hair fell over one shoulder, barely brushing the tip of her right breast.

The robe was short and sheer, barely covering the curve of her upper thighs. Jake figured the robe would be hard-pressed to provide her with enough warmth in the drafty halls of the castle.

But Vivian Sheffield was rarely concerned with comfort when it came to fashion. Whatever shocked and titillated was her typical MO. Or so it seemed to Jake.

"Good evening, Vivian," he said dryly. "Not dressing for dinner, I see."

The psychiatrist's wife yawned and stretched, the robe moving up a few more tantalizing inches to showcase a skimpy pair of black bikini panties. They were little more than a scrap of lace string. "I was just about to when I thought I'd come look for you and see if you were interested in a cocktail before dinner." She hit him with what he was sure she thought was a smoldering glance. "Something recreational."

"No, thanks." He sat back, shooting her a quick cool glance. It was a glance meant to warn her to turn down the sexual heat a few notches. Her antics were wasted on him. But then, Vivian had never shown much ability to grasp subtleties.

Sure enough. Right on cue, she reached around and pulled the doors closed. The left door caught on the track and stayed open a crack, but Vivian didn't waste any time trying to fix it—she obviously had an agenda. She sauntered over to his desk.

She settled one hip on the edge of his desk and reached out to run a perfectly painted red nail down the length of the pen in his desk set. "Daniel is terrible company. One or two drinks and he's out snoring like a bull walrus." She glanced up from beneath spiky eyelashes, hitting him with full wattage.

Jeez, the woman didn't have time to dress before coming downstairs, but she had enough time to get the makeup on.

"Something tells me that you would have the ability to hold your own. So I came down to offer to share a drink or two before dinner."

"Thanks, but no thanks, Vivian. I'm not much of a drinker."

She stuck out her lower lip in a child's pout. It would have been laughable if she wasn't leaning down, practically draping herself across his desk. "Oh, I could remedy that."

He closed the file on his desk and shoved it into the drawer next to him. Best to nip this little seduction play in the bud before it had a chance to go any further. If there was one thing he didn't need right now, it was Daniel Sheffield wrapping his poor excuse for an analytical mind around the idea that Jake was in the least bit interested in his bored, undersexed wife.

CORA GLANCED AROUND the kitchen. A rack of lamb was finishing up in the oven, the seasoned potatoes sat in the juices toasting a delightful brown, and the crisp green asparagus was waiting to be steamed and covered with her special Hollandaise sauce.

She checked the clock. Dinner in less than twenty, and she finally had a free moment. She'd already retrieved the lunch dishes from Mr. Mackenzie's bedroom several hours earlier. Or at least she'd taken them from his dour-faced nurse, Beatrice Crane. The rude woman had practically slammed the door in Cora's face after shoving the tray into her hands.

Not much food had been eaten off the tray, signaling to Cora that Jake's father didn't have an appetite. But instead of discouraging her, Cora took it as a challenge. Somehow she'd find a way to entice the man to eat.

Sighing, she settled in to scour the pan she'd used earlier to make sticky buns. She was fairly certain she could have gotten the pan clean in the huge state-of-the-art industrial dishwasher situated in one corner of the kitchen, but she'd always found scrubbing pots a form of therapy when trying to work out a problem. And the weird, unexpected little flutter that Jake Mackenzie created in her whenever he was within a few feet of her qualified as a problem.

She sighed heavily. Time to be honest. The guy didn't even have to stand a few feet away to start the flutter from beating against the sides of her stomach. Even now, up to her elbows in suds and dishwater, she could feel the quiver deep in the pit of her belly, and all she'd done was think about the man.

She scrubbed harder, running the scouring pad roughly over the caramelized butter, sugar and cinnamon sticking to the bottom of the pan. How was she supposed to concentrate on her job and keep her senses on full alert when the man's taunting, undeniably sexy smile kept creeping into her thoughts?

She straightened up and tossed the pad into the other sink to soak longer. Damn, she needed to figure out how to handle Jake's request for her driver's license and Social Security card, not the sexy quality of his smile.

She reached up and grabbed down a large mixing bowl, the base hitting the countertop with a dull thud. Turning toward the pantry, she almost fell over Caesar's sprawled-out body. He glanced up at her, his brown eyes immediately alert.

Resisting the urge to retreat, she tentatively poked one beefy haunch with the tip of her toe. "Come on, pooch, move your carcass."

He grunted and pulled himself up, lumbering over to sit near the fireplace. His eyes never left her. After her encounter with him the first night, the dog had taken an unexpected and sudden attachment to her. He followed her everywhere, and it was more than a little creepy.

But Cora didn't dare try to shoo him out of the kitchen. Something told her it wouldn't be advisable to cross this particular dog. Hopefully, he'd get tired of hanging around her and wander off.

She entered the pantry and pulled down sacks of flour, sugar and a few other staples. It was time to destress and get her mind on something other than Jake Mackenzie. She lined the dry goods up on the granite-topped island in the middle of the kitchen.

If pot scrubbing didn't work, then her only other recourse was to make a pan of something decadent and sinful. Maybe if she made it sinful enough, Mr. Too-Sexy-for-His-Own-Good Jake Mackenzie would eat the entire pan and put on a few extra pounds. That should take care of any lustful thought she was having about the man.

She shook her head. Who was she kidding? The guy was built like the ultimate calorie burning machine—tall, lean and with enough tightly carved muscles to send most women into a swoon of sexual need. He could probably consume ten pans of her Death by Chocolate Brownies and still come back for more. It was like pouring a thimbleful of water on a raging inferno.

She dumped flour into the sifter and quickly filled the bowl. What was wrong with her? The man had essentially admitted that he planned on poking around in her private life, and she was consumed with thoughts about how attractive he was. Pathetic.

Disgusted with herself, she dumped in the sugar and cocoa. Turning to the refrigerator, she pulled a carton of eggs and grabbed the can of thick fudge syrup she'd spied in there earlier.

What had happened to the caution she'd carefully culti-
vated after Erik's attack? She'd made sure the word *trust*
didn't even exist in her vocabulary anymore. Even Jeffery
Greene had discovered that fact when he'd tried to gain her
cooperation for the trial. She'd freaked him out when she'd
hightailed it out of California without telling him where she
was headed. And the assistant D.A. had been one of the good
guys.

She paused, an egg poised over the edge of the mixing bowl.
Maybe she was being unreasonable. Maybe it was time for her
to work on developing some trust. Could be she needed to learn
how to confide in someone. She had to admit that she was getting weary of running. She wasn't sure how much longer she
could maintain this level of vigilance. This level of distrust.

Taking Jake Mackenzie up on his offer to confide in him
might be exactly what she needed. But was his claim to look
out for his employees genuine? And if it was, could he really
provide her with the protection she needed?

But what about the suspicions surrounding Jake's wife's
death? Could she truly ignore the whispered talk of his possible involvement? Was she running from one danger only to
step into something even more treacherous? More risky?

Her heart told her that he was a hard man. A man who got
what he wanted out of life. But the fear that he would hurt a
woman, kill her because she was no longer of use to him,
seemed out of character. She was so confused.

She closed her eyes a moment. God, it would feel good to
open up to someone. To share her enormous burden. She
wanted to testify at Erik's trial. Wanted to put him away for
a very long time. But she also wanted to be safe.

She opened her eyes and cracked the egg with a flick of
her wrist. The insides plopped into the center of the mixture.

She added five more and then selected a spoon from the drawer, mixing and folding the eggs into the dry ingredients.

Maybe it wouldn't hurt for her to have someone else on the lookout for Erik. Someone like Jake. Someone taller, bigger and more powerful than the maniac who had vowed to come back for her.

She reached down and wiped her palms on the towel as she glanced at the clock. She'd seen Jake go into the library a few minutes earlier. Perhaps he was still in there. If she did this quickly without overanalyzing everything, then maybe she wouldn't have time to stop herself.

She walked over to the table and rummaged through her purse for her wallet. Pulling out her license and Social Security card, she took a fortifying breath and slipped them into her pocket. She'd give him the identification information he'd requested and take the chance. A dangerous chance.

She would try to convince him to help her with this mess. A mess that was getting more dangerous and life threatening by the minute.

VIVIAN TRAILED the tips of her fingers down the line of Jake's jaw as she moved in close. "I like a man with a bit of reserve," Vivian purred.

She slid one arm up around his neck and coyly pressed her sleek body to his, taking particular care to grind her pelvis against his. Jake felt nothing but irritation. Vivian seemed to have a difficult time getting the message. "Don't you ever tire of playing games, Vivian?

She laughed, something deep and throaty. "Not by a long shot, sugar. I'm looking to pick up where we left off in New York six months ago. You're an evasive little cuss."

"Oh, you mean when you conveniently showed up in my

hotel room without Daniel in tow?" He was tempted to add how he'd also thrown her shapely oversexed butt out of the room less than five minutes later, but he figured he didn't need to rub the rejection in.

"Oh, I'm not so clueless that I don't know when a man wants me but feels duty-bound to say no."

Perhaps he *did* need to rub the rejection in. "I guess maybe you—"

He was cut off by the sound of the door opening. Over Vivian's shoulder, he caught a glimpse of Cora as she started to step into the room. Her expression wavered between embarrassment and something else—something that looked remarkably like regret.

But she recovered quickly, the familiar, aloof expression slipping across her elfin face with lightning speed. "Oh, excuse me, Mr. Mackenzie, I didn't realize you were otherwise occupied."

He almost had to smile at her wording—"otherwise occupied." Hell, she'd walked in on him in a compromising position, and even though Vivian was the aggressor, he was pretty sure that wasn't what Ms. Shelly judged to be happening.

He slipped out of Vivian's hold. "Not a problem, Cora. Mrs. Sheffield was just leaving. Weren't you, Vivian?"

"Not by a long shot." She shot a barracuda smile in Cora's direction and slinked over to one of the chairs, artfully draping her long body over it. "And who might this be?"

"I might be the cook," Cora said, her voice and posture speaking loudly of her disapproval of what she'd walked in on. A tigress, Jake thought. A moral little tigress to boot.

Vivian tilted her head back so she could see Jake. "You really should train your staff better." Her amusement vanished as she swung her gaze back toward Cora. "Helpful hint, sweetie—never ever walk in on your boss when the doors are shut."

"I'll certainly keep that little hint in mind." She turned to Jake. "I was just about to see if your stepmother and Mrs. Sheffield's husband wanted a cocktail before dinner. I was wondering if perhaps you'd like one?"

Jake struggled to keep from grinning. "Mrs. Sheffield's husband." She wasn't above providing him with that little reminder. Apparently, Cora Shelly wasn't just moral—she was feisty. "No, we're fine. But thanks for thinking of us. As I said, Vivian was just on her way upstairs to finish dressing."

The wry look she shot him told him that she thought he was doing less than "fine" but that she had expected nothing less of a man of his caliber. No doubt he'd slipped more than a few notches in her book. Ah well, perhaps it was best that she realized early what his true colors were.

She turned to go, but he stopped her. "Were you able to dig up those documents I requested earlier?"

Her small shoulders stiffened beneath the starch of her chef's shirt, and she didn't answer for a moment. One hand slipped into her pocket as if to check something.

"No, I'm sorry, I've been busy acclimating myself to the new kitchen. I haven't had time to get them."

"Perhaps I should accompany you back out into the kitchen while you look for them."

Her expression tightened with concern. "That won't be necessary. I'll have them to you by morning."

"I'll be waiting with great anticipation."

She opened her mouth to say something else but then closed it, as if she'd reconsidered. As she turned to go, she almost tripped over Caesar. She shot him a scowl. "I'd appreciate it if you'd see that your dog didn't get under my feet every minute."

Jake snapped his fingers and whistled softly through his teeth. Caesar glanced in his direction briefly and then away again. His alert brown eyes focused intently on Cora.

Strange. The beast never disobeyed.

Sighing in exasperation, Cora stepped around the dog and headed back down the hall. Caesar shot Jake a quick look of apology and then trotted out after Cora.

As the door shut on her slight frame, Jake fought against an unfamiliar feeling of regret, as though he'd lost an opportunity of some kind.

THE REST OF THE EVENING passed relatively uneventfully for Cora. She made a conscious effort to stay out of Jake Mackenzie's way, and she avoided any direct confrontations with Amanda.

Despite Caesar being constantly underfoot, Cora managed to pull off dinner without a hitch. Her food selections seemed to go over well; at least, no one complained. Dr. Sheffield went back for seconds and thirds, and he even managed to mumble a compliment around a mouthful of succulent peach tort.

By midnight Cora was exhausted. Once the last dish was put away, the counters cleaned off and the coffeepot filled for the morning, she climbed the back stairs to her room. Unfortunately, Caesar climbed them right along with her.

She tried slipping into her room by only opening the door a crack, but the persistent beast immediately tried to nudge her aside. Cora blocked him and shut the door in his face. She heard his big body hit the floor outside the door with a thud. Apparently, he wasn't about to leave even if he wasn't welcome inside.

With barely enough energy to wash her face and slip into her nightgown, Cora struggled to keep her eyes open. But as soon as she lay down in bed, she was wide awake. Her gaze fell on the sleeping pills sitting on top of her dresser. For a brief moment, she considered taking one as a means of avoiding the nightmares that visited her during sleep.

But she turned away. She didn't need them. She was tired enough to do this on her own. She snuggled deeper beneath the down comforter, but as her eyes started to close, there was a light knock on the door.

"Who is it?" she called.

"It's Alice Benson, dear."

Sighing, Cora climbed out of bed and padded across the floor. When she reached the door, she glanced over her shoulder to check and see if her knife was hidden safely beneath her pillow. She didn't need to scare Mrs. Benson with the knowledge that the new cook slept with a knife under her pillow.

She unlocked the door.

The kindly housekeeper stood in the hall with a cup and saucer balanced in the center of a delicately etched silver tray. "Mrs. Mackenzie thought you might like a soothing cup of herbal tea to help you sleep. She wanted to be sure you had a restful sleep after last night's scare. She thought this might help."

"How thoughtful," Cora said, opening the door wider. "Please come in."

"No, that's all right. I'm sure you're tired and I'm feeling a bit worn-out, too. Cleaning a room from top to bottom according to Mrs. Mackenzie's standards isn't easy at my age." She handed Cora the tray. "Enjoy the tea. I'll see you in the morning."

Cora accepted the tray and watched as the stout housekeeper wearily headed back down the hall toward the back stairs.

Wisps of steam from the cup curled up to tickle the ends of Cora's nose, the smell enticingly mellow. Perhaps a few sips wouldn't hurt. She closed the door and almost stumbled over Caesar. "How'd you get in here?"

He grunted and moved over to lie down next to her bed. She considered trying to shove him out the door, but then she realized how ridiculous that idea was. The mutt probably outweighed her.

Instead, she climbed over him into bed. Maybe having the slobbering beast in the room wasn't such a bad idea. He might warn her if anyone tried to get into her room.

Settling back against the pillow, she took a few sips of the tea. Sweet and thick it slid down the back of her throat with ease. She could taste the honey.

A few more sips and she could barely keep her eyes open. Her eyelids drooped, and her brain reeled.

She reached out to put the cup back on the tray, and her fingers couldn't hold it. The delicate cup fell from her nerveless fingers, crashing onto the hardwood floor. She tried to sit up, but she couldn't lift her head off the pillow.

What was wrong?

Darkness set in, rolling over her like a relentless cloud, obscuring her vision and pulling her under. She slipped into a heavy sleep.

Chapter Six

Jake entered the back door to the kitchen and slid off his jacket, reaching up to hang it on one of the pegs next to the door. Water rolled off the slick outer skin of the coat and pooled at his feet. Cleo added to the puddle with a quick shake of her sleek, muscular body.

"Wonder where Caesar is?" Jake said as he ran a hand through his hair, pushing the damp strands back away from his face. "Not like him to miss one of our late-night walks."

Cleo grunted and stalked off, her nose in the air. She clearly wasn't happy with Caesar's recent desertion, either.

Moving over to the counter, Jake poured himself a cup of black coffee and eyed the sinfully rich brownies sitting enticingly on a platter next to the coffee. Unable to resist, he unwrapped one corner of the plastic and carefully slid one off the edge of the plate.

Cora was treating them all entirely too well. If he didn't watch out, he was going to have to double up on his exercise routine to account for the increased calories.

Bending down, he threw another log on the fire and then poked the coals a bit to get things crackling again. He set his dish and mug on the table and settled into a chair.

The kitchen was his favorite room in the house. In any

house, for that matter. It didn't matter where he was or whose house he was in, for as long as he could remember, he always sought out the kitchen.

Perhaps it was the warmth or the variety of smells. Or maybe the sounds of pots and pans banging about were part of the attraction. All he knew was that he didn't enjoy anything better than sitting around a large table, laughing and exchanging lighthearted barbs with friends while he ate. But then, sometimes, he simply liked being there alone, sipping coffee and staring into the fire.

He knew on some level that it brought back memories of his childhood and his mother. Images of him sitting on a grown-up's chair, his short, toddler legs swinging back and forth as he watched her prepare supper.

His mother never believed in hiring people to do the cooking, in spite of his dad always having the money to make that a reality. Sara Mackenzie didn't believe in hiring someone to cook for her men.

Jake smiled sadly. She always called them "her men," as if he'd been a giant of a man rather than a tiny child who toddled around the tiled kitchen, sucking his thumb. He had adored her, worshipped her every word, and he'd known without question that she adored him right back.

Maybe if she hadn't died when he was so young, he would have been able to reconcile that adoration with the reality that everyone was human. But she'd died when he was seven, confusing him. Abandoning him when he needed her most.

It wouldn't have been so bad if he'd understood what was going on. But Sara had been convinced that he didn't need to see her ravaged by her illness. She simply disappeared, never to return.

He took a healthy bite of the brownie and chewed. Her

death had broken his father's heart, and it wasn't until he was in his sixties, and after his heart attack, that he'd actually stopped being consumed with work and started to date again. A short time later he'd married Amanda.

Jake sat back. Maybe his mother's abandonment set the stage for his troubles with Natalie. He never really understood why he'd married Natalie. She had never valued any of the things he'd held close to his heart. She hated cooking and refused to even contemplate learning. *Why should I waste my time learning to cook, Jake? You're rich enough to hire someone to take care of boring stuff like that.*

When they had stayed in the city at their apartment in Manhattan, Natalie had refused to even consider eating in for any meal. It didn't matter if he hired someone to do the cooking or not. To her, wealth meant eating in the best restaurants and drinking the finest wines. It meant being seen at the most fashionable restaurants and consistently finding her name featured prominently in the society columns.

There were times when Jake would have preferred a simple cheese sandwich and a glass of cold milk, eaten in front of the television while watching some inane, forgettable comedy show. But Natalie would have none of that.

When he finally put his foot down and simply refused to go out, Natalie had shrugged and gone out on her own, returning late at night with several friends in tow to party into the wee hours of the morning.

He took another bite out of the brownie, washing it down with a sip of hot coffee. When he finally insisted they return to Midnight Castle, she had bucked him all the way, hating the isolation, calling it her prison.

And then she'd found someone else, someone right under his nose, and walked out on him.

FROM SOMEWHERE FAR AWAY, Cora heard her mother calling, *Time to get up, Cora. Time to get ready for school. Hurry, pumpkin, or you'll be late.* Her mother's voice was a soft singsongy rush of familiar words. Sweet sounds, childhood sounds.

Cora snuggled deeper beneath the weight of her blankets and pulled her knees closer to her tummy. Maybe she could get away with a few more minutes of sleep. She felt a little lightheaded. Fuzzy. A little sick to her stomach. Maybe she was sick and her mother would let her stay home from school today.

From the direction of the bathroom, she could hear the water drum loudly against the tub. Mommy was running her bath for her. She smiled sleepily and pulled the covers tighter around her body. A few more precious moments, perhaps.

But then she decided she'd better not stall any longer, and she got up, wandering across the floor to the bathroom half-asleep. She stumbled slightly, feeling her way in the darkness. Why hadn't Mom turned on the light? She tried to focus, but her brain seemed turned inside out. Confused. She swayed a little but caught herself before she fell.

Twice she stubbed her toe, pain zinging up the length of her foot. She whimpered and rubbed her eyes. God, she felt funny. Woozy. Disconnected.

She fumbled for the bathroom switch. Not there. Confused, she ran her hand along the wall until she found it. Strange. It was on the wrong side of the door.

She flicked it up and down.

Nothing.

She stumbled in the direction of the sink and the other switch, but instead, her knee hit the side of the tub. How did the tub come to be in the wrong place?

Water poured out of the faucet, splashing and spraying over the sides. It was going to overflow. Where was Mommy? What time was it?

Dazed and disorientated, she groped for the tub facet, and as she bent over, a hand hit her between her shoulder blades, sending her tumbling over the side of the tub.

She tried to catch herself, but she was off balance. The hand hit her again. Hard. Her legs hit the rim of the tub as she went over and water splashed up. She groped for something to hold on to and her palm smacked the wall on the opposite side of the tub. But she slipped and went in. The water was cold. Bone-chilling cold. It rushed to suck her in, pulling her under.

She thrashed and struggled, but a hand pushed her beneath the surface. She gasped for air and water rushed into her mouth, choking her, the cold seemed to sear her lungs with frost.

The water churned, and she struggled to lift her head. But the hand between her shoulder blades pushed harder, holding her down. Her knees and elbows thudded wildly against the sides of the tub, sending stinging jolts of pain racing through her body.

She twisted onto her back and shoved with her feet, slipping away from the hand that tried to hold her down. Her head popped above the surface and she gulped in a mouthful of air. She coughed and sputtered. She shoved her hair out of her face, but her wet nightgown held her down. She grabbed the edge of the tub and pulled herself up.

Frantically she searched the darkness. Where was she? Who was in here with her? Her head ached and her vision was blurred. Water dripped off her head into her eyes.

The tiny bathroom was pitch-dark, the door closed. On the

other side, the dog howled and threw himself against the door, his body hitting the wood with one crash after another.

"Did the water wake you up, little Cora?" a voice whispered in her ear.

Her heart leaped to the back of her throat, and she whirled around, water splashing over the sides of the tub.

Erik! He was here somewhere!

She opened her mouth and screamed. And as she screamed, Cora thought she'd never be able to stop.

THE SCREAM and Caesar's frantic howls shot down the back stairwell. Jake jumped to his feet, his chair toppling over and hitting the floor with a crash.

What the hell? He ran for the stairs, taking them two at a time. He reached Cora's door in under ten seconds. He tried it. Locked.

The screams—Cora's terrifying screams—reached a crescendo, a long high-pitched wail that trailed off and abruptly stopped.

Jake smashed a shoulder into the door, crashing it open. He stumbled into the room.

Caesar was on the other side of the room, throwing his huge body against the bathroom door. His jaws dripped saliva, and his front paws scratched and clawed frantically at the wood. He was in an absolute frenzy.

Striding across the room, Jake shoved the dog out of the way and yanked open the door. The bathroom was dark but the light from the bedroom filtered in. Water poured over the sides of the tub and onto the tiles.

Cora lay huddled in one corner of the tub, submerged up to her small chin in water. Her screams had subsided to choked whimpers. Her nightgown was plastered to her skin. Her hair clung to her face, hanging limply in her eyes.

He bent down, shut off the taps and then pulled the plug. Grabbing a towel off one of the racks, he reached for her, but when his hand touched one frail shoulder, she screamed and jerked away, huddling closer against the opposite side of the tub.

"Don't hurt me," she begged. "Please don't hurt me."

"It's me, Cora—Jake. It's okay. No one is going to hurt you." He leaned over the side and quickly scooped her out of the water. Damn, the water was cold.

Her cries softened as he held her to him, and one of her small hands reached up, tightly clinging to his neck. Her shoulders shook as she sobbed, and water streamed off her body, soaking his. She was shivering so hard he thought her bones might break into a thousand pieces.

"What in heaven's name is going on, Jake?"

Jake turned to see almost the entire household assembled outside the bathroom door—Amanda, Dr. Sheffield, Nurse Crane, Mrs. Benson and an infinitely amused Vivian. All five were in bathrobes, their hair slightly tousled from sleep. Amanda's expression of horror spoke volumes on what she thought might be going on in the new cook's bedroom.

Jake brushed past them and carried Cora to her bed. She was shaking at this point, her entire body trembling. She hadn't lifted her head from its place against his shoulder.

"I heard Cora screaming and came to see what was happening. I found her huddled in the tub, the water running over the side."

"She got into the bath with her clothes on?" Amanda asked, her tone sharp.

Jake lifted his hand and made an abrupt slashing motion, trying to tell his stepmother to hold her tongue for a minute. She shot him a miffed look through tightly clenched lips, but she didn't say anything.

"What happened, Cora?" Jake asked gently.

She raised tragic, soft brown eyes to meet his, and he could see a terrible fear cramping every inch of her delicate features. He could almost feel the terror rolling off her in huge crashing waves.

"The door locked on me and I couldn't get it to open. The lights wouldn't work," she sobbed.

Her voice was breathless and strained, and Jake could tell she was struggling to regain some semblance of composure. But she was failing miserably. Sobs tore at her body.

He started to lay her down on the bed, but she continued to cling to him, letting him know without speaking that she didn't want him to let go. So instead, he sat on the edge of the bed and pulled the comforter over the two of them, trying to warm her body and stop the terrible trembling racking her small frame.

Amanda reached behind her and flicked the bathroom switch. Light flooded the tiny bathroom, illuminating the water running across the tiles and soaking the thick bath mat. "I guess the light is working fine now," she said dryly, only able to stay silent for a brief moment.

"It...it wasn't working a f-few minutes ago," Cora said. "I heard the water running and went in to check. Someone slammed the door closed and p-pushed me into the tub. H-he held me down. I thought I was drowning."

"You think someone was in your room and pushed you into the tub?" As much as he wanted to believe her, even Jake had a hard time keeping the disbelief out of his voice. "Are you sure you didn't just trip and fall into the tub?"

"I...I know someone was in there. There had to be someone in there. I couldn't get up. He held me down." But even as she spoke, her head lolled slightly and she blinked as if she was having a hard time focusing. For the first time since entering the room, Jake noticed that her pupils were the size of a pin and she seemed to be struggling to keep her head up.

"Cora, are you all right? Are you on any medication?" Jake asked.

Dr. Sheffield moved closer and reached out to take her chin in his pudgy hand. He turned her to face him, studying her pupils. "What did you take, girl? Sleeping pills? Did you take sleeping pills?"

"N-nothing. I didn't take anything," Cora protested.

Jake glanced at the doctor, and the man shook his head. "She's on something," he said.

Vivian snorted in disgust. "You mean she's stoned? Good grief, you mean the bimbo cook can't keep her sleeping pill dosage right. Wonderful. All right, I've had enough for one night. I'm out of here." She stormed out of the room.

"I…I'm not stoned," Cora protested weakly.

"Daniel, do you mind staying a moment and seeing that she gets safely back to bed? I don't have time for this kind of nonsense," Amanda said, following Vivian out of the room. The nurse shot a disgusted look in Cora's direction and took her leave, too.

Cora lifted her head again, her eyes seeking out his. "I swear to you, I didn't take anything."

"But you've admitted to all of us that you've had trouble sleeping, Cora," Dr. Sheffield said. He wandered over to her dresser and lifted up a pill bottle sitting on top next to a container of lotion. "This prescription has your name on it, Cora. Did you take some of this?" In answer to Jake's inquiring look, he added, "It's a strong sleeping pill."

Cora stiffened in Jake's arms and her eyes flashed anger.

"I told you, I didn't take anything. Someone pushed me! Why won't any of you believe me?"

But even as she gathered her strength to argue, fatigue or the effects of medication seemed to hit her and her head fell back against him. She felt boneless in his arms, weak and defenseless. His heart went out to her. No one needed to be grilled like this when they were this confused. This frightened.

"Perhaps you were sleepwalking," Sheffield pressed.

"I wasn't sleepwalking." She paused and then tried again. "But I was dreaming right before I got out of bed. I…I heard the water running and I dreamed I was back in school—that my mother was getting my bath ready for me."

Jake smiled down at her and gently brushed back several strands of damp hair off her forehead. Her skin was chilled. "So it was a pleasant dream. One with your mom in it."

She nodded, her dark lashes brushing the curve of her cheek. He watched the anger and stubbornness drain from her face. She was left looking slightly bewildered, as if now even she wasn't quite sure what had happened.

But it was the terrible vulnerability haunting her delicate features that made Jake want to pull her closer. Made him want to comfort and protect her from whatever it was that made her question herself.

"I know I was awake when I got up to go to the bathroom," she reiterated. "And I *know* someone was in the bathroom with me. I felt him push me and then hold my head under the water."

"But no one was in there when I opened the door, Cora," Jake said. "You were huddled in the tub all alone. No one tried to get past me. And if the person had left already, Caesar was right outside the door. He would have torn anyone apart who tried to leave."

Her eyes dropped away from his, despair coloring their depths, and she pressed her face against his chest. "B-but I felt someone touch me. I heard him speak to me."

Her voice was soft and weak against the cloth of his shirt, but he could feel the whisper-soft movements of her lips on his skin beneath.

"What did he say to you, Cora?" Sheffield asked, his tone indicating that he was only humoring her.

She didn't answer. She simply shook her head and wouldn't look at him.

Jake shot a hard look at Sheffield and jerked his chin in the direction of the door. He wanted the quack out of her room. He was only making things worse.

The doctor shrugged. "You're not going to get any coherent answers from her tonight. She's still under the influence of the drug." He pointed to the small knot on Cora's forehead. "She must have hit her head on the side of the tub. No doubt scrambled her brains a bit. Nothing major. Just a little bump."

He tightened the belt of his robe and headed for the door. "I'll check in on her in the morning. She just needs to sleep off the effects of the drug. Good night, all."

He brushed past Mrs. Benson.

"So much for the good doctor's bedside manner," Jake said dryly.

"I don't care if he leaves," Cora said softly. "I don't want him touching me. He gives me the creeps."

Jake smiled at her. "Me, too." He looked at Mrs. Benson. "Would you mind helping Cora get into some dry clothes. I'm afraid the bed will have to be changed, too."

"I'll take care of it, Mr. Mackenzie." The housekeeper moved closer, reaching out to help Cora stand. But Cora shrank from the woman's grasp, tightening her hold on him, her fingers digging into the flesh of his shoulder.

"Please don't go yet."

He stood up and gently set her on her feet, his hand sweeping back several strands of damp hair off her forehead and smiled. "I'm not going anywhere, but as delightful as I might find it to be the one to help you change your clothes, I'm not sure that's entirely appropriate. Once you're changed, I'll come back in and stay with you for a bit. At least until you're settled."

She nodded and the motion almost sent her over backward. Jake reached out and held her, his fingers cupping her elbow. Her eyes met his and he felt her gratitude and relief wash over him like a wave of clear water.

In that single second, their connection deepened, and Jake knew he had stepped over a small line. He was no longer simply her employer. He had stepped into the realm of something more, and a small part of him worried that he'd only succeeded in making things even more complicated than before.

RELUCTANTLY Cora moved away from Jake, struggling to understand this sudden change in feeling toward him, this sudden need for her to have him stay close by. It had to be the shock. Or it could be the bump on the head. But whatever the reason, she didn't care.

But whatever the explanation, she wanted him close by and that frightened her. A little voice inside her head was screaming at her to slow down. To proceed with caution. Had she forgotten that Jake's own sister had accused him of murdering his wife? And hadn't she witnessed him trying to seduce the wife of one of his own guests?

But even these thoughts did nothing to dispel the intense

feeling that she was safer with him close by. Despite her ve-
hement protests, perhaps Dr. Sheffield was right. Maybe she
had ingested the pills and just didn't remember doing so. It
would go a long way in explaining her impaired judgment.

Cora rubbed a spot directly between her eyes. She couldn't
think straight. She shook her head trying to clear the cobwebs.
But it didn't help.

Jake went to stand in the doorway, his back to the room.
She knew it was his way of giving her a bit of privacy but also
honoring her request that he stay close by.

She stared at his muscular back and the broad, capable
shoulders. A big man. Strong and powerful. Someone who
wasn't afraid of anything, not even things that bump in the
night. So unlike herself. She glanced down at her hands, tightening them into fists. He probably thought she was nuts—totally whacked.

Numbly she peeled off the wet nightgown and took the dry
nightgown Mrs. Benson handed her. She shivered violently
as the room air hit her skin.

As she finished changing, Mrs. Benson efficiently stripped
the bed and started to remake it with fresh linens from the
closet. She didn't speak the entire time, but from her expression, Cora could see she was deeply troubled.

"I must have been sleepwalking like they said," Cora
said softly, trying to explain her behavior. "I'm sorry I
frightened you."

Mrs. Benson snapped the top sheet to spread it over the bed
and then glanced over her shoulder at Jake. She leaned closer
to Cora and whispered, "Strange things have been happening
at Midnight Castle, dear. Don't be too quick to dismiss what
happened to you as a dream."

"What other choice do I have?" Cora asked, stepping to the

other side of the bed to help tuck in the bottom sheet. "There's no other explanation. The door was locked and Caesar was out here. No one got past Jake when he broke through the door."

"Perhaps it was our visitor, The Mournful Lady, again."

Cora pulled the two new blankets over the top of the sheet and smoothed out the folds. "As much as I'd like to believe that a ghost was responsible, I can't buy that, Mrs. Benson."

"Well, I'm glad to hear that someone other than me has finally stepped forward to say they aren't buying this ghost story nonsense," Jake said, stepping back into the room. "You probably tripped in the dark and fell. That would explain the bump on your head and your confusion."

She reached up and cautiously explored the outer edge of the bruise. Was that really what happened? "But I don't understand how the water got in the tub. I was already in bed. I wasn't bathing or even planning to take a bath."

"Maybe you forgot to turn the water off when you went to bed. You fell asleep and started to dream. Sometimes the real world pushes its way into our dreams." His met her gaze, his eyes revealing a gentleness that seemed oddly touching, as if even he wasn't used to this kind of territory, this degree of tenderness. "It's possible that you heard the water running, started dreaming about your mom and then got things mixed up when you stumbled into the bathroom half-asleep."

Cora frowned. Was what he was suggesting possible? Her stubborn pride didn't want to buy it, but the rational side of her warned her that it was a probable explanation.

Hadn't she been thinking about Erik all day? Worrying about him and the fact that he'd escaped? Perhaps her brain, in its exhausted half-asleep condition, had used her own fears

to frighten her. Dreams were supposed to be a person's re-
lease, weren't they?

She nodded slowly. "Perhaps you're right. I'm really sorry
I ended up waking the entire household."

"No need to apologize, dear," Mrs. Benson reassured her.
She squeezed Cora's arm and then headed for the door. "I'll
say good-night now. Sleep well."

Suddenly she was alone in the room with Jake. He stood
just inches from her. She could smell the clean, tangy scent
of his aftershave and feel the heat that seemed to radiate off
his big frame. She still felt cold and the thought of snuggling
up against that warmth and strength flitted across her con-
sciousness. She quickly dismissed it.

He watched her silently, his expression closed, a total
enigma. He had rolled up the sleeves of his shirt, the dark hair
on his tanned forearms visible in the soft glow of the lamp.
The portion of his shirt covering his chest, the spot where
she'd pressed her head not too long ago, was still damp. The
pristine white cloth clung to him like a second skin, outlin-
ing the hard muscles of his upper chest and the dark circles
of his nipples.

Her gaze went lower. Heat fanned her face. His face might
be expressionless. Emotionless. But he wasn't able to hide his
blatant arousal.

She was suddenly very conscious of the fact that the nightgown Mrs. Benson had grabbed out of her dresser was her
sheer white one. Her own excitement was evident in the tightness of her own breasts. She folded her arms and shifted her
bare feet restlessly on the rug.

"Would you like me to leave?" he asked.

"Perhaps that would be best." But as soon as the words
were out of her mouth, her brain screamed at her, telling her

that she was a fool and a liar. She didn't want him to leave. She wanted him to stay right here with her.

He nodded, his eyes never leaving her face, the intensity of his gaze searing her and telling her he knew of her attempt to hide how she truly felt about him.

He waited, as if giving her a chance to reconsider, to re-think what she already said. But Cora couldn't. Despite what her heart told her—the tiny voice that whispered Jake Mackenzie might be just what she wanted—she knew bet-ter. He was a complication in an already complicated situ-ation. He was a mistake she couldn't make at this point in her life.

Finally, as if sensing the finality of her decision, he turned to go, and Cora fought a sudden and overwhelming feeling of panic. Unable to stop herself, she reached out, her fingers curling around his forearm, touching the strength and power that seemed to pulse directly beneath the warmth of his skin. It was the barest, briefest of touches, but he paused, one dark eyebrow raised as he waited for her to speak.

She pulled her hand back, but lifted her gaze to meet his. "I want you to know how much I appreciate your coming to my rescue. You have no idea how scared I was. How fright-ened I was by everything."

"I'm glad I heard you call out."

His tone was deep…and so rich that it seemed to wash over her in velvety waves, cocooning her in its seductive warmth. She felt dizzy, slightly disorientated. What was wrong? Was it the aftereffect of the pills she didn't recall taking—or some-thing else?

And then, as if sensing her indecision, her total vulnera-bility and openness, Jake bent his head and lightly brushed his lips across hers. It was a caress so soft and sweet that for the briefest of moments, Cora wondered if perhaps she had only imagined that he had actually kissed her.

But then, before she could step back and gather her wits about her, he slid a hand around her waist and pulled her roughly to him, pressing her to his rock-hard body with a fierceness that was frightening but strangely welcome at the same time.

A bolt of fire swept through her blood with the speed of a wave hitting the rocks of the island, and when she tried to speak, to tell him to stop, to give her a moment to get her head straight, she found she couldn't. She found that she didn't want to.

Her mouth went dry, and the words clamoring in her head to get out seemed to disappear. And when she tried to speak, no words came out. Instead a soft moan escaped, startling her with its blatant display of need.

"You've wanted this," he said, his lips going to her neck and leaving a trail of hot kisses from the lobe of her ear to the hollow of her throat. "You've wanted it as much as I have."

His hand, large, capable, commanding, slid up over her ribs, his fingers seeming to count each indentation as they sent thrills of delight racing through her.

When he touched the underside of her breast, Cora thought her heart might surely pound through the wall of her chest. But she leaned back anyway, allowing his hand to reach up to cup her breast, his thumb gently rubbing the taut bud of her nipple. She thought for a moment that if he wasn't holding her up, she might surely melt into a puddle of liquid need at his feet.

She didn't deny she wanted him. But she didn't agree, either. She just allowed him to do what he wanted to her mouth and her body, taking what he wanted as she poured out her need through tiny moans of pleasure.

But deep down, Cora knew her refusal to answer was a technicality. She knew that the way she wrapped her arm around his neck and pulled him closer, the way she threaded her fingers into and through his thick dark hair, and the way she opened her mouth and gave him access to her warmth, told him all he needed to know. She desired him, she wanted him as much as, maybe even more than, he desired her.

Her head spun and she felt dizzier and more disconnected than she had earlier. They stumbled backward until she found herself pressed tight against the wall, his large, powerful body seeming to overwhelm her. He pushed closer, lifting her onto her toes, her feet barely touching the floor, and then he picked her up and moved sideways toward the bed, his lips never leaving hers.

She knew what was happening, and an urgent little voice in her head demanded she stop. Demanded that she stop him. But she couldn't. Wouldn't. She was in a fever, responding to a need so powerful, so great that she couldn't have stopped him if she wanted to. Her brush with death made her want this. Made her seek out his heat and power.

Her fingers tore at the buttons of his shirt, burrowing beneath the expensive cloth to touch and explore the finely drawn lines of his chest muscles. And as he lowered his head, gently kissing and caressing her breasts with a clever tongue, she explored lower, her fingers brushing across the steel ridge of his flat stomach to the hardness of his desire. She reached up to work the buckle of his belt as they fell backward together onto the bed, and he rose up over her, his length and bulk almost too overpowering, but she welcomed him, wanted him.

Suddenly Caesar growled, a long, ugly, threatening sound from deep within his barrel chest. And then he started barking, the sound urgent. Belligerent. Demanding.

Cora froze, her fingers tangled in Jake's belt. With a muffled curse, Jake rolled off her and they both turned toward the dog.

Caesar stood in the middle of her room, his legs splayed wide in a fighting stance, his hackles standing on end. He stared in the direction of the bathroom, an ugly growl rolling out from between his giant jaws.

Jake sat up. "What's the matter, old boy?"

Cora scrambled to a sitting position, her hand sliding beneath her pillow to grab the knife. As her fingers curled around the handle, she pressed her body up against the headboard of her bed. "What's he growling at?" she asked, her voice shaky.

Jake glanced over his shoulder at her, and his concern was immediately evident. "Jeez, Cora, a knife? For pity's sake, relax. He's growling at a mouse or something. The damn things get in the walls all the time."

Cora shook her head and backed up into the corner of the bed, her knife in front of her. "Someone's in there, Jake. I told you someone was in there. Caesar knows. He hears him."

"No one is in there." Jake held out a hand. "Come on, I'll show you." She shook her head, refusing to accept his hand. He sighed. "Okay, I'll go check myself."

He got up and walked into the bathroom, flicking on the light switch. He turned around and smiled at her, spreading his hands. "See, nothing. No one is in here. No boogie men hiding." He bent down and grabbed a few of the drenched towels off the floor that Mrs. Benson had put down to absorb the water and threw them into the tub. They hit the sides with a wet splat.

Cora stayed pressed up against the far wall of the bed, watching. Her heart was beating frantically. In the center of the room, Caesar turned away from the bathroom and looked in her direction. He glared, his hair seeming to rise straight up off his back. His growl built and his jaw dripped saliva. Hatred gleamed in his dark eyes.

Next to her head, Cora heard a soft rustling sound directly behind the wall. She jumped toward the middle of the bed.

"Oh God, someone's behind the wall!" Her feet tangled in the comforter as she scrambled to get off the bed. She almost fell off the side as she shook off the covers and then jumped off the bed. Jake came out of the bathroom and caught her in his arms as she raced for the door.

"Where the hell are you going?" he demanded.

She pointed toward the bed. "Someone's behind the wall. I heard them. Caesar heard them." She turned toward Caesar, but the damn beast was now sitting in the middle of the floor, looking at her like she'd lost her mind. "He was growling a minute ago. He heard something. He…he was staring at the wall, and right then I heard something behind the wall—a…a soft rustling sound."

Jake raised an eyebrow, and even she knew what she was saying sounded ridiculously paranoid. "I heard something," she insisted.

"You heard mice. Like I said, the damn things crawl around in the walls all the time. It's the problem with stone—the little thieves can get in between the cracks and get into the walls. Haven't you seen the mice traps in the pantry?"

Cora nodded, but she knew in her heart of hearts that it hadn't been a mouse scurrying behind the wall. Someone or something had passed directly behind the wall near her head.

And something told her that that very person had been in the bathroom a few minutes ago, watching Jake kiss her and touch her intimately on the bed.

A cold, terrifying chill crept up the center of her spine and settled deep in the marrow of her bones. She wasn't crazy. She wasn't wrong about this…was she?

Chapter Seven

After Jake had calmed her down, Cora had refused to sleep in the room. Jake hadn't argued. He had simply grabbed a few of her things out of the closet and taken her to his room. He'd turned on every light in the room, pulled back the covers of his bed and opened the door between his room and the bedroom next door.

He'd told her he'd sleep in the adjoining bedroom, and Cora had agreed only when he promised to keep the door between the two rooms open. Part of her had simply wanted him to crawl into bed with her, but she didn't dare ask.

Instead she settled for Caesar lying down next to the bed. Cora didn't complain. In fact, after tonight, the mutt was welcome to sleep in the bed right next to her if he wanted. Especially since his master didn't seem interested.

She had climbed wearily into Jake's bed, and as he tucked the blankets around her, Cora had found herself wrapped up in warmth and the reassuring scent of Jake. It clung to everything, the sheets, the pillowcase, the blankets. It was as good as having him lying next to her, holding her in his arms. Almost, but not quite.

He'd said good-night and disappeared into the next room. No kiss, no show of affection. It was as if their earlier encounter had never even happened. But Cora didn't blame him. What man wanted to get involved with a neurotic? A crazy woman who screamed that people were crawling around in the walls of his house.

Whatever they had shared earlier had been replaced by the cold reality of her fears. As she closed her eyes trying to sleep, a certain sadness settled over her. She had ruined the one chance she might have had to be happy. And safe.

The next morning, Cora awoke sore. Every bone, joint and muscle seemed to ache with a special twinge. It was a solid reminder of last night. Caesar waited at the end of the bed for her, but a quick check of the adjoining room told her that Jake was already up and about. Just as well. Meeting in the cold brightness of the morning would have been awkward. It was best that she dress and get to work. She would ask Amanda for a new room this morning and be out of Jake's hair.

But as the morning unfolded, Cora realized that facing Jake was only half the battle. Dealing with the other residents of Midnight Castle turned out to be just as disconcerting.

It was as if every glance in her direction held the hint of a question or a tinge of smugness. The kind of smugness people got when they knew something about you that was personal and not particularly attractive.

Not that anyone actually said anything. Instead they seemed content to shoot covert little glances in her direction, as if expecting her to burst into some kind of crazed laughter or shrieks of madness.

At least no one said anything until Vivian joined the group for breakfast. She went immediately to the sideboard and grabbed a piece of whole-wheat toast, her head turning in Cora's direction. A tiny smile played at the corner of her perfectly colored lips.

"Well, you seemed to have recovered admirably," she said, applying a pat of low-cal margarine to her toast. Her knife stayed poised over her toast as she asked, "No hangover? No ill effects?"

"I'm fine. But thank you for asking," Cora said stiffly.

Vivian laughed and deposited her toast on a plate. "Lighten up, Cora. Everyone has a bad trip once in a while."

"Leave the woman alone, Vivian," Jake ordered. "She's already told us that she didn't take anything. We don't need to beat this thing until it's dead."

Cora glanced in Jake's direction, a part of her wanting to thank him for coming to her defense. But when her eyes met his, she felt her face redden and she looked away again.

Had she really allowed him to kiss her and touch her so intimately last night? Had she really explored that big, powerful body so brazenly with her own hands? Her cheeks blazed with color. Yes indeed, she had. In fact, she'd encouraged him and enjoyed every minute of it.

As soon as he'd entered the dining room earlier, she had felt the potency of his gaze hit her. An inquiring glance told her he was trying to determine whether or not she regretted her brief moment of sexual surrender. As if he wasn't sure how he felt about it, either. Although, she had a feeling he probably regretted it on some level. How many millionaires wanted to roll around in the hay with their crazy, unbalanced cook?

Grabbing a pot holder, she moved the plate of bacon closer to the eggs. She knew she was fussing needlessly, but she couldn't stop. As much as she knew she shouldn't have encouraged Jake, she had to admit to herself she'd enjoyed— no, reveled in—the erotic taste of him.

Even now she could feel his lips on hers, the quick dart of his clever tongue as it slid between her lips and plunged deep into her mouth. Whether she liked it or not, Jake Mackenzie had made a lasting impression on her, one that she wasn't about to forget anytime soon.

Cora sucked in a shaky breath, surprised at how just thinking about the man and what his mouth did to her reduced her insides to mush.

At the table, Vivian seemed mildly amused by Jake's rebuke. She grinned and sashayed over to slide into the chair next to him. She patted his upper arm. "Relax, tiger. I'm just having a bit of fun."

"Well, save it," Jake said curtly. "None of us is in the mood."

"Are you sure you're up to working this morning, Cora?" Amanda broke in smoothly. "That's a nasty bruise on your forehead and you're looking awfully pale. If you need to take the day off, please, speak up. I'm sure Mrs. Benson could handle your kitchen duties for today."

Cora shook her head. "I'm fine, ma'am. No need for Mrs. Benson to do my work."

Amanda looked her up and down with an assessing glance. "All right, if you're sure you're all right. But please, let me know immediately if you're not feeling well. The last thing we need is to have you suffer a nervous breakdown your first week on the job."

Cora stiffened. *Nervous breakdown?* Did Amanda and everyone else on the island actually believe that she might be that unstable? For pity sakes, she'd had one lousy nightmare. At least that's what she hoped it was. It wasn't if she'd run naked through the castle screaming that an ax murderer was after her.

Okay, maybe she'd gone a little off the deep end later when Jake was in the room—her comment about the person being behind the wall—but none of them knew anything about that. Did they? She turned and studied Jake. He gazed back at her, his expression blank. A knot of anxiety settled in her belly. Maybe he wasn't an ally any more than Amanda or Vivian was.

"I appreciate your concern, Mrs. Mackenzie, but I'll be just fine," she said stiffly.

"Well, in any case, I'd feel better if Dr. Sheffield took a look at you just to make sure. Perhaps a little chat with him will help reassure me that everything is okay." Amanda glanced at the portly doctor as he shoveled another forkful of the broccoli-and-cheese quiche into his mouth. "You'll do that for me, won't you, Daniel?"

Sheffield dabbed at his thick lips with the edge of his napkin. "Of course, Amanda. After breakfast Cora and I will chat for a bit."

Cora gritted her teeth. Over her dead body she'd converse with the portly toad. "I'm fi—"

"Let him check you out, Cora. He's a doctor," Jake interrupted. He turned toward Sheffield. "You *are* a real doctor, aren't you, Sheffield?"

Anger flashed across Sheffield's pudgy face, but he quickly erased it. "You seem to have a great need to insult me, Jake. Perhaps you and I should discuss these hidden feelings of resentment you seem to harbor toward me."

Jake laughed, his dark eyes lighting up with amusement. "I wasn't aware that I was hiding my disdain, Doctor. I thought I was being pretty open about it." He winked at Cora and the slightly teasing smile playing at one corner of his mouth sent a jolt of something wickedly delicious shooting through her. "Do me a favor, Cora—let Sheffield check the bump on your head. Even he can't screw that up, can he?"

She bit her lip and nodded. At this point, she'd do whatever he asked as long as they all stopped discussing last night. She wanted to put that entire fiasco out of her head as quickly as possible. Especially the memory of his lips moving over hers, sending wild, hot sensations across the surface of her skin. Sensations that threatened to send her over the edge.

And she especially didn't want to think about what would have happened if the two of them had continued to explore those delicious sensations. Better to keep her mind on work.

"That'll be fine," she said stiffly, turning away. "Excuse me, I have some bread in the oven."

She turned and left, very conscious of the fact that Jake's eyes followed her out of the dinning room. She didn't think she could stay unaffected by that penetrating gaze too much longer. She couldn't help but wonder if he, too, thought she was unstable, about to tip over the edge of sanity. The thought saddened her.

"Okay, Cora, let's have a look at that nasty bruise of yours."

Cora glanced up to see Sheffield standing in the doorway of the kitchen. He had spilled a bit of cranberry juice on his tie, and there were several generous sprinkles of powdered sugar clinging to his beard.

He didn't present an appearance she'd find confidence building if she was meeting him for the first time on a professional basis. In fact, nothing about the man appealed to her. She didn't want him near her.

"I didn't want to make a fuss in the dining room, Dr. Sheffield, but I'm really okay," she said.

He swung a smart leather medical bag up onto the table. "Of course you are," he said condescendingly. "But Amanda has asked me to take a look at that bruise and talk with you a bit to make sure you're fit to be working. And since she's your employer and my host, we'll humor her, won't we?"

"Most definitely," another voice chimed in.

Cora's gaze flicked to the doorway, not in the least surprised to see Jake standing there. She sighed inwardly. Apparently everyone was going to get in on this evaluation.

"I really am fine," she protested.

But Jake ignored her by pulling out a chair and motioning for her to sit down. Cora complied reluctantly.

Sheffield probed the bruise, shone a light in her eyes and had her touch her fingers to her nose with her eyes shut. Finally he snapped his bag shut and announced, "You're fine. A little knock on the head is all."

"I could have told you that," Cora said, shooting a told-you-so glance in Jake's direction. He merely smiled, the stretch of his lips sending a flutter of desire so intense through Cora that she had to look away again. Damn the man, he was like a walking hormone enhancer.

Sheffield settled into the chair across from her and folded his hands across his ample belly. "So, if your head is fine and you're feeling right as rain, why are you having nightmares?"

Out of the corner of her eye, Cora watched Jake lean forward, his face intent. This had been what he'd been waiting to hear. His eagerness irritated her almost as much as Sheffield's questioning.

"I had a nightmare," she said through tight lips, realizing it was futile to vocalize her suspicions about what truly happened any longer. No one believed her and *she* wasn't even sure what to believe any longer. "Everyone has nightmares once in a while. What's the big deal?"

"Not everyone wakes up the entire household with their screaming, claiming someone tried to drown them in a tub."

Cora played with the buttons on the collar of her shirt. She wasn't going to get into this again with Sheffield. She waited him out.

"Have you ever been in treatment or been hospitalized, Cora?" Sheffield asked, his voice deceivingly soft and supportive.

"What do you mean?" She knew what he meant but she wasn't about to admit that to this toad.

"Have you ever had a nervous breakdown or been to see a doctor about your nerves? Have you ever suffered from anxiety attacks?"

His gentle probing didn't fool Cora. The muscles in her shoulders tightened until her neck screamed in protest. People like him knew how to ask questions like that—their voices all warm and gushy. But then when they got the answer they wanted, they turned judgmental and harsh. They waited to tear you into pieces because of what happened to you.

She knew that because Jeffery Greene had told her what to expect when she testified in court. He'd said that the defense team would try to discredit her with the fact that she'd been hospitalized after the attack—that they would go after her mental status.

He had tried to reassure her that people on the jury would understand, sympathize with her ordeal. But Cora wasn't stupid, she knew that the further it was from the time that she was attacked, the less sympathetic people would be.

"I…I don't see why any of this is your business."

Sheffield leaned forward, his pudgy hands touching her arm. "I'm just trying to help you, Cora. You need to tell me if you've ever received psychiatric treatment for a nervous disorder."

Her skin crawled beneath the touch of his sweaty hand. She shook him off. "Please don't touch me," she said from between clenched teeth. "I'm perfectly fine. I wish everyone would stop asking me about last night. It's over with. I'm okay. Why can't people just accept that fact?"

Irritation flooded Sheffield's face. He didn't like her evasiveness. "Look, little lady, you need—"

"She doesn't *need* anything, Sheffield. But you definitely need to back off," Jake said, stepping forward to stand next to Cora, his hand dropping down to lightly touch her shoulder.

Cora fought the urge to lay her cheek against his hand. She wanted to cry, she was so relieved that he stepped in and stopped the questioning. She hated lying to him, hated not being able to tell him what had happened to her. But she couldn't talk about it in front of Sheffield. She knew without question that the psychiatrist would take what she said and turn it into something shameful.

Maybe if it was just Jake standing in front of her asking the questions, she would be able to admit the truth, tell him about the time she spent in the hospital, trying to put her life back together. But not now, not in front of Sheffield. She didn't trust the psychiatrist. Something told Cora that he'd use the information to hurt her in some way.

"Come on, Doc," Jake said. "You and I are going to go find Amanda and report your findings to her. We're going to let her know that Cora is perfectly capable of performing her duties here on Midnight Island."

"But I—" Sheffield protested.

"But nothing, Doc. Get up." Jake glanced down at Cora. "I'm sorry for agreeing to this in the first place. I should have known better. Whatever happened to you in the past is no one's business but your own. I apologize for pressuring you."

"Thank you," Cora said gratefully. "I appreciate that."

"You won't be so apologetic if she ends up hurting herself or someone here in the house," Sheffield said as he lumbered to his feet. "The woman has problems, and your stepmother simply wanted to make sure she was mentally sound."

"Oh, and you're the one who is going to determine that?" Jake asked sarcastically. "Dream on, Doc. I didn't mind you taking a look at that bruise of hers, but the psycho mumbo-jumbo has gotta go. You couldn't analyze your way out of a paper sack."

"I don't need to put up with this," Sheffield mumbled as he stalked out of the kitchen.

Jake hung back for a minute. "I hope that whatever happened to you, Cora, you're able to talk about it someday."

His dark eyes held hers for a moment, and the sincerity and compassion in them was so poignant that Cora wanted to beg him to sit down and allow her to tell him everything.

But before she could open her mouth, he left, leaving her alone with her memories. She wondered what it would be like to actually trust someone enough to tell them what she'd gone through. What she'd suffered at the hands of Erik Dubane.

Would Jake Mackenzie understand?

LATER THAT SAME EVENING Cora set a tiny vase with a handful of miniature sunflowers on a tray. She stood back and surveyed the overall effect. Nice. She grinned. More than nice. It was homey. Comforting.

She had pilfered the flowers from one of the large bouquets in one of the three formal living rooms in the front of the castle. According to Mrs. Benson, Amanda had a standing order for fresh flowers to be delivered to the castle every third day. With her demands for fresh fruit and fresh flowers, the poor groundskeeper, Gracy, was no doubt making daily trips over to the mainland.

Cora carefully straightened the edge of the woven place mat and aligned the cheerful dishes that were shaped and glazed with giant sunflowers. They had been a recent discovery, found while she was cleaning off one of the bottom shelves of the pantry.

She could tell that they had been lovingly made by hand, the edges slightly irregular and the glaze brilliant in color. Between the vase of sunflowers and the colorful dinnerware, the effect of the tray was truly festive. If Mr. Mackenzie, Sr., wasn't enticed by the tantalizing aroma of the thick Irish stew she'd prepared especially for him, perhaps he'd find some solace in the cheerfulness of how his food looked. Hopefully it would convince him to eat more than a few measly morsels.

As she picked up the tray, Caesar scrambled to his feet, all legs and clicking toenails.

"Stay," she said, trying to use the same self-assured tone Jake used when addressing the animal. But the beast ignored her and trotted gracefully to the door, glancing back over one beefy shoulder as if to tell her to hurry things up a tad.

Sighing, she followed, shouldering open the door. Caesar moved out ahead of her, leading the way to the staircase.

Cora grinned and nudged open the elevator door. She ducked inside, kicking the grate closed just as the dog's head appeared in the doorway. "Sorry, pooch, no dogs allowed."

The door slid shut on Caesar's accusing brown eyes. She used her elbow to hit the second-floor button and braced herself as the claustrophobic box chugged upward at an agonizingly slow pace.

She hated the damn thing, but it was easier to maneuver the tray inside the tight space than it was to navigate the stairs. Plus it gave her a good way to dodge Caesar. Even though she'd found his company comforting last night, he was still a nuisance.

The cubicle jerked to a halt, and she nudged open the grate with her foot. As the outer door slid open, Caesar stuck his head in. Cora jumped and the dishes rattled. So much for dodging him.

He glared at her and his jaw hung open, his white teeth gleaming in the hall light. He blocked her exit for several seconds before turning and trotting off down the hall in the direction of Mr. Mackenzie's room.

Cora followed, duly warned by the dog that she'd better not try to ditch him again. As she walked down the hall, she passed a door slightly ajar.

"I will *not* stay if these types of things continue to happen," a woman said, her sharp tone drifting out into the hall. "You've got people screaming at all hours of the night. Dogs barking like the hounds from hell. And to make matters worse, things continue to go missing from my room. I shouldn't have to live like this."

"I realize things have been a little unsettled lately, Bea," another voice said, one Cora identified as Jake's. "But things are bound to improve."

"How do you know that? Can you promise me that none of this will continue to happen?" Cora realized that the voice belonged to Mr. Mackenzie's nurse, Beatrice Crane.

"Now, Beatrice, you need to be more patient. We seem to have a new employee who is a bit unsettled. A little unstable perhaps. You need to give us some time to deal with things."

Cora cringed. The new voice belonged to Amanda, and the three of them appeared to be discussing her. She backed up a few steps and glanced into the room. Jake, the nurse and Mrs. Mackenzie stood in a tight little circle.

An expression of irritation flashed across Jake's face. "We've already discussed this issue, Amanda. No one is unstable. And I don't appreciate you bringing it up in front of one of the other employees."

He shot his stepmother a cautionary glance, and Cora smiled. He was actually defending her again.

"Oh, for heaven's sake, Jacob, everyone in the house knows the new cook is more than a bit odd. In case you've forgotten, the woman woke up the entire house last night with her screaming. I'm hardly breaking any confidences here," Amanda said caustically. "The woman is a certifiable loon. Even Dr. Sheffield thinks I made a mistake hiring her."

"Because a person has a terrible nightmare in a strange, unfamiliar place, they're certifiable? No wonder I question that quack's professional license," Jake said, his voice cold with anger.

Cora frowned. Why was Amanda so determined to paint her out to be some kind of crazed nutcase?

"Excuse me," Bea said, interrupting the two of them. "I'm really not interested in anyone else's problems. I'd simply like to know what you're planning on doing about the items missing from my room."

Jake turned away from Amanda, focusing on the nurse. "Look, just make up a list of the things missing and give me an estimate of their replacement cost. I'll see that you're fully reimbursed."

He paused and then asked, "You're positive the items are gone, not simply moved or misplaced?"

The skinny nurse's frame tightened another notch. "Are you insinuating that I don't keep track of my personal belongings, Mr. Mackenzie?"

Jake held up a hand, his expression exasperated. Cora could tell he was fighting to stay calm. "Nothing of the sort,

Bea. I'm simply suggesting that there might be another explanation. I don't want to jump to the conclusion that someone is sneaking into your room at night and stealing things."

Intrigued, Cora shifted the heavy tray and tried to get closer to the partially opened door. What was this about? She fought the twinge of guilt that grated at her for eavesdropping, but she couldn't resist. Had she not had a nightmare? Was it possible that someone really had been in her room that night? Did someone in the house suspect that there was a person sneaking in and out of the rooms?

"I was tolerant of the perfume and lotion coming up missing," Bea said. "But I will not stand by while someone sneaks into my bedroom drawers and steals my underwear." She folded her arms. "I'm totally creeped out by this. And if the culprit isn't found soon, you'll be getting my resignation. And you can forget about getting two weeks' notice. I'll just leave."

Personal items. Missing underwear. A cramp of fear tightened in the pit of Cora's stomach, and her hands started to shake. The teacup on the tray rattled softly in its saucer.

She shakily set the tray on the hall table and leaned against the wall, pressing her spine flat. Oh God, please tell me this isn't happening, she thought, her head falling back to gently bump the wall.

For months before Erik's attack, she and Jennifer had complained of personal items disappearing. Favored toiletries, stuffed animals and little trinkets given to them by past boyfriends came up missing. Small things. Insignificant things. Things that could be easily lost or misplaced.

But suddenly the missing items became more intimate. More personal. Sexy lace panties and slips in their dresser drawers simply up and disappeared.

At first Cora and Jennifer hadn't given the missing items

a second thought. They'd chalked it up to misplacing them or losing them in the laundry room. But after a while, even that explanation didn't seem fit.

It wasn't until after Jennifer's death, when the police searched Erik's apartment, that they had found all the items. Little trophies saved up by him to fondle and enjoy while he contemplated his next move.

Cora shuddered. Was it possible that Erik was here on Midnight Island? Had he somehow found her hiding place?

She wiped her damp palms on her apron and straightened up. No, she was spooking herself. It wasn't possible. Erik had no way of knowing where she was.

She had left the state of California and headed east without notifying anyone she knew where she was going. Even Erik couldn't follow a nonexistent trail. Could he?

Chapter Eight

STRAIGHTENING UP and willing her legs to hold her weight, Cora picked up Mr. Mackenzie's tray and proceeded down the hall. Behind her, she continued to hear Bea Crane, Amanda and Jake talking in heated tones. But somehow she no longer had the heart or the will to hear what they were saying. She knew Jake was angry at the threat Bea had made about leaving. That he didn't like the thought of his father without a trained nurse. But she couldn't handle any more information.

She found the older man's door open a crack, and when she peeked in, she saw Mr. Mackenzie asleep in a hospital-style bed. She hesitated in the doorway, unsure what to do.

But as she started to withdraw, a pair of startlingly familiar brown eyes opened and stared at her from across the room. There was no missing the man's relationship to Jake. The bold features beneath the paper-thin skin spoke of a former handsomeness. A strikingly defiant look that fought valiantly against whatever illness racked his thin body. It was a battle that was being slowly and painfully lost.

"Don't stand there gawking. Come in." His voice was weak, almost hoarse and slightly less than a whisper, but there was no missing the underlying tone of command. This was a man used to getting his own way. He lifted a thin arm off the bed and his skeletonlike fingers beckoned for her to enter.

"Ms. Crane is just down the hall, sir. I'm sure she'll be along shortly."

The old man waved an impatient hand. "No doubt preparing some sort of torture for me. The woman is a sadist."

Not sure how to respond to that particular comment, Cora stepped inside. "I brought your dinner."

"It smells good. What did you bring?"

"Some Irish stew and freshly baked bread, sir."

"William. The name is William." He smiled, a painful stretch of thin lips within sunken cheeks. "Bless you for not bringing me another dish of tasteless mush. The other cook couldn't boil water."

Cora smiled. "I had a hard time telling if you liked what I was preparing for you. Both the breakfast and lunch trays have been coming back virtually untouched."

He waved a hand weakly. "I've been feeling a bit peaked the past few days. But the smell seems to have revived my appetite this evening." He lifted his head, wincing slightly as he shot her a sly smile. "What did you bring for dessert?"

She set the tray on the hospital table next to the bed. "Sorry, sir, no dessert. Mrs. Mackenzie was quite clear in her instructions that I wasn't to put any sweets on your tray—not even fresh fruit."

The paper-thin skin of his forehead gathered into a frown. "My Amanda is a hard woman."

He reached out and curled his fingers around Cora's forearm. She could feel the deep tremors that racked his rail-thin body. "You'll bring me some pie next time, won't you?" A dreamy expression flickered across his gaunt face, and his eyes closed partially. "A homemade cherry pie with big, plump red cherries. Topped with a generous glob of real whipped cream." He opened his eyes again. "Promise me that you'll bring that next time."

"Cora won't be bringing you pie," a voice interrupted.

Cora whirled around. Jake stood in the doorway.

He was dressed in dinner clothes, his standard uniform of neatly pressed slacks, white shirt and dark, richly woven wool jacket. His shoes were shined to a high gloss.

The neatness of his clothes contrasted sharply with the unshaven bluish black line that shaded his jaw. Somehow he managed to pull off the look of sophistication and decadence with ease. He carried a thick leather-bound book under one arm.

As much as Cora hated to admit it, she was pretty sure his appearance would be a big hit on the cover of *GQ*. She steeled herself against the sharp stab of need that shot through her, threatening to knock her to her knees with a whimper of surrender. Her body's blatant betrayal irritated her. She knew without question that her body's reaction was due to the memory of those magnificent lips on her own. Her body ached for a return to that moment.

The old man's hand tightened on hers. "Steady, gal," he said, his amusement unmistakable. "Come in, Jake, meet the delightful creature who has promised to bake me a cherry pie with real, honest-to-goodness whipped cream."

"I promised no such thing," Cora scolded. "Don't be making up stories and getting me into trouble."

"Trouble? You think Jake would tattle on you?" The old man snorted. "Sweetheart, he's the one who sneaks me a candy bar whenever he can." He reached beneath his covers and pulled out several telltale red and silver crumpled candy wrappers.

Cora shot Jake a glare. Was the man nuts or did he truly intend to kill off his father, too?

He caught the look, and a faintly amused expression flickered across his classic features. He spread his hands and shrugged elegantly, his muscles moving effortlessly beneath the expensive cloth of his jacket. "Hey, I only sneak him one once in a great while."

"Well, it can't be good for him if your stepmother has said no sweets."

"Phooey, if my wife had her way she'd have me eating brown rice, bean sprouts and that disgusting fiber mix twenty-four hours a day." He grinned up at her. "Jake understands that a man needs an occasional indulgence."

"I have no doubt that Jake understands a man's need to indulge." Cora grabbed the cloth napkin off the tray and opened it with a quick snap. She shot a knowing glance in Jake's direction, letting him know exactly what type of activities she knew he had a tendency to indulge in—the kind that combined forbidden kisses with clever touches meant to send a woman over the edge.

She shivered, and humor sparkled in his beautifully expressive eyes, as if he knew exactly what she was thinking. He opened his mouth as if to protest, but Cora turned away and carefully draped the napkin across William's thin chest. Reaching down, she pushed a button and raised the head of his bed.

"Cora doesn't think much of me, Pop," Jake said. "Somehow she's developed this mistaken impression that I'm a useless, good-for-nothing womanizer."

"She looks like a pretty perceptive young woman to me," William teased, his eyes twinkling with humor. "You sure she doesn't have you pegged right?"

Cora shot Jake a triumphant look, but he only grinned. He walked around the end of the bed and reached over to gently pry the candy wrapper from his father's hand.

Stuffing it into his pocket; he leaning down and kissed his father's forehead, whispering, "Watch out, old man, or your candy supply will be permanently cut off."

"Pah, I have too much dirt on you, boy. Don't even try to threaten me."

Jake laughed and rearranged the napkin higher on his father's chest, tenderly tucking the ends along the top edge of his nightshirt. "You've got nothing on me. Well, nothing compared to what I have on you."

He sat on the side of the bed, putting one long leg up on the mattress. His posture was relaxed. Comfortable, as if this was how he spent every evening.

But then his gaze settled on the tray. He glanced up at Cora, his expression taut, angry, the playfulness gone in an instant. "Where did you get those dishes?" he demanded.

Cora stepped back, surprised by the sudden animosity in his voice. How had the mood changed so quickly? "I found them in the pantry, stuck way back on the bottom shelf." She glanced anxiously back and forth between the two men. "I was cleaning up and thought they might cheer your father up. I'm sorry—did I do something wrong?"

"Of course not." William reached up and patted her hand. "You surprised Jake, that's all. We haven't seen these dishes in quite some time." The old man smiled up at her, his eyes genuinely pleased. "I'm glad you found them. Seeing them has been a welcome treat."

Cora nodded but then glanced over at Jake. He seemed oblivious to what his father was saying, the incident definitely not in the "treat" category for him.

He reached out and touched the rim of the bright yellow mug sitting next to the teapot. He ran the tip of his finger along the edge, and then he picked the cup up, turning it over.

In the bottom of the mug, etched directly into the clay, someone had drawn a heart and the letters "WM + SM."

Cora watched as Jake slowly traced the letters. A shadow of pain passed through his dark eyes like a flash of heat lightning on a hot summer's day.

"My first wife made them," Mr. Mackenzie explained as if reading her confusion. "She was an artist. It was one of her first gifts to me."

"How romantic," Cora said. "Something to be treasured."

William nodded. "My Sarah was a true romantic." He glanced at Jake, his expression softening. "It's something she passed on to Jake."

Jake seemed to hear him for the first time and he snorted dismissively. "Me, the romantic? I don't think so." He set the cup down, and the haunted look still lingered. Cora knew without him admitting it that Jake had been shaken by the appearance of his mother's dishes.

"You're the romantic, Pop," he said. "I'm the perpetual cynic, remember?"

"Oh, yeah, the cynic. I guess I need to get everyone's role straight around here," William said, his disbelief obvious.

Unsure what to say, Cora arranged the tray closer to the elderly man, making sure the utensils were all within his reach. He reached out for the spoon, but as he tried to scoop up a bit of the stew, the tremor in his hand became so pronounced that the liquid spilled before he'd got it halfway to his mouth. Irritation flickered across his face.

Cora gently took the spoon. "Here, let me help."

He relinquished the utensil with a sigh of resignation and glanced up at his son. "What book did you bring to read tonight?"

Cora struggled to keep the astonishment off her face.

Would wonders never cease? Apparently the hardened flirt read to his father every night. Perhaps people really were wrong in their assessment of the man.

The elderly Mackenzie swallowed a small spoonful of the stew before adding, "I hope it's something exciting, adventurous and wildly sexy."

Jake laughed. "I'd hardly call *Caesar, the Reign of Julius Caesar's Legion* sexy. But there's plenty of adventure."

"Bah, you have the worst taste in books. Hard to believe you're my son." He winked at Cora as he opened for another taste of the stew. A teasing sparkle of something jumped into his eyes, something she'd seen before in his son's eyes. "I bet Cora could pick out a book fitting for this old man's tastes. What would you choose, Cora?"

She paused and thought about it for a minute. "Knowing me, it would probably be some kind of cookbook."

"Bah." The old man waved a hand in disgust. "The two of you deserve each other. You'd bore an old man half to death."

Jake laughed and reached out to take the spoon from Cora's hand. "Here, let me take over. I know you have things to do."

His fingers brushed the back of her hand, sending a jolt of awareness ripping through her. She glanced up at him, frightened to meet those hypnotic eyes but unable to stop herself.

As she expected, their startling darkness and depth bored into her with breath-stealing sharpness. The effect threatened to flatten her. How was it that she was so vulnerable around this man? What was it about him that attracted her so?

"I don't mind," she said, barely aware that she was still holding on to the spoon's handle as he gently tugged on it. For a brief second they wrestled, his fingers cradling her hand. The warmth and pure strength of his fingers seemed to burn her to the core.

"I don't mind, either," he said, his voice suddenly huskier than a few moment ago, as if he, too, felt the strange power that seemed to hover between them. Her breath caught in the back of her throat, and she struggled to catch her breath.

"Watching the two of you fight over who's going to feed me is a pretty good substitute for some of that sexy reading I was talking about just a moment ago," William said, his amusement obvious.

Flustered, her color heightening, Cora practically shoved the spoon into Jake's hand and stepped back. But it was as if a golden thread of awareness unraveled between them, keeping them intimately connected on another level.

Jake watched as Cora raised a hand to her cheek and touched it, as if surprised at her reaction. He knew without her saying anything that she was confused by the heat, bewildered by the sensations rushing through her body. He knew because he was experiencing some of the very same feelings himself.

"I…I'd best get back to work," she stammered. "I hope you enjoy the stew, Mr. Mackenzie." She headed for the door, her entire body rigid, as inflexible as her opinion of him.

The door shut after her, and his father's voice cut into his musings. "Cute little thing. You picked a winner this time."

"I didn't hire her—Amanda did."

"I wasn't referring to her cooking abilities, although they appear to be first rate. I was referring to the attraction she seems to hold for you." He paused and then added, "And the attraction you seem to hold for her."

Jake managed a laugh. "You're reading that wrong. She's already dismissed me as a hopeless womanizer."

His father merely chuckled. "Doesn't change the fact that she's attracted to you." He frowned. "I admit, however, that I'm somewhat surprised that Amanda was the one to hire her. It's not like Amanda to allow anyone that young and pretty to walk through the front door. She has a thing about youth, you know."

"You think?" Jake quipped. He scooped up another spoonful of the thick stew and lifted it to his father's lips. He waited patiently as his father took a small bite, hardly enough food to nourish a hummingbird. The fact that his father's appetite declined daily worried Jake more than he cared to admit even to himself.

"I'm guessing that you've already run one of your infamous checks on poor Cora, huh?" his father asked. "Sicced those watchdogs of yours on that poor defenseless little girl."

Jake ignored the baiting tone of his father's voice and scooped up another spoonful of Cora's stew. "It's in the process of being completed."

His father sighed. "I've failed you somehow. I never was able to help you with that all-important issue of trust, was I?"

"Trust has nothing to do with background checks. I'm simply employing good hiring practices. Practices you taught me."

"Practices that weren't meant to be used in one's personal life, Jake. I wasn't looking to hire Amanda when you started running that background check on her. She was already working for me. I was looking to marry her."

Jake sighed. They were back on this subject again. His father still hadn't forgiven him for digging into Amanda's past. He'd taken it as a personal affront to his ability to choose a mate. "The decision wasn't personal. I did it to protect you."

"It might not have been personal to you, but it had the potential to create a whole lot of hard feelings."

Jake bit back an angry reply. When his father had asked him to stop his investigation of Amanda, he had immediately honored that request. And he had never told his father what he'd found. Never revealed that the prim, proper and self-righteous Amanda had battled the State Child Welfare system. A system that had branded her an unfit mother.

"Perhaps you still haven't learned that relationships are based on trust?" William pressed, seemingly unwilling to give up the current conversation.

"Trust? What's that? You seem to forget that my wife walked out on me," Jake said. "Maybe if I'd done a better background check on that damn gardener, Connery, Natalie might have stuck around a little longer. At least long enough for us to get a legal divorce."

His father shook his head sadly. "You still haven't stopped nursing that wound, have you?"

"I'm not nursing anything. I'm simply pointing out the fact that I have reason to be cautious. Maybe if I'd been more cautious in my hiring practices, I wouldn't have been surprised when Natalie left."

"So what you're saying is that you are more upset about being caught by surprise than by her actual desertion? Kind of like when your mother died and you found yourself unprepared. Right?"

Jake paused, the spoon halfway to his father's mouth. Damn, when the old man went for the jugular, he went for it full force. His assessment stung. He'd never really thought about Natalie's desertion in quite those terms before. He'd always told himself that he had resented her leaving because she'd given up on the marriage. But in reality, he'd been more resentful of her taking him by surprise, leaving him behind to fix the mess.

The two of them had certainly talked enough times about their marriage not working, of the possibility of them getting a divorce and going their separate ways. And in his heart, Jake had known they weren't going to make it as a couple. Their differences had been too deep, too dividing.

But when Natalie had taken off with his money and never told him where she was going, Jake had found himself left to deal with the messy aftermath. And his anger had been immense. Not too different from the rage he'd felt when his mother had died without him ever knowing why or where she'd gone.

"You're a clever old man," he said softly.

His father touched his hand. "I miss your mother, too, Jake. But in her defense, she believed she was doing the right thing when she didn't allow you to see her in the hospital. She thought her appearance would only frighten you."

Jake swallowed against the thick rush of emotion that threatened to choke him. "I know that."

"Do you really?" His father's eyes sought out his. "As hard as it was for you and Natalie to make it as a couple, she wasn't a bad person—insensitive, perhaps. Naive and immature, most definitely. People make mistakes, and whatever happened between the two of you, Natalie would have wanted you to get on with your life."

Jake nodded, and his father's hand dropped away. He closed his eyes and heaved a weary sigh. "Now go away. I'm tired and want to sleep. Go find that pretty cook and give her a kiss for me."

Jake pushed the tray aside and stood up, carefully rearranging the blankets around his father's frail shoulders. He bent down and kissed the old man's pale cheek. But he was already breathing softly, shallowly, the blue veins in his forehead looking terribly small and vulnerable beneath paper-thin skin.

"Thanks, Pop," he said softly.

He left his father's room, thinking perhaps he really did need to have a more open conversation with Cora, get a few things straight between them. But first he needed to locate Bea and make sure she returned to his father's bedside.

The old guy looked even more fragile than usual, and Jake wanted Bea tending to him, not out making threats about quitting because a few personal items were missing from her room.

CORA TOOK ANOTHER apple and cored it with a quick, professional twist. Then she dunked the utensil under running water to clean if off.

Silly romantic fool, she berated herself softly as she set the apple corer aside and picked up her paring knife. *Think he's interested in you? Get a grip, woman. He's out of your league.*

On the other side of the wooden island, Caesar whimpered in agreement and stared up at her from his position next to the fire.

"And you, you big mutt, you don't have to agree with me," she scolded.

Caesar grunted and rolled over onto his back, his expression seeming to say, *Women.*

She peeled the apple in one swift single strip, flipped the skin into the garbage disposal and cut the fruit into perfect slices. She plopped the slices onto the already overflowing pile occupying the center of the pie plate. A single glance told her that if she sliced any more apples, she wouldn't be able to get the top crust on.

Sighing, she set aside her knife and sprinkled the dry ingredients generously over the apples, followed by the wedges of butter. Lifting the crust off the marble pastry board, she set it on the pie and efficiently cut off the excess edge, using her fork to expertly seal the pie.

Then she lifted the plate and carried it over to the oven, placing it in the center of the rack. She glanced at the clock. Just enough time to take a walk in the cold night air to cool down. Something told her that the walk would be better even than a cold shower.

She shut the oven door, turned on the timer and grabbed her coat off the hook by the door. Several flashlights sat on a shelf and she slipped one into her pocket. Although there was a moon out, she knew the trail wasn't lit and she might need the extra light.

Caesar jumped up, his big body fairly dancing with anticipation. "Not this time, big guy. I need some time alone. Go find Cleo."

She opened the door a crack and squeezed out. Caesar whined and clawed the door, but Cora ignored him.

An icy wind hit her as she stepped out onto the back porch, and the outside light spilled a weak pool of yellow light a few feet into the yard. Off in the distance she could hear the clang of one of the channel markers and the crash of the waves hitting the shore.

Stepping off the porch, she avoided the path to the boathouse. No way was she traveling back down through that thicket of bushes, even with a flashlight to guide her.

Better to take the path that Mrs. Benson had told her led to the northern tip of the island. A path that was supposedly open all the way to an area that served as the family's private beach during the summer months. According to Mrs. Benson, Jake often used the path to jog on when he was looking for something other than a treadmill to get some exercise.

She glanced skyward. For the first time since she'd set foot on the island, the thick, ominous clouds overhead seemed to part, and a thin shaft of moonlight spilled out onto the packed dirt. It gave off enough brightness to allow her to clearly see the narrow strip of path without the use of a flashlight.

The breeze eased some as she started out, but the temperature stayed fairly frigid. She wished she'd remembered to bring gloves. Getting used to the cold north wasn't easy. She burrowed her hands deeper into her pockets, ignoring the stinging chill in her fingers.

Turning, she looked behind her. The shrubs around the castle blocked her view of the lower floor. But the other four floors were dark, the stones, wet from an earlier rain, fairly glistened in the moonlight. Around her, the trees' ice-encrusted branches snapped and cracked.

She pushed on, rounding a small curve in the path. She stopped short. Several yards ahead a person stood in the middle of the path. The figure beckoned to her, as if urging her to catch up.

Cora squinted. It was a woman, but she couldn't quite make out the face to tell who it was. Her hair, thick and waist long, blew in the wind that rose up off the river. Her white gown billowed, seeming to float and dance about her like a shimmering wave of satin.

"Hello," Cora called, quickening her step. "Is something wrong? Do you need help?"

The woman waved again, her motion even more urgent. But she didn't speak, and before Cora could reach her, she turned and disappeared into the trees bordering the path.

An intense wave of fear rushed over Cora. She cupped her hands over her mouth and called again, "Where are you? Are you in trouble?"

The ice in the tree cracked louder as the wind built, pushing whip-thin branches against each other like hissing snakes. Suddenly Cora wasn't so sure she wanted to venture any farther. Perhaps it would be better to go back and get someone from the house to accompany her.

She turned to go back, but a cry rose from the woods. A haunting, high-pitched cry of despair, a wail so desolate and sad that the hair on the back of her neck rose.

Suddenly unsure, Cora paused, her teeth worrying her lower lip. If she ran, she'd reach the castle in less than three minutes flat. But her feet seemed frozen to the dirt path, unable to take her in the direction she wanted so desperately to go.

What if the woman had slipped and fallen in the darkness? What if she truly needed help? She couldn't just leave her alone out there.

Swallowing her fear and bracing herself, Cora walked toward the edge of the woods. Her heart crowded the back of her throat and her blood whistled in her ear.

As she neared the spot, she peered into the darkness, catching a glimpse of shimmering white as it flitted in and out between the thin trees.

She reached into her pocket and pulled out the flashlight. She snapped it on, and the beam of light weakly lit the surrounding area. She shook the heavy metal. The light flickered but stayed on.

"Just my luck," she mumbled to herself. "I picked up the one flashlight with crummy batteries." She stepped off the path and cautiously entered the wooded area. She followed the soft, desolate sounds of someone sobbing.

The crash of the waves hitting the shore got louder, telling Cora she was close to the riverbank. Somewhere off in the darkness, a channel marker clanged more urgently.

She reached up and brushed aside the scrawny branches that whipped her body and the sides of her face, making her skin sting.

The crying increased, the sound heartrending. It pulled at her and she started to run.

A chill raced up Cora's spine. It sounded like the same cry she'd heard in the library. Was she following The Mournful Lady, the ghost of Midnight Castle?

Just when she thought she could go no further, her breath harsh and raspy to her own ears, the tree line ended and she burst out onto a rocky shoreline. She glanced right just as a snatch of frothy white cloth disappeared, fluttering around a bend up ahead.

Her feet slipped on the wet stones as she followed. Rounding the point, she reached out and grabbed the trunk of a small tree and scrambled to get over the pile of rocks. Her foot slipped on one and she fell forward, her ankle slipping between two boulders.

Her flashlight fell from her hand as her knees hit. She lifted her head. Her flashlight lay a few inches away, throwing a thin beam of light out across the tiny bog she'd fallen into. She pulled her foot out of the crevice and struggled to stand in the cold, wet mud. It was then that she saw it—the body of a woman lying stretched out on the ground a few yards away.

She scrambled backward, falling flat on her back. Her head hit the mud with a dull thud. She gasped for breath. Images of Jennifer lying spread-eagle on the bed in San Francisco flashed through her.

She shook herself, forcing herself to breath normally. *Don't panic. You are not back in the apartment. You're here on Midnight Island. That's not Jennifer. Focus, dammit.*

She sat up. A few feet away, lying on her back, was Beatrice Crane. Her angular face was frozen, her expression a mask of fear. Her mouth was open as if giving forth a silent scream.

Cora squeezed her eyes shut and then opened them again. It hadn't been a dream. The woman was still there. *Please God, let her be okay,* she prayed as she crawled closer. Beatrice's head was cocked at an odd angle and her arms and legs were thrown wide as if she'd given herself up in some kind of strange offer of sacrifice.

For the first time, Cora realized that the night had turned quiet. No crying. No wind. No ice-encrusted branches bending or crackling. Instead, a deep silence blanketed the entire area. The silence seemed to weigh down on her, almost deadly in its heaviness.

Her heart hit the sides of her ribs as she reached forward to touch the woman's neck. Her fingers frantically searched for something. Anything.

The skin below the line of the woman's jaw was cold and hard, as if frozen to the bones beneath. She was so pale her skin seemed translucent.

Cora pressed harder, but nothing moved beneath the tips of her fingers. No pulse. No flutter of life.

"Are you all right?"

Trembling, Cora looked up to see Jake standing in the clearing, his dark face creased with concern. He immediately crossed the space between them, seemingly oblivious to the fact that he was dressed in evening clothes. Mud splashed and splattered on the neatly creased trousers.

He was at her side a few seconds later, reaching down and lifting her to her feet. He pulled her to him, clutching her trembling body to his powerful frame.

Cora buried her face in the softness of his jacket, her nose savoring the smell of damp wool and the faint scent of him. The touch of his hand against her back was rock hard, steady and strangely comforting.

She hadn't realized until that moment just how reassuring the touch of him would be to her. How welcome. It was if the terror gnawing its way into the center of her heart vanished in a single second, chased away by his mere presence.

"What happened? Are you hurt?" His deep tones flowed over and into her like a rich, soothing balm.

"I…I thought I saw someone running. I followed them and then the next thing I knew, I tripped. When I looked up, I saw Beatrice." Her voice wavered. "I…I think she's dead. I checked for a pulse and—" A sob caught in the back of her throat, cutting off her voice, and his fingers tightened on her elbow. It was as if with that single movement he could will his own superior strength and composure into her nerveless body.

She soaked the feeling in and savored the feel of its warmth. "I…I checked, but I couldn't feel anything. I was too late."

He stroked her back, and his other hand gently touched the back of her head, stroking her curls as if she were a small, inconsolable child needing comfort. And she was. She drew on his calmness, sucking in deep frantic breaths of cold air.

"Easy, now. Take slower breaths. You're okay. You're safe. No one is here to hurt you."

Air shuddered in and out of her lungs, and slowly her breathing returned to normal. But she didn't move. Didn't step away from him. Instead, she clung to him as if he were her last possession. As if he were her very own lifeline.

After a few moments he seemed to sense that she had calmed a bit and he stepped back. Concerned, she reached out to maintain contact with him. This was not a time when she wanted to be alone.

He steadied her again with a light touch of his hand to her shoulders. "Stay right here. I just need to check on Beatrice."

She didn't want to let him go, but she knew she needed to let him check on the nurse. She nodded and clenched her arms tightly around herself, trying to keep from shaking into a thousand pieces.

He stepped into the bog, oblivious to the mud oozing up over the sides of his shoes. He moved over to Beatrice's body and bent down, his powerful shoulders bunching beneath the cloth of his jacket. His fingers, long and elegant, sought out a place on the side of the nurse's neck. He moved them across her skin searching for a pulse.

A few seconds later he straightened up, a resigned expression crossing his face. Overhead, the clouds parted a fraction, and cool moonlight bathed the small clearing. From across the short distance, his eyes locked with hers, and she didn't miss the tinge of regret in their depths.

He shook his head, and several strands of dark, silky hair swept across the sharp blade of his high cheekbones. But then, her gaze settled on a deep scratch running the length of his neck and disappearing beneath the collar of his pristine white shirt.

Fear rose in her throat. Where had that come from? She didn't remember seeing it there earlier in his father's room.

Her gaze dropped down to his feet. Dried mud caked the hem of his pants. His shoes were now covered with the dark fresh mud from his recent foray into the bog. How had he gotten the dried mud on his pants? It hadn't been there earlier. Had he been out here already? Perhaps stalking Beatrice Crane?

Her pulse kicked up a beat, and she struggled to keep her concern from registering on her face. She couldn't let him see her suspicions. Not when she stood on the very tip of the island, totally out of earshot of the castle. If she called for help now, no one would hear her.

Was it possible that Jake's earlier confrontation with the hard-nosed nurse had led to something more deadly than a simple disagreement between employer and employee? She stared at the raw, jagged scratch on the side of his neck. It had the appearance of fingernail gouge, as if someone had dug into him as she fought for her life.

Suddenly Jake's large capable hands didn't seem quite so comforting. Quite so welcoming.

Chapter Nine

The local cops swarmed over the island like ants on a thick trail of fresh honey. From his spot near the windows in the living room, Jake stared at the glow of lights down at the point. The police had set up some kind of temporary lighting to aide in their investigation of the site where Beatrice's body was found. The harsh yellow glow pushed against the night sky.

They had removed the body a few minutes ago, carrying it over the rough, frozen terrain in a metal basket, the body covered by a plastic body bag. It was stored in the back of the police cruiser moored at the dock. Jake knew the boat only too well. It was the same one they'd used to pull up to the dock two years ago when he had reported Natalie missing. Over the following year, the cruiser had made frequent trips to the island, talking to him and searching for clues to Natalie's whereabouts. All to no avail.

"Okay, Jake, tell me what happened?"

Jake turned to face Red LaPlant, the local chief of police. The man's bulk filled the doorway of the dining room, his ruddy face composed into an expression of outward calm. There was no missing, however, the shrewd questioning look that lurked deeper.

Jake knew it was there because Red was nobody's fool. Although he knew which side his bread was buttered on, namely that of the Mackenzie money that supported the little town of Myst Inlet, he wasn't about to overlook anything in this investigation. The man had a reputation for being honest and fair.

"Your guess is as good as mine, Red. We found her right where you picked her up—in the bog, face up," Jake said.

"Any idea what the hell she was doing out there in the first place?"

Jake shrugged. "From what Mrs. Benson said, the woman liked to take a late-night walk before settling in for the night."

"Alone?" The police chief's tone was skeptical.

"Sure alone. Why the hell not? This is a private island, Red, not New York City. No one on the island except family and invited friends."

"Yet a woman turns up dead. Her skull caved in on one side."

"Is…is that how she died?" a voice asked, the sound so soft it was almost strangled.

Jake shifted his gaze to the small figure standing in one corner of the room. Cora.

He'd lost track of her in the excitement of returning to the house and contacting the police. He'd left her sitting in the kitchen, her face pale, a stunned mask of shock. After seeing Beatrice's body, she had seemed to revert to automatic pilot.

Now she stood opposite him, blending into the wood paneling of the room, a tiny speck of dust against the rich wood. She was hidden behind one of the chairs, her hands clamped so tightly onto the back cushion that her knuckles stood out stark white against the dark cloth of the chair. It was if the chair was her fortress, her protection against some expected onslaught.

Her eyes were wide with fear, the color so deep and soul-ful that they looked as though they might well up with tears at any moment. But they didn't. She pulled on that incredible strength she seemed to have, that inner core of steel that kept her standing and in the game. But Jake had gotten to know her well enough to know that she was teetering on the edge, holding on with her fingernails.

"And you are?" Red asked.

"This is the new cook—Cora Shelly. Cora, Chief LaPlant," Jake said. "Cora was the one who stumbled upon Bea first."

Red pulled a narrow notebook and pen out of his jacket pocket. "About what time did you find the body, Ms. Shelly?"

Small lines of concentration popped up between Cora's chocolate brown eyes, but she didn't glance in his direction. It was if she used the thickness of lashes to shield herself from him. To keep herself separate, as if the mere act of making eye contact with him was too much for her.

"I'm not sure exactly, but it had to be around 9:30 or so. I just went out for a short walk when I saw the gho—" Her gaze flicked toward him and then away again. She swallowed and started again. "When I thought I saw someone in the woods. I followed her—I know it was a woman because she was wearing a dress. When I broke through the clearing, I stumbled and fell. That's when I saw Beatrice."

"Did you move her or touch her in any way?"

"I…I touched her neck to see if she had a pulse." She glanced around in alarm. "Was that okay? I mean I just wanted to see if I could help her. To see if she was still alive."

Red held up a hand, his expression reassuring. "You did fine, Ms. Shelly. Was she breathing? Did she say anything?"

Cora shook her head, her upper teeth working her lower lip hard. "No, she was already dead."

Jake figured that her lip would be raw before morning if she kept that up. She looked as though she was barely hanging on to that last shred of sanity that kept her from being reduced to total hysteria.

He suppressed the urge to tell Red to lay off. To let her regain her composure before questioning her any further. But he knew it was better that the questioning was finished.

As he watched, her hand went to her throat, and she unconsciously traced the thin scar cutting across her throat.

"Was the woman you saw wandering around in the woods Ms. Crane?" Red asked.

"No. I...I don't think so anyway. She was dressed in something very long and flowing. Ms. Crane had on pants and a heavy coat." She frowned as if struggling to conjure up a clearer visual image. "The woman's dress was gauzy. Almost as if it floated around her body. Maybe the wind made it seem that way. She had long, dark hair."

Red scowled and glanced up from his notes. "Something long and gauzy on a night like this? She must have been freezing her a—" he glanced guiltily in Amanda's direction "—butt off.

"I thought the same thing. But that's what she was wearing." She looked at each of them in turn, as if she could convince them to believe her simply through the force of her sincerity. Something told Jake that she desperately needed them to believe her.

Her gaze settled on him and her eyes beseeched him, her need clawing at him. "I swear to you, I really saw her."

Jake tried not to let his exasperation show, but the fact that the stupid ghost story was reappearing yet again irritated the heck out of him. What the hell was wrong with Cora? Did she really believe some ghostly apparition was wandering around the castle trying to make contact with her?

As if sensing his disbelief, Cora dropped her gaze, and her body seemed to fold in on itself. "I thought I saw her." Her voice trailed off.

Red raised an eyebrow. "Anyone else see this woman in a white dress wandering around the island?"

Amanda exhaled loudly, a sharp sound of impatience.

"I'm guessing you have something you want to add, Mrs. Mackenzie," Red said.

"Only that Ms. Shelly has been a bit confused since her arrival on the island four days ago." She directed a half-hearted, apologetic smile in Cora's direction. "I'm sorry, Cora, but I feel that Chief LaPlant needs to hear all the facts." She brushed an imaginary piece of lint off her fashionable sheath dress and addressed the chief again. "Cora thought someone tried to break into her room the first night she was here, and then she reported that someone pushed her into her bathtub and tried to hold her head under water."

"She was attacked?" Red looked alarmed. "Why wasn't any of this reported?"

Amanda's lips tightened in disapproval. "Because as far as we can tell, none of it happened. Jake heard Cora scream-ing and broke down her door. When he got inside, he found her alone in the bathroom. The only logical explanation is that she took too many sleeping pills, had a nightmare and ended up waking up the entire household." She glanced at Sheffield. "At least, that's what Dr. Sheffield feels happened."

Red turned toward Sheffield. "Is that true, Dr. Sheffield?"

Jake felt the hot sprawl of anger crawl up the back of his neck. In a matter of seconds Amanda had reduced Cora's credibility to zero.

"In my professional opinion, Cora is an overwrought, overly emotional young woman," Sheffield said. "She hasn't been able to tell me what's bothering her, but since her arrival on the island, she's gotten even more highly strung. She has admitted that her doctor out in California prescribed some tranquilizers—something to help settle her nerves. I believe that she took too many of them on the night she woke everyone up." He nodded solemnly. "Perhaps it's a good thing she did awaken us with her screaming because there's no saying what might have happened if she slipped beneath the bathwater with a bellyful of sleeping pills."

Across the room, Cora seemed to get even smaller, her shoulders sagging and her eyes blinking rapidly to block the tears.

"All right, that's enough," Jake said. "Cora doesn't remember taking any of the pills that night so we're not really sure what happened. Besides, anyone can get overwrought coming to a new place."

"Of course they can, Jake," Sheffield said smoothly. "But you have to admit that Cora's behavior has made her ability to report things accurately a bit suspect."

"No one is blaming Cora," Amanda added smoothly. "I'm sure Cora is telling us what she *believes* to be true. But it is imperative that we take into consideration the fact that she's been under a lot of pressure and seems to be a bit fragile emotionally."

"But I wasn't dreaming or imagining things when I was out taking a walk," Cora protested, her voice shaking. "I haven't taken any pills today and I saw a woman on the path."

"Of course you did, dear," Amanda said, exchanging a careful look with Red, letting him know exactly how much stock he should put in what Cora was saying.

"So, no one else saw this woman Ms. Shelly reports seeing?" the chief pressed.

Everyone, Jake included, had to shake their heads. He couldn't even glance in Cora's direction when he shook his head. He felt as though he was betraying her, and somehow he couldn't deal with the sorrow he knew would be in those soft brown eyes.

"All right. That'll do for now." Red snapped his notebook shut. "I'll need you to come into the village tomorrow to sign a statement."

"I'll have Mr. Gracy take her over," Amanda said.

"No need to do that," Jake said. "I'll take Cora over. You need me to sign a statement, too, I suppose?"

Red nodded. "If you come around ten, I'll have it drawn up for your signatures."

"I thought you were leaving for New York early tomorrow," Amanda said, her expression revealing her displeasure with this change in plans. "Won't this interfere with your schedule?"

"I've decided to stay the rest of the week. I have a few things I want to finish up here on the island before winter sets in."

Amanda frowned and then turned to Cora, "Would you mind getting us all some coffee, Cora? I think we could use something hot to warm us all up."

Jake knew from her tone that Amanda didn't appreciate him discussing his change in plans in front of the staff. But he really didn't care. He wasn't about to allow Cora to go into town to sign a police report without him along to check things out first. He owed that to her, at least, especially after not being able to support her story about the woman in the woods.

Cora seemed eager to take his stepmother up on the request for coffee. No doubt she saw it as a convenient excuse to escape from all of them, him included.

She hurried out, her slender frame stiff with unreleased tension. Jake knew without asking that she felt strangely betrayed. And more than mildly confused. Her eyes held a frightened, almost haunted look, making him wish he could go after her.

He needed to find an opportunity to talk to her alone, to explain why he'd been out on the point and why he hadn't been able to support her story about the woman. But it would come later. First he needed to deal with Amanda.

CORA POURED COLD WATER into the large silver coffee urn, measured the right amount of coffee into the filter and then flicked on the switch. She focused on the tiny light on the side of the pot, willing it to turn red quickly.

Somehow the thought of that light coming on was comforting. Familiar. And she needed something familiar right now. She didn't think she could handle anymore excitement. If anything else happened tonight, she was sure she'd shatter into a million tiny little fragments of herself.

If Mrs. Mackenzie hadn't given her something to do right when she had, Cora was fairly certain she would have become a quivering pile of raw nerves. She smiled grimly. That would have certainly sealed the police chief's doubts about her credibility.

She tightened her hands into fists, closed her eyes and counted to twenty. God, give me strength, she thought. Somehow she needed to prevent the shakes from settling in.

The thought of running upstairs and grabbing two tranquilizers flashed through her mind, but she immediately shoved it aside. That particular thought had already gotten her in trouble once. No pills. No artificial help. She could handle this, with or without Jake's help.

She paused. That was part of her anguish, wasn't it? The fact that he hadn't supported her when the police chief had questioned her.

She swallowed against the pain that rose in the back of her throat. How could she expect him to support her when she sounded so irrational, so crazy?

"Are you all right?"

Startled, she looked up to see one of the policemen standing in the doorway. It was the younger one. The one with the angry expression and the intense eyes that had seemed ready to burn a hole through Jake Mackenzie. He hadn't said anything, but even in her distraught frame of mind, Cora had picked up on the animosity that seemed to seethe in the air between the two men.

She willed her hands to unclench. It was bad enough that the inhabitants of Midnight Castle thought she was driving straight for the edge of sanity. She didn't need the police questioning her stability, too.

"Thank you, I'm fine." She reached into the cupboard and lifted down a handful of mugs. "The coffee will be ready in a few minutes."

"No hurry," he said softly. "The name is Bobby. Bobby Knight."

Cora smiled a greeting and then set the mugs on the tray. They rattled against each other as she set them down, and she hoped the young policeman had missed the slight tremor in her hands. But from the quick assessing look he shot her when he lifted his gaze to meet hers, Cora knew he hadn't.

"Finding someone dead can be a pretty frightening experience," he said.

She nodded but didn't speak. She didn't trust her voice.

He stepped into the kitchen, allowing the door to swing

shut behind him. "An experience like that can stay with a person. Give them nightmares."

Cora nodded, swallowing back the tears that threatened to spill. She would not cry. She refused to cry. What were a few more nightmares when her life had become one giant nightmare after another.

She moved over to a shelf near the pantry and pulled down a small pitcher for cream and a sugar bowl, filling each and setting them on the tray. She stole another glance at the coffeepot. Why hadn't the damn light gone on? If she had to stand here much longer, she knew the cop would start asking questions. Questions she didn't want to answer.

"How long have you been working for the Mackenzies?"

Here it comes, she thought. "I'm brand-new actually. Been here less than a week." She busied herself grabbing a handful of napkins and carefully arranging them on the tray.

"Guess you've heard all about the trouble they've had out here on Midnight Island."

"No, I'm sorry, I'm not very familiar with the island's history. I'm from San Diego." There, she'd gotten the question about where she was from out of the way before he even asked. Hopefully that would satisfy him, keep him from prying even more.

"You're a long way from home."

Cora nodded and checked the coffeepot again. Oh God, it still wasn't done. She was going to be trapped out here forever answering his questions, getting picked apart piece by piece.

She grabbed a tub filled with oatmeal cookies and quickly arranged them on a plate and then added it to the tray.

He moved closer, the leather of his holster creaking with every move. "What made you decide to come east?"

"I thought I needed a change, and I've always wanted to see the change of seasons." She shrugged. "Besides, the Mackenzies pay well and the duties are light compared to restaurant work."

"Well, you'll certainly get a taste of how the seasons change around here." He laughed, and she smiled in return. "How's Jake Mackenzie as a boss?"

Cora hid her surprise. "What do you mean?"

"Is he fair? Does he treat you well?"

"He's very fair." She grabbed two coffee carafes and filled them with hot water, warming the insides in preparation for the fresh coffee. He was fair except he didn't stand up for her in the living room, she thought.

"I've heard rumors that he likes the ladies a little too much. That he's a player. I've also heard that he likes things to go his way."

"You've heard a lot, haven't you?" Cora tried to figure out why the cop was trying to get dirt on Jake. There obviously was some bad blood between them. "I'd have to say that I haven't seen those sides of him. He's been more than fair with me."

Knight had moved up to stand next to the island, leaning one hip against it, folding his arms conversationally. He was settling in for one long interrogation. "Anyone mention that his wife disappeared a few years back?"

"I heard something along those lines."

"People think he's responsible."

"Really?" Great, not only was the guy nosy, he was a gossip hound, too.

"Yeah, some say that he killed his wife and dumped her body somewhere here on the island."

"Sounds like an ugly rumor to me." She hit him with an

innocent, wide-eyed look. "Do the police actually believe he's responsible?"

Knight's scowl deepened. "Actually, I'm the only one convinced of it. But that's because Mackenzie has the town officials and the chief of police in his back pocket."

"Did you know Natalie Mackenzie?"

He nodded. "Yeah, we were good friends. Grew up together, actually."

"I didn't realize Natalie grew up in Myst Inlet." She hadn't figured Jake Mackenzie the type to marry a local girl. Not with his money and sophistication. Somehow it didn't fit the profile she'd formed of the man, or the woman, for that matter.

"Born and raised in Myst Inlet, both of us. Natalie would have never left except she got swept off her feet by Jake Mackenzie."

"You sound as if you weren't too happy with her decision." The coffeepot's light kicked on, and Cora almost sobbed with relief.

But Knight wasn't done with her. "Do you blame me? Look what happened to her. Mackenzie destroyed her." There was no mistaking the bitterness in his voice.

"You sound as though you've got some evidence that Mr. Mackenzie is responsible for her disappearance. I was under the impression that people thought she'd taken off with someone."

"Mackenzie was the one who spread the rumor that she took off with the gardener, Tyler Connery. But that was just a little too convenient if you ask me." Knight rounded the end of the cutting block and came to stand next to her. He reached out and took the heavy coffeepot out of her hands and poured the hot liquid into the two carafes.

"Why convenient?"

"Because Jake Mackenzie didn't believe in divorce, and Natalie had asked him for one less than a week before she up and disappeared."

"How do you know she asked him for a divorce?"

Knight set the coffeepot down and used a damp sponge to carefully wipe the dark drops of liquid that had run down the side of the carafe. He threw the stained sponge back in the sink and then looked up and stared across the short distance between them, the intensity in his eyes feverish. "Because she loved me and asked for the divorce so she could be with me."

Cora swallowed hard. Natalie had been having an affair with her childhood friend. How would Jake Mackenzie have reacted to that? Would it have thrown him into a jealous rage? Enough of a rage for him to actually retaliate by killing her?

"She only married Jake because of his money. He seduced her with it. But after a while she smartened up, realized she was getting a raw deal—an absent and inattentive husband. So she demanded a divorce."

"Why wouldn't he give her one?"

Knight shrugged. "Who knows. The thought of turning over half his money? The fact that he was a possessive man who wasn't willing to share the woman he loved with someone else?"

"Hate to break it to you, Bobby, but Natalie didn't have any plans to leave me to run off with you. She had other fish to fry, namely Connery."

Cora turned to see Jake standing in the doorway to the kitchen. His gaze met hers across the length of the kitchen, and she was struck by the infinite sadness in the depths of his dark eyes. Sorrow seemed to infuse every bone in his lean, powerful body.

Beside her, Bobby Knight stiffened, and the testosterone level in the air rose to a suffocating height.

Jake walked into the kitchen. "Hell, she laughed at you just as she laughed at the rest of us. We all danced to her tune, Bobby. But if you want to know the truth, we bored her to tears."

Knight's hands tightened into fists, his massive shoulders tensing with anger. "That's a crock and you know it, Mackenzie. You couldn't stand the fact that she loved me more than you."

Cora reached out and put a hand on his arm. "Maybe she did see it all as an amusing game. You don't know for sure. You didn't live with her."

"I know that she wanted out, and he wouldn't let her go. I know that she promised to marry me once she got away from him." He shook her hand off, and his face twisted with anger. "But go ahead and listen to his lies. It's obvious that you're as sweet on him as all the other women who have ever met him. Natalie told me about the affairs—the women who called at all hours. You believe what you want."

Knight brushed past Jake, bumping him slightly with his shoulder as he pushed open the kitchen door.

The door swung shut after him.

"I'm sorry, Jake," Cora said softly. "We shouldn't have been discussing something so personal as your marriage."

"Why not? Everyone else seems to get a kick out of it." His tone was bitter, his expression brooding. "I just wanted to set the record straight. Natalie had no intention of running off with Bobby. She obviously had other plans."

Cora didn't want to be so crass as to ask what those plans had been, but she couldn't deny that the question burned on the tip of her tongue. She wanted to believe that he had nothing to do with his wife's disappearance—that Natalie, not him, had been the one unable to commit.

But the scowl on his face and the thick cloud of anger hanging over him made her think there was more to this than he was willing to reveal.

"Amanda sent me out to get the coffee. She's getting impatient."

He stepped forward as she reached for the tray, and their hands touched, their fingers becoming tangled on the handle of the tray. The brush of his skin against hers sent a familiar hot ripple of awareness up her arm and into her chest.

She didn't pull away or step back. She stared up at him, her eyes searching his, taking in the raw pain etched into the sharp planes of his face. "I'm sorry, Jake. I'm sorry that none of it worked out for you."

He nodded brusquely, and for a moment she thought he might brush her off, reject her overture of kindness. Of friendship. But then finally he smiled, giving her the barest hint that he accepted her offer. "I'd like to tell you about it sometime. Explain things. Talk about it some."

"I'd like that," she said softly but in her heart knowing that the day would never come.

"Maybe tomorrow—when I take you into town to sign the statement. We'll get to talk then. I'll tell you about Natalie, and you can tell me a little about yourself." He smiled and reached up to touch her cheek, his hand sending a thrill of anticipation through her. "It'll be a chance for us to get to know each other." His smile widened. "Maybe we can even figure out what these strange feelings are that we keep experiencing whenever we're around each other."

Cora swallowed against the swell of bitter regret that clung to the back of her throat. She had longed for him to say something like this since the day they'd met. Words acknowledging the fact that he, too, felt what she felt.

And now that he'd said them, Cora knew that what he wanted was impossible. There would be no sharing. No exchange of memories. No quiet talks that would blossom into something more. It wasn't possible. Not with Erik on the loose. Not when Erik had promised to come back for her and anyone else she cared about.

Better to just let the relationship die before it was even born. She bit back her refusal. Jake wouldn't understand. No one would. No one had ever dealt with an entity like Erik before.

Oblivious to the storm raging inside her, Jake lifted the tray and headed for the living room. Cora watched him go, remorse washing over her with the speed and power of an unchecked storm. She had reached out to him, and he had reciprocated.

But now she had to turn away, keep him at arm's length.

She refused to put his life in danger.

Chapter Ten

The next morning, an unfamiliar sense of unease circled the pit of Jake's stomach as he watched Cora and Megan make their way down the path to the dock. A voice inside his head wanted to know what the hell he thought he was doing getting close to Cora.

Even now, as he watched her step out onto the dock, her hand reaching back to gently guide a chattering Megan out onto the sun-bleached planks, he felt a strong, undeniable pull. Something powerful and unexplainable. It was an attraction that seemed to come out of nowhere, uncurling in the pit of his belly and raising its persistent head whenever he thought of her or came in contact with her.

He couldn't give a reason, a good explanation for the attraction. She certainly wasn't the most beautiful woman he'd ever met. Far from it. The curl of her hair was too wild, too undisciplined. Definitely not like the classy, sophisticated styles worn by most of the woman who ran in his social circle.

And her face, small and inquisitive, missed beautiful by a hairbreath, the mouth too wide and the features too delicate.

It bothered him that he couldn't figure out what the magnetic force was that constantly drew his eye to her. The thing that sent the deep shiver of desire racing through his blood whenever she was near.

He puzzled over it as he watched Megan chatter on about how much money she'd brought with her and what she was going to spend it on once she reached town. Cora's pixie face was composed into an expression of intense interest, as if she was truly enraptured with what Megan was saying.

Jake smiled. He knew without even asking why Megan was coming. Cora was using Megan to keep him at a distance. She knew he had wanted this opportunity for them to be alone, to get to know each other better.

Perhaps Cora was afraid of him. Not afraid in the sense that she feared for her life. More than likely she was confused by the attraction between them.

At some point he'd have to step in and rescue Cora from the sea of words flowing from Megan's mouth. But for now, he decided to let her swim in them. It served her right. Perhaps she'd think twice next time before inviting someone along.

He bent down to untie one of the mooring ropes looped over the weathered piling. A single day in town with his stepsister would cure Cora of her do-gooder mentality. He needed only one glance in Megan's direction to see that she was in rare form, dressed in full regalia—a flowing skirt with baggy knee socks and a pair of scuffed black pumps with chunky heels. Her midriff shirt, showcasing a plump belly, was worn under an unzipped, billowy red ski jacket.

Jake was fairly certain Amanda hadn't gotten a load of her outfit before Megan had ducked out of the house. Amanda wouldn't have allowed her to leave for town dressed like that. She had a thing about the family not presenting themselves in anything less than perfection in public. Of course, they were probably lucky Amanda had missed the fashion show. If she'd said anything, Megan would have pitched a fit, and he wasn't in any mood to break the two of them up.

He moved to the side and helped Megan aboard. As she stepped clumsily aboard, he tried to guide her toward the cabin, but she shook his hand off. "No, Cora and I want to sit outside."

She marched past him toward the bench seats lining the back end of the big cruiser. Sighing, Jake turned and offered a hand to Cora.

He watched the immediate indecisiveness enter her eyes, a slight flash of something worrisome and anxious. But as quickly as it appeared, she conquered it and reached out to slip her small hand into his. Her cold fingers caressed the palm of his hand.

She leaped nimbly aboard, both feet landing solidly in front of him. She looked up at him and smiled her thanks, the stretch of her lips enticingly sweet and shy.

"You're freezing," he said, his hand still holding hers.

She shook her head, the breeze off the river ruffling her unruly curls and sending them tumbling riotously about her face. She swept them back. "No, I'm fine. I'm really getting used to the cold here."

"Sure you are."

She seemed to sense his cynicism, and she pulled on her hand. "Can I have my hand back, please?"

Jake reluctantly opened his hand, and her eyes widened a little, the pupils dilating, as he allowed his fingers to lightly caress the palm of her hand as she pulled away. He knew his message was clear.

She swallowed, her throat making a small clicking sound as she shoved both hands into the pocket of her coat as if they'd been burned. "I...I'll just go sit with Megan."

"You do that," he said softly.

He watched as she turned and walked over to sit next to Megan, the gentle sway of her hips beneath the thin cloth of her coat enticingly and unintentionally sexy.

He pulled his gaze away to nod at Gracy to start the cruiser's engine. But as the boat's engine rumbled to life, he saw Mrs. Benson rush out onto the dock, waving a hand and cheerfully calling after them, "Yoo-hoo! Don't you dare leave without me!"

Jake shot a quick glance in Cora's direction. Sure enough, her eyes met his and she shrugged, a tiny smile touching her exquisite lips. No need for him to ask. He knew immediately that she had invited Mrs. Benson along, too. Her attraction to him was even stronger than he'd originally thought. She felt the need for another layer of insulation, another person to keep him safely at bay.

Amused, he shook his head and moved to the side of the boat to assist Mrs. Benson aboard. At the rate they were going, the entire household would be down on the dock making the trip into town.

The three women settled in the back of the boat, on the cushioned bench, their coat collars pulled up against the breeze ripping across the river. Cora's small nose and cheeks were already pink, and she had shoved her hands deep into her pockets. Her shoulders, looking small and frail inside her coat, hunched forward as her teeth chattered.

He sighed. They hadn't even hit the open water yet. At this rate he'd be chipping ice off her before they reached the Hidden Harbor Marina in Myst Inlet.

Shaking his head, he lifted the lid of a storage box and grabbed three heavy blankets. He handed one to Mrs. Benson and one to Megan. Then he reached down and pulled Cora to her feet. She squeaked slightly in surprise, but her teeth were chattering too hard for her to even speak.

"Stand still a minute," he said. "You're going to shatter into a thousand pieces if you continue shaking like that. You should be sitting inside the cabin where it's heated."

"No," Megan said petulantly, folding her arms. "I want to sit outside, and Cora promised to sit with me." She nodded her head at Mrs. Benson. "If she's cold she can go inside."

"It's not Mrs. Benson I'm worried about, Megan. Cora isn't used to the cold weather here. She's been living in sunny California."

Cora rested a hand on his forearm. "It's okay. I'm fine. I promised Megan I'd sit outside with her."

"And you never break a promise, do you?" he said.

She smiled, the warmth of her eyes reaching in to touch his black soul, searing it with an honesty so sharp and sweet it was almost unbearable. "I try to keep my promises."

The cruiser's engine surged and the craft lurched slightly as it entered open water. Cora tightened her grip on his arm, attempting to stay upright. He reached out and steadied her with a hand to the small of her back. She nodded her appreciation.

He draped the blanket over her shoulders and pulled it close around her neck. "An admirable quality—the ability to keep one's promises. It's not a quality I'm real familiar with," he said gruffly, not sure why she was so capable of reaching in and twisting his emotions so effortlessly.

"You had best sit down," he said. "The ride might get a little rough from here on out."

She did as he suggested, and Jake crouched down in front of her, carefully wrapping the blanket around her and tucking it in along the side. He felt the heat of her thighs soak-through the wool of the blanket, and he smoothed his hands down the length of her legs as if making sure she was completely covered. But in reality, all he wanted was to stay connected to her, to touch her bare skin beneath the blanket.

He was surprised at the intensity of his passion, the sudden overwhelming surge of heat that hit him hard enough to make it difficult to breathe.

His housekeeper and stepsister sat a few inches from him and yet he felt something so fierce that he hardly cared who was near them. If he'd been alone, he would have gathered Cora up in his arms and taken her into the cabin, laying her down on the small narrow bunk and making wild passionate love to her.

But he knew better. Instead, he rested his hands on either side of her and glanced up. He was intrigued. A passion so searing had never hit him like this before. What was it about this woman?

Cora's own eyes shimmered with amusement, telling him without question that she knew exactly what he was thinking—what he was feeling.

But he could also tell from the pinkness in her cheeks that she was feeling much the same thing.

Her gaze dropped away, but he didn't let her retreat. He leaned in. "I'm guessing that someone who is so careful about keeping their promises is also meticulously honest," he said. "Am I right?"

She lifted her eyes to his, the tiniest shadow of caution entering them. "I try to be honest."

He pitched his voice low, "So, why the parade?"

She cocked her head questioningly.

"Why the parade of people into town?"

She gnawed her bottom lip. "There wasn't any need.

Megan simply asked to go with us. I didn't see any harm in her coming."

He grinned. "I'm getting the distinct feeling that you're being evasive. Why all these layers of protection?"

She opened her mouth to answer, but he held up a hand. "Remember, you said you always try to be honest."

She laughed, and a dozen lights danced in her warm brown eyes. He watched them with fascination.

"Okay, you got me." She held up her hands. "I was dodging you. Satisfied?"

He nodded. "I find myself immensely relieved. I like a woman who can admit when she's playing games. It means she's honest." He glanced over at Mrs. Benson who was watching their whispered exchange with interest. "You wouldn't mind seeing that Megan gets over to Pandora Record Store, would you, Mrs. Benson? That way I can take Cora over to the police station and have her sign her statement."

"Of course, Mr. Mackenzie."

"But Cora promised to go to the record store with me," Megan whined.

Cora opened her mouth to protest, but Jake shook his head in warning. His hand gently squeezed her arm, telling her not to speak. She closed her mouth.

Mrs. Benson smiled and patted Megan's arm absently. "Cora will meet up with us later. We'll have a grand old time just you and me. And I think I might even have a bit of extra change to take you for a nice hot chocolate with real whipped cream at the Darlin's Dairy Twist."

"Can I have a triple scoop sundae instead?" Megan asked, recognizing the bribe for what it was and going in for the kill.

Mrs. Benson laughed. "As long as you don't tell your mother I allowed you to eat ice cream at ten in the morning."

"I'm old enough to decide if I want ice cream or not," Megan grumbled.

"So you are, dear. So you are," Mrs. Benson said, winking at Jake.

But in the end Megan agreed and Jake shot Cora a small grin of triumph. She answered the grin with her own soft, tentative smile, but it wasn't hard to see the slight trepidation hidden in that smile.

He wanted to tell her to relax, that he might have gotten around her wall of protection, but he had no intention of hurting her. But she turned away to talk to Megan, dismissing him as easily as she'd just shared that brief moment of intimacy with him. Shrugging, Jake stood up and moved to the front of the boat. No matter. He'd have her alone soon enough. And when he did, Jake intended to delve a bit deeper into those secrets she seemed to guard so closely.

WHEN THEY ARRIVED at the quaint little building that served as Myst Inlet's local police station, they found their typed statements on Chief LaPlant's desk, waiting for their signatures. In short order the documents were signed and filed away.

Cora waited patiently as Jake questioned the chief, asking if anything new had been discovered since last night. LaPlant was apologetic, but stated it would be a couple of days before the autopsy was complete.

"I have to contact her family," LaPlant said, taking off his cap and scratching the top of his head. His expression told just how unpleasant that task was going to be for him. "According to the file you gave me last night, Jake, her only living relative is an elderly aunt in Toronto. Would you mind sticking around while I make that call? It might help in case she has any questions I can't answer."

Jake nodded. "Sure, Red, I'll stay. I want to reassure her aunt that all the expenses for the funeral will be taken care of, anyway. It's the least we can do."

Cora saw her chance and edged her way toward the door. "I think I'll wander around town while you make that call."

Jake turned. "Chickening out already, Cora? Forgetting that promise you made?"

Red frowned, glancing back and forth between the two of them. "Chickening out? Promises? Did I interrupt something?"

"Oh, it's nothing, Red," Jake said. "You go ahead, Cora. I'll catch up to you at the Myst Inlet Diner for brunch in about a half hour or so." He grinned, letting her know that he knew exactly what she was up to. "I'm sure we'll still have plenty of time to talk before taking the boat back to the island."

Cora nodded, her hand already on the door. If she hurried, she'd be able to find Megan and Mrs. Benson before he was done. If she was able to convince them to accompany her to the diner, Jake wouldn't be able to force her into revealing anything.

She edged her way out the door, and a few minutes later she found herself on the quiet, almost vacant main street. Like most resort towns, Myst Inlet might as well have rolled up the sidewalks once the summer ended.

Most of the little gift and curio shops that lined the street were closed up tight. Everyone either fled to a warmer climate during the winter months or didn't bother opening up until later in the day.

She crossed her arms, trying to keep out the chill and walked along, looking for the record shop Megan had talked about earlier on the boat. She walked up to several men, huddled deep in their scarves and hats, talking about the weather.

"Excuse me," she said. "Could you tell me where Pandora's Record Store is?"

"Take a right at the next corner, miss. Cut through the alley, and you'll see Pandora's on the next street over. Little shop with a giant CD sign hanging over the door," the younger of the two said.

She nodded her thanks and hurried along the sidewalk to the next corner. Before ducking into the alleyway, she glanced up at the sky. Thick, angry clouds had rolled in, blotting out the early-morning sun. She shivered. Did the sun ever shine for longer than a few minutes here in the northeast?

The alley was short and narrow, too small for vehicular traffic. It was a pedestrian walkway, but the closeness of the buildings made it seem dark and claustrophobic.

She hurried, eager to get to the other end, and as she neared the middle of the alley, a man came from behind. His shoulder roughly hit hers as he brushed past, and Cora stumbled, falling clumsily to the right, hitting her other shoulder on the wall.

Sharp pain radiated down her arm.

"Hey!" She caught herself before she pitched forward onto her knees. "Watch where you're going!"

The man didn't stop but continued on. Cora stared after him, a tiny nudge of something tickling the back of her brain. Something about the man's walk—about the shine of his blond hair beneath his black watch cap seemed familiar.

She frowned. Did she know the man?

Suddenly a ripple of fear shot through her. She stumbled backward. *Oh God, it was Dubane.* He'd found her. Somehow he'd tracked her down.

The man stopped, his back to her.

Her hands scraped the side of the brick building as she

fought for balance. She swallowed against the bitter taste of fear flooding the back of her mouth.

She stepped back, tripping on the uneven pavement. Her hat flew off and landed in a puddle. She didn't bend down to pick it up.

She continued to back away, unwilling to turn and run. Unwilling to let the man out of her sight.

He started to turn.

"Stay away from me," she screamed.

She turned and ran. By the time she reached the end of the alleyway, she was openly sobbing.

She stumbled out onto the sidewalk, her nose running and her hair in disarray, curls hanging in her face and obscuring her vision.

She tripped and would have fallen, but someone caught her. Strong arms closed around her, lifting her up and Cora sobbed with relief. She didn't need to see to know who it was that held her. She knew his touch. It was Jake. Somehow he had known she needed him, and he'd followed her.

She clung to him, wrapping her arms around him and pressing her face against the softness of his down jacket. He dipped his head, his lips caressing the side of her cheek and sliding intimately to kiss the side of her neck. She leaned into him, soaking in the searing heat he generated in her, reveling in his warmth and protection. This is what she wanted. What she needed. All thoughts of him as dangerous or threatening vanished. He was her protector. Her savior. He would not let Erik harm her.

"He's in the alley. He followed me here."

"It's okay. You're all right." Jake stroked her back, pressing her head and whispering soft words of comfort. "Take some deep breaths. No one is going to hurt you. I can't understand what you're saying."

Cora knew she was babbling, but she couldn't seem to slow her breathing. Her fingers clawed the slick material of his jacket.

Finally, her crying slowed and she was able to lift her head. She was surprised to see a small group of people clustered around them, their faces filled with concern. Mrs. Benson and Megan stood on either side of Jake, Megan looking frightened by all the commotion.

Jake tucked a finger under her chin and gently lifted her face. "Are you all right?"

She nodded but held on to him. Hiccuping, she glanced over her shoulder in the direction of the alley.

"I thought you were staying with the Chief to make the call?"

"The line was busy, and I got worried about you." He smiled something surprisingly gentle and reassuring. "I figured the Chief could handle things on his own."

Again the sensation of being safe and protected washed over her.

"What happened?" he asked. "What scared you?"

"S-someone followed me into the alley. He tried to knock me down."

"By accident?" Jake asked. "Or do you think he was trying to hurt you?"

"I…I think he wanted to hurt me." Her voice was barely above a whisper. "It was someone I knew from California. Someone who must have followed me here."

Jake frowned. She could tell he was thinking that it all sounded a little far-fetched. He glanced at Mrs. Benson. "You came out of the alley right after Cora. Did you see anyone in there?"

Mrs. Benson shook her head. "No one, Mr. Mackenzie. I

saw Cora running out this end and I tried to call to her. I could tell something was wrong. But she was gone before I could get the words out." She glanced apologetically in Cora's direction. "I'm sorry, dear, but I didn't see anyone else in the alleyway. It was empty except for you."

"He was there," Cora insisted. "He must have hidden when you came into the alley." She straightened up, using the back of her hand to angrily swipe at the tears still spilling from her swollen eyes.

This couldn't be happening to her. She wasn't seeing things. Dubane had been in the alleyway. He had tried to knock her down. He had wanted her to know he was here in Myst Inlet.

A slow creeping feeling of dread rose up inside her. What if he hadn't been in the alley? What if she was seeing things? What if her mind was playing tricks on her again?

She swallowed against the taste of fear that washed into the back of her throat and glanced at Jake, trying not to see the glimmer of disbelief lingering in his eyes. She wanted to roll up into a little ball. He didn't believe her. He thought she was making it up. Or worse, he thought she was stark raving mad.

"He was in the alley," she said, her hands tightening into fists. She grasped her lower lip between her teeth to keep it from trembling. "I swear to you, he was in the alley."

"It's okay, we believe you." He glanced at the people standing around them. "Okay, everything is all right. No one was hurt."

He tucked her up against his side and nodded to Mrs. Benson. "We'd better get everyone home. We'll have brunch at the diner another time."

"I don't want to go home now," Megan pouted. "You promised me an ice cream sundae."

"Shhhhhhh, gal," Mrs. Benson said. "Do what your brother says. We have ice cream at home. I'll make you one when we get back."

"It won't be the same," Megan grumbled.

Cora agreed. Nothing was the same as it was a little while ago. Not too long ago she felt pretty secure in the knowledge that Jake believed she was honest. That she was someone he wanted to get to know better. Now he couldn't get her back to the island fast enough.

They followed the two women down to the marina in silence. Gracy saw them coming and had the motor of the big cruiser started before they had even climbed aboard.

When Jake tried to help her climb over the side, Cora ignored his offered hand and climbed aboard alone. She brushed past him without a word and made her way to the cabin. She wouldn't sit on the cold deck for the return trip home. She refused to give him an excuse to try and wrap a blanket around her.

But as she sat down alone at the tiny table inside the cabin, she admitted to herself that she was even more afraid that he wouldn't try to put a blanket around her. Everything had changed. What had happened in town had somehow cemented the idea in Jake's head that she was a fruitcake, jumping at the slightest provocation. It was obvious that he now believed Amanda's less-than-favorable assessment of her mental status.

A small tear slipped from between her lashes and splashed on the table in front of her. Maybe they were right about her. Maybe she was slightly crazy. What if it hadn't been Erik in the alley this morning? If she was losing touch with reality, perhaps she was truly seeing things now.

Frightened, Cora folded her arms and leaned forward to cradle her head. She sobbed silently, her shoulders shaking slightly with the pain of isolation. She had no one to depend on.

Chapter Eleven

For the rest of the day, Cora stayed clear of Jake, angry that he seemed unable to believe her description of what had happened in town. Although he tried several times to get her alone, she dodged his efforts.

She had decided that his disbelief was a good thing. It proved to her exactly where she stood with him. Besides, she told herself, the less Jake knew about her and her life up to this point, the less chance there was that Dubane could hurt him. It meant that she wasn't about to put anyone, Jake included, in danger by sharing anything about her life.

Her duties were light most of the day as Amanda and her guests, Dr. Sheffield and Vivian, had left the island for the day. They took the boat ashore and hired a car to drive them to Syracuse for dinner and the symphony. Their plans included an overnight stay at a hotel.

Mrs. Benson and Cora readily agreed to look after Mr. Mackenzie until a new nurse could be found to fill Beatrice's shoes. But despite her light duties, by nightfall Cora was exhausted.

She stood in front of the bathroom mirror in Jake's room and stared critically at her reflection. She sighed. Things were not looking good. Not good at all.

Dark smudges hugged her lower eyelids, and her hair, wild and unruly, gave her a slightly deranged look. Definitely not the image she wanted to present. If Amanda was looking for a solid reason to classify her as Looney Tunes, she only needed to get a look at her now. She'd win the argument hands down.

She rolled her shoulders, and a stab of pain shot up the middle of her back to the base of her skull. She grimaced. Not good in that department, either. Every bone and muscle ached, but her nerves seemed to hum with unused nervous energy.

Getting to sleep would be a problem if she couldn't get her body to relax. She was exhausted but at the same time wide-awake.

She glanced over her shoulder at the delicately painted teapot sitting on the bedside table. Alice had delivered it a few minutes ago, telling her that Amanda Mackenzie had insisted she bring it up, even preparing the special mixture of tea leaves before leaving for the evening, and then instructing Alice to steep the tea before bringing it up to Cora at bedtime. Several cinnamon graham crackers were arranged neatly on a small plate next to the teapot.

Cora smiled. Graham crackers and sweet tea. Her mother used to serve that very same thing to her when she was a child and home sick with a cold. Her mother and Amanda Mackenzie didn't have much in common, one being warm and nurturing and the other cold and distant, but perhaps she was wrong in her assessment of the woman. The tea and crackers were thoughtful.

She picked up her brush and absently drew it through her thick curls, trying to tame them. Perhaps the tea would help her relax. She shuddered. Did she really want to sleep? The thought of having another nightmare was enough to convince her she never wanted to close her eyes again.

But she knew she wouldn't survive if she didn't get some rest. She'd try the tea.

Squaring her shoulders, she marched over to the table and poured herself a generous cup of the hot liquid. The familiar tang of the herbs curled up on the wisps of steam and swept into her nose. Cora smiled.

She lifted the cup to her lips and sipped, savoring the taste. Delicious. Turning, she walked over to the cushioned chair angled close to the fire and sat down. Someone had thoughtfully built up the fire in the hearth. Jake, no doubt, anxious to make her comfortable.

But the door between their two rooms remained shut, a reminder that he was determined to fight the pull between them. No doubt worried about her sanity or lack of it.

Heat poured through the iron screen, bathing her body with warmth. She pulled her bare toes up beneath the hem of her nightgown and watched the fire crackle. The tea soothed her tummy, and she leaned back, resting her head on the cushion. Maybe sleep wasn't as far off as she originally thought.

She took a few more sips, delighting in the rich taste of the tea. Time passed and her eyelids drifted downward, her lashes brushing her cheeks. Her breathing quieted, whispering in and out.

Her muscles melted, fusing with the softness of the cushion at her back, and the knot cramping the back of her neck seemed to evaporate. Everything, all the tightness and tension racking her body, seemed to slide down the length of her arms and out the tips of her fingers. Her mind floated free.

"Cora. Oh, Cora." Her name seemed to ride the slight breeze of coolness that reached out to caress her warm cheeks.

Cora tried to lift her head, to open her eyes, but for some reason she couldn't. It was as if she were asleep but still aware of everything going on around her. She wondered if this was what being paralyzed felt like.

"Coooooooora," the voice called again.

The Mournful Lady? No, the voice was too deep.

Cora struggled to lift her head, to open her mouth and ask who was calling to her, but none of her muscles seemed willing to cooperate. It was if someone had crept into the room and sucked every ounce of strength and energy out of her body, leaving her limp. Boneless.

"Cooooora. Oh, Cora," the disembodied voice drifted along the air current again, the sound light and eerie, raising the hair on the back of her neck.

She lifted her head. Was Jake calling her?

She forced her body to obey, pulling herself to the edge of the chair and stumbling to her feet. She swayed back and forth for a moment as waves of dizziness attacked her head and stomach. But she pushed it aside and concentrated on staying upright.

Her eyes seemed veiled with a strange mist, and she couldn't seem to think or focus. It was if her head and ears had suddenly become stuffed with just enough cotton to make everything seem unreachable. Far off.

But through it all, she could hear the voice continue to call to her, beckoning her. Urgent. Commanding.

She stumbled to the door, her fingers fumbling with the lock. She pushed the door and almost fell face first into the hall when it swung open. The corridor was dark, but her vision was so poor it hardly mattered.

"Help me, Cora," the voice pleaded.

Cora squinted, trying to see down the dark hall. Someone needed her help. She forced one foot in front of the other. Her body swayed slightly as she weaved down the hall, and she trailed her fingers along the wall to keep her balance.

She rounded the corner and saw the elevator. The door yawned open, the gate pushed aside. It was totally dark inside. Funny, the overhead light must have blown. She tried to see if anyone stood in the doorway, but it looked empty.

Cora rubbed a hand over her eyes. It felt as though grit was under her eyelids, scratching her sensitive eyes. Why couldn't she see right? Was she dreaming again?

Exhaustion pulled at her, weighting down her body. She glanced over her shoulder. Maybe she should go back to her room and crawl into bed. She felt as though she could sleep for a century.

"Oh, Coooooora," the voice called again.

She jumped. The voice she heard wasn't inside her head. It was coming from inside the elevator.

Her heart beat faster, and she curled her bare toes under, gripping the carpet.

One floor below, the grandfather clock bonged midnight. Everything else was eerily silent, everyone asleep. She was the only one awake, wandering around in the dark, hearing voices. Perhaps this was the aftereffects of Erik's assault four months ago, appearing only now.

The elevator doorway beckoned. She tried to see inside, but it looked empty. Why did she think someone needed her help? She was overtired. She only *thought* someone had called to her.

She straightened her shoulders. Her head was a little clearer, not as cloudy. No doubt the adrenaline zipping through her blood had helped.

The best solution was to go and check the elevator and then head back to her room. She felt silly, but she didn't want to walk away if someone truly needed her help.

She approached the elevator and poked her head into the small, cramped space. Just as she thought, empty.

The overhead light was out, but the operations panel was backlit and the numbers glowed bright red. Someone had pushed the button leaving the door in the open position. It kept the elevator from moving off the second floor if someone hit the call button on one of the other floors.

Strange. She stepped inside and a cold draft of air hit her full in the face. Odd. She reached out a hand, feeling for the back wall. Her heart pounded. There was nothing there. The entire back wall of the elevator was gone. Vanished.

She snatched her hand back. Something was wrong. Terribly wrong. How could an entire wall just disappear. She swallowed her fear and reached out again, cautiously waving a hand in the area where the wall should have been. It was totally open, as if someone had removed the back wall of the elevator and then the wall to the elevator shaft.

Cautiously, she stepped through the opening and found herself on a stone floor. The chill from the stones beneath her bare feet soaked up through the soles. Cobwebs pulled at her skin and hair and she frantically brushed them aside.

She ran a hand along the stone wall and her toes bumped up against a step. She peered into the darkness, barely making out the outline of steps rising up into darkness.

Another secret passageway? It had to be. But how had the door opened? And where did the steps lead? A terrible coldness hit the back of her neck, raising goose bumps, and her nerves tingled with anticipation. Something or someone was behind her. Slowly she turned.

A few feet away, in the middle of the castle hall where Cora had come from, stood a woman in a white gown. The dress flowed around her, seeming pale and wispy, almost transparent. Her long hair fell forward to obscure her features, but she lifted a hand, pale white and delicate, and motioned for Cora to follow her. Cora knew without question that this was The Mournful Lady.

Icy fingers played the bones of her spine. She stepped back, pressing her body against the stone wall. Behind her, a voice, soft and haunting, filtered down the stone steps from above. "Ooooo, Cora, where are you?"

The icy fingers spread out, encasing Cora's entire body in a mind-numbing chill. Who was calling to her? The voice wasn't coming from the ghost. It came from somewhere above, from the top of the stairs.

The Mournful Lady motioned to her again, her gesture seemed frantic. Desperate, as if she was afraid that Cora might not follow her. Something told Cora that The Mournful Lady did not want her to go up the staircase.

She felt trapped, frozen in place, unable to go in either direction. Perhaps if she didn't move, if she stayed right where she was, the ghost would disappear and the disembodied voice from above would cease calling to her.

But the voice called again, "Cora. Sweet Cora, come upstairs."

The hair on the back of Cora's neck rose. She was dreaming. This wasn't happening. The voice wasn't Jake's. It sounded eerily like Erik's. Oh God, she truly was going insane. She was hearing Erik's voice and seeing ghosts.

Frantic, she moved back toward the elevator. She needed to get back to the main hall. But just as her toe touched the threshold, the elevator's engine whirled to life and the tiny cage shuddered.

She jumped as the elevator started downward. For one brief, terrifying moment, Cora teetered on the edge. But then, she threw herself backward, her heart hammering in her chest and her breath catching in the back of her throat.

"Are you all right?"

Cora looked up across the empty chasm to see Jake standing in the hall outside his room, his hair rumpled, his expression confused. The noise of the elevator had awakened him.

He started toward her, his face registering concern.

Cora scrambled to her feet. "Wait, Jake! Don't come any closer!"

He stopped just short of the doorway and looked down. His concern turned to horror, and his eyes met hers across the width of the shaft. "My God, what happened? Where's the elevator?"

"I…I don't know. I thought I heard you calling me, asking for help. But when I got into the elevator this whole wall was gone." She used one hand to indicate the small alcove she stood in. "Then when I tried to get back to the hall, the elevator just dropped away. I…I almost fell into the shaft."

She opened her mouth to tell him about the appearance of The Mournful Lady, but at the last minute she bit the words back. He already suspected she was a little strange. No sense in cementing that impression with tales of a ghost he didn't believe in.

"My father and I knew the castle had secret passageways," Jake said in amazement, his gaze probing all angles of the empty shaft and the room beyond. "We were always too busy to search for them. But every now and then one would pop up."

"H-how do I get back over there?" Cora asked.

"Hang on a minute." He disappeared back into his room, and Cora, finding herself alone again, glanced nervously over her shoulder into the darkness cloaking the stairwell. Would the voice call to her again? And if it did, would Jake hear it, too? But Jake reappeared a moment later, a pair of heavy rag socks in his hand, a sweater and a flashlight.

"Back up a little," he said. "I'm coming over."

Cora did as he said, flattening herself against the wall. Jake backed up and took a running start. When he reached the elevator door, he launched his body across the four-foot shaft, landing next to her. His body nudged up against hers, crowding her and pressing her up against the hard stone.

His nearness was comforting. Warmth and a familiar feeling of safety and protectedness washed over her. Cora found herself wishing he would never step away again, that he'd stay pressed up against her forever. Something told her she'd never be afraid of Erik Dubane coming for her if Jake was always at her side.

But he did move away, his strong, capable hands reaching out to grasp her upper arms to steady her as he straightened up and stepped back. "Sorry. Space is a little smaller than I thought."

He handed her the socks and motioned for her to put them on. She did, her relief instantaneous as the socks' heaviness encased her frozen toes.

As she stood up, Jake slipped the sweater over her head and helped her into it. It was large, sagging to her knees, but the wool smelled faintly of him, and Cora burrowed her chin into its thickness, savoring the familiar scent.

Jake flicked on the flashlight, and his dark eyes sought out the staircase, as if he couldn't wait to see what lay beyond. "Game to see where it leads?"

Cora suppressed a shudder and nodded her head. She was determined not to let him see how much the very thought of going up those stairs frightened her. But if he was at her side, she was willing to go. Besides, she wasn't about to stay behind while he investigated. Not after what had just happened.

He started up the stairs, and Cora crowded in behind him.

Although she felt as though she was almost on top of him, she didn't care. The staircase narrowed as they climbed upward, and Jake's big body seemed to block the light, leaving her in almost total darkness.

"How much further?" she asked, glancing nervously over her shoulder.

"I think I see some light up ahead."

Sure enough, a few seconds later, they reached a small landing. Light filtered down through an overhead hatch with iron hinges. Jake tried the latch, but the hatch only opened a crack. He jammed one muscular shoulder against the wood and pushed, the cords in his neck bulging with effort.

Finally the hatch swung open, and light from the room above spilled down over them.

Jake hoisted himself up over the lip and then reached down, offering Cora a hand up. She grabbed hold and he lifted her up next to him. He draped an arm over her shoulder and pulled her close. She glanced up at him, surprised at the protective gesture. But his gaze was fixed on the room beyond, his expression filled with surprise.

"What the hell?" he said, stepping further into the room.

Cora stifled a cry of wonderment. It was a tower room, completely circular. She was sure that in daylight the windows lining the walls of the room would give a spectacular panoramic view of the river below.

A large, king-size bed occupied much of the space, but there was also a dresser and a small table with a lamp on it. The lamp was lit, responsible for the light they had seen seeping beneath the opening to the passageway.

Cora envied whoever was lucky enough to have such a beautiful room. "Who sleeps here? "

"No one. The room is unoccupied."

Cora laughed and walked over to the bed, sitting on the side and bouncing up and down lightly. "Sure looks like someone uses it." She pulled back the comforter and showed him the sheets. "See, fresh sheets." She lay back and stared up at the ceiling, delighted to see the stars through a perfectly situated skylight.

"Oh, Jake, this is absolutely glorious. You should use this room."

"No, thanks," he said gruffly. "No one has used this room in years."

For the first time Cora noticed the anger playing roughly with the corners of his mouth. She sat up, suddenly ashamed that she hadn't picked up on his mood "I'm sorry. Was this Natalie's room? Is that why you're angry? Why no one uses it anymore?"

He shook his head. "No, she slept in the room I'm sleeping in now. When she slept in her own bed, that is." He walked over and touched the comb and wooden-handled brush sitting on top of the dresser. His expression was a mixture of anger and pain. The pure rawness of the emotions surprised Cora. He always seemed like such a controlled man, so careful about what emotion he permitted people to see.

"Then who slept here?"

"A gardener who used to work for us. A guy by the name of Tyler Connery."

Cora immediately stood up, brushing off the seat of her nightgown. She knew who he was talking about—the man who had supposedly taken off with Natalie. No doubt he'd slept with Natalie in this very bed. Suddenly the pain in Jake's eyes was understandable.

She stepped away from the bed. "I'm sorry, I guess this isn't a place that holds too many fond memories for you."

He nodded in agreement. "I thought my stepmother had cleaned the place out. But it almost looks as though the guy never left."

Jake opened one of the dresser drawers, but the inside was empty, the bottom covered with a piece of scented liner paper.

He closed the drawer and then angrily swept his hand across the top of the dresser. The comb and brush tumbled into the small wastebasket, hitting the bottom with a satisfying thud.

"Come on," he said, holding out a hand. "Let's go downstairs." He used the tip of his foot to slam the hatch to the passageway shut. He nodded at the door. "We'll take the regular stairs this time."

A SHORT TIME LATER Jake managed to get the elevator door on the second floor to shut. The car was still stuck on the first floor, but he planned on warning everyone in the morning not to use the damn thing until he had someone out to fix it.

He straightened up. "That'll hold until I can get it repaired."

Cora stood behind him, her toes curled under and her hand worrying the collar of his oversize sweater. She hadn't moved since they'd come downstairs, studying him with solemn eyes.

He could tell she was reluctant to go to bed. Wherever he moved, her soft eyes sought him out, brimming with questions. He knew what she wanted. She was afraid to fall asleep alone. But she was too afraid to ask him to sit with her. Afraid of rejection. Of ridicule.

"You want to tell me what happened earlier?" he asked, putting his tools away in his toolbox.

Cora shook her head.

"Why not?"

"Because you won't believe me, and I'm tired of not being believed." She scrubbed her face with her hands, and fatigue seemed to roll off her in one giant wave of exhaustion. "Tired of everyone thinking I'm nuts.

"Besides," she added, "I'm not even sure I believe myself anymore."

She turned as if to walk away from him, but Jake stopped her, putting a hand out to block her from leaving.

"Don't," she said. "Just let me go."

"No, I need to talk to you. You've got this all wrong. I never said you were crazy," he insisted. "In fact, you know very well that I've stood up for you every time Amanda or Sheffield has tried to insinuate that you were unstable."

She didn't look up, keeping her eyes carefully averted. "But you didn't believe me when I told you what happened in that alley."

"How do you know what I believe or don't believe? You shut down so tightly and quickly you couldn't have heard a single thing I wanted to say to you." He moved closer, his hand reaching down to lightly touch her shoulder. He stroked the cinnamon curls resting there.

She stepped away, refusing his touch.

He tried again. "I was worried about you, Cora. You were so distraught. So frightened. I didn't think we should stay in town when you were that upset. I wanted to bring you back to the island—I wanted to talk to you here. But you froze me out. You did everything in your power to keep me at a distance today."

She looked up, a single fleeting glance, but one that showed she'd actually heard him. That she was actually listening to him. She gnawed at her bottom lip, her eyes revealing her distrust. Her hesitancy. She wanted to believe him, but she was struggling.

"Do you believe that someone tried to hurt me today in town?"

"Definitely. No one could have been as frightened as you were without seeing something horrible."

She smiled, a single small upturn at one corner of her luscious lips. But it was enough to tell him that she was beginning to thaw.

"Thank you for saying that."

"So what happened this evening?"

She took a deep breath. "I had another nightmare... At least I think it was a nightmare. I'm not really sure. I heard someone calling to me, and when I got out here, I found the passageway."

"You heard someone calling to you? They were calling your name?"

She nodded.

"Did you see anyone?"

He saw the hesitancy in her eyes again. She was holding something back. Finally she blurted out, "I saw The Mournful Lady again. She tried to call me back. She didn't want me to go up the stairs."

"That damn ghost again," he said, an unavoidable note of resignation in his voice.

Cora stiffened and he immediately reached out and pulled her to him. "Look, don't even think about going all prickly on me again. I might not believe in ghosts, but I believe that you saw something. We just won't be able to come to an agreement of what it was exactly."

He felt her fragile frame shake with silent laughter, and he sucked in a quick breath as her arms came up to encircle his waist. She held him and said softly, "I guess I'll have to be content with that."

"Tomorrow you'll tell me the story of what happened to you in California. And then you'll tell me about this guy that is stalking you. But right now, you need sleep. You're about ready to drop right here in the hall."

She started to protest, but he ignored her, picking her up as effortlessly as he would pick up a kitten. He shouldered open the door to his bedroom and carried her to his bed, gently depositing her in the middle.

She looked so tiny in the center of his huge bed. Her dark ringlets spread out against the stark white pillowcase, his oversize sweater seeming to swallow her slight body in the thickness of the heavy wool, and her small feet swimming in his oversize socks.

She looked defenseless. Vulnerable. And, oh, so desirable. A need, so sharp and sweet that it almost doubled him over, hit Jake, and he knew he had to possess her. Right then. Right there.

"I have to explain a few things, Jake," she said, staring up at him. "I…I know honesty is important to you, and I wanted to tell you that—"

"Not now, Cora," he said. Her eyes were so large and warm that he thought he might fall into them and drown in them. "You'll tell me, but later."

She nodded, her eyes never leaving his face. Her anticipation raw and open.

He reached down and pulled off her socks, his hand lingering for a moment to caress her ankle and then higher to the delicate curve of her calf, the swell of her thighs and then higher still.

Her lips parted and a soft moan escaped. Her eyes filled

instantly with hot passion, and she lifted her arms, welcoming him. He dropped down beside her, pulling her into his arms.

The heat from the fireplace poured into the room, but it was nothing compared to the heat between them. Scorching hot. Totally unquenchable. Jake thought he'd found what he was looking for all these years and he bowed his head to drink her in and swallow her whole.

Cora surrendered herself with total honesty. Her lips met his with a fierceness and eagerness that took his breath away. She pulled at his shirt, loosening it from his pants and yanking it over his head. Her slender hands moved over his chest, touching him, caressing him with a boldness that amazed and excited him.

He slid his own hands up the sides of her body, pushing aside the oversize sweater and the thin nightgown beneath. The golden light spilling out from the fireplace gave her pale skin a soft glow, and the perfect curve of her high breasts and small waist were a sight to savor.

Her nipples were taut with desire, and Jake bent his head, gently circling one and then the other, lapping gently, and then smiling slightly as her spine arched upward to meet his mouth, a soft moan slipping from between her lush lips.

He lifted his head. "More?"

She reached up and wrapped her arms around his neck, pulling him down to her. "Do you even need to ask?" she whispered, her lips sliding down the side of his neck and sending a sharp shiver of anticipation through him.

His hand moved over her flat stomach to the tight curls at the base of her belly. She opened her legs with a soft sigh, telling him without words that she trusted him at that moment. At that time. He touched her skillfully, intimately, until her body seemed to vibrate and shake with need. Her moistness and heat told him she was ready for him.

Her hands worked his belt as he leaned over to the bedside table and fumbled with one hand to open the drawer. He pulled out the foil package, a package he hadn't thought he'd need or use anytime in the near future.

He kicked off his shoes and shucked his pants off the side of the bed. Cora reached out and took the foil package from him, her grin playfully passionate. "Let me."

He sat back on his heels and allowed her to rip open the package and slowly, erotically slide the condom over him. His breath hissed in the back of his throat as her small hands touched the length and width of his hardness. He needed her then—he couldn't wait any longer—and she seemed to understand and want the same thing.

She lay back, her body open to him. Ready for him. He touched the apex of her opening, pausing for a minute to stare into the depth of those brown eyes, those eyes that seemed to see into his very soul. Their sweet honesty and trust sang to him, telling him that he was doing the right thing. That they were right for each other. Belonged together.

He slid into her, and she sighed his name, a tiny whisper of ecstasy before she wrapped her legs around him and drew him closer. He bent his head and kissed her, deepening the connection, and he felt her body move beneath him, her movements telling him of her want and need.

He was gentle at first, moving with caution, but then as their passion ignited to a high level, their movements became more frantic, more frenzied. She cried out, the sound wild and free, an open expression of such joy it brought a smile to his lips. He whispered her name in her ear, and she tightened her arms around his neck.

"Don't stop," she said. "Don't ever stop."

And he didn't. He gave her what she asked for. Loved her and cherished the feel of her beneath him and surrounding him. How wonderful to make love to a person who saw it as so joyous, so spontaneous.

Suddenly, her entire body shuddered and trembled beneath him, and Jake pulled her tight to him, clutching her small bottom with his hands. He gave every last bit of himself to her, following close behind as they both soared to reach shattering heights.

Chapter Twelve

The next morning Cora woke in Jake's arms. She moved cautiously, sitting up to glance down at his sleeping form. The morning light filtered in through the sheer drapes of his room and fell across his bed, bathing them both in its weak yellow light.

She grinned. His dark hair was mussed and his lips were slightly parted as he breathed softly against her naked skin.

He slept on his side, his strong powerful body curled around hers, as if he meant to keep her pressed against him forever. She fit so perfectly that she felt as though she was born to lie right where she was at that very moment.

She didn't want to get up, but it was already later than usual. She slipped out from beneath his arm and waited a minute as he mumbled sleepily and moved restlessly, seeking out the warm spot she had vacated. He turned over onto his stomach and buried his face in his pillow. In a few moments his breathing was deep and even.

She tiptoed into the bathroom, conscious of the fact that the fire had gone out at some point during the night, leaving the room almost cold. Her bare skin rippled with goose bumps, and she relished the thought of a hot, steamy shower.

A few minutes later, her hair washed and her body warmed

from a hot shower and a brisk towel drying, Cora stepped out of the bathroom. She was surprised to see Jake sitting up, bare-chested and the phone to his ear.

He grinned at her and held up a hand, letting her know he'd be just a minute. But then, from across the room, she saw his face change. One minute he was engaged in a thoughtful conversation with someone on the phone, and the next, his imposing frame seemed to seethe with anger. His responses to the person were terse.

Finally he set the receiver down. Cora could tell he was struggling not to explode. Bad news, obviously, and from the dark look he threw her, whatever was bothering him had something to do with her.

"What's wrong, Jake?" she asked, pulling the fluffy towel off her head and draping it over her shoulders.

He stared across the room, silent for a moment, as if he was trying to decide how he was going to say whatever it was he needed to say.

"That was my security chief." His voice was flat.

Her heart squeezed with frightened anticipation. Confession time was near. His security expert, his hired snoop, the man assigned to get the goods on her. Cora waited, but for some reason, Jake didn't continue. It was as if he wished the moment hadn't come, that if he spoke, the magic between them would be gone.

She sank into the chair next to her. "From your face, I'd say he had some concerns. Am I right?"

"Good guess."

She waited.

Finally he spoke again, "I want to know why you lied to me."

"What did I lie about?" she stalled. Oh God, even now she was skirting around the truth, prolonging her confession.

Sparks of anger fired in the depths of his eyes. "Just answer the question, dammit."

Heartrending sadness rushed through her. How did she answer him when there were so many lies, she wasn't sure where to start? Did she just confess to them all and lose him straight-out? Or did she wait and see if she could salvage something of what they had been trying to build—a fragile trust between two people unable to trust?

She trapped several strands of her hair between the ends of the towel and carefully rubbed them dry. She glanced up at him. "I can't answer your question, Jake, if I don't know what you're talking about. What have I lied about?"

"Marty tells me that your IDs are bogus. Fakes. Not even good fakes, at that."

She didn't answer. How could she? His snoop was right. They were lousy fakes.

"Well?" His voice was impatient, curt. He was waiting for an answer, but Cora already knew that anything she said would be rejected. The tone of his voice told her that he'd already judged her and found her guilty.

Not that she was surprised at his reaction. How could she be? He'd told her at the start how he deplored lies. How he had no ability to tolerate lies in a relationship.

She'd known that going in and still had allowed something to build on that foundation of lies. She had planned on telling him, planned on telling him last night. But they'd gotten caught up in a moment of passion, and somehow the explanation hadn't seemed so important last night.

As terrible as her lies had been, she'd done it for a reason. He had to understand. He had to realize there wasn't any other way she could have done it.

She faced him, her hands folded loosely in front of her, her shoulders braced. "He's right. My identification is fake."

Pain flickered across Jake's face, just a brief flash and then it was gone. It told her that he'd hoped, for one brief moment, that his security chief had been wrong.

Finally he nodded abruptly as if what she'd revealed was what he'd expected. His expression went blank. "Any particular reason for lying? Or was it simply a lark? An opportunity to see if you could get away with it? What were you trying to pull?"

"Jake." She moved closer. "I don't know how to explain this to you in any other way than to say that I never meant to hurt you. I had my reasons for hiding. I wanted to tell you, I—"

"Save the sentimental explanations and cut to the chase. Why?"

Cora opened her mouth to tell him, to simply blurt it all out. But the words wouldn't come. She loved him and she knew the risk she put him and his entire family in by telling him. Every instinct told Cora that she was better off leaving. If she got off the island—removed herself from anything that had to do with Jake and his family—they would remain safe.

If she told him what she was up against, Jake would need to be her protector; it was his nature. His lot in life. He would try to go after Dubane, and Jake had no idea of the insanity that drove Erik. The rage and hatred that ripped at his soul and made him unbeatable. A demon who knew no limits.

Cora couldn't bear the thought of not having Jake in her life. But even worse, she couldn't bear the guilt and pain that would come from losing him should Erik find him.

Better to keep silent and walk away. To leave behind something that she could never have because one man was bent on killing her and anyone who came in contact with her. If she left now, Erik would leave Jake alone. He would be out of her reach, but he would be safe.

He saw her hesitation and the anger flared again. But he got it under control as quickly as before. He held up a hand. "You know what, don't even bother. I've heard my fill of excuses. Just make sure you're off the island by tomorrow."

Cora nodded, trying to ignore the rip of pain that tore through her body. He was dismissing her. Rejecting everything they had meant to each other, and she couldn't fight it. She had to comply. Had to do what he said in order to protect him.

He turned and stalked for the door, his back and shoulders stiff and unforgiving.

Desperation slammed against her chest wall. She stepped toward him. She couldn't do this. She loved him. She needed him so desperately that it ate at the edges of her very soul. "Jake, wait!"

He stopped but didn't turn around. His hand rested on the door knob.

She swallowed against the thick veil of fear that coated her throat. She had to tell him. She had to reveal her true identity and make him understand. Make him believe that she never meant to deceive him.

But Erik's final words to her sang sweetly in her ear. *I'll be back for you, sweet Cora. Back for you and anyone else you care about. Wait for me.*

Her hand dropped to her side. No, she was right the first time. If she told him who she was she'd only put him in more danger. She needed to get off the island and as far away from Jake as she could possibly get. But the thought of leaving, of never seeing him again, hurt more than she thought her heart could bear.

"I…I'm sorry," she choked. "I never meant to hurt you. I'll leave in the morning."

He nodded without speaking, without turning to look at her. Cora wanted desperately to add something—anything just to let him know how much she loved him. But he shoved the door open and left before the words could leave her lips.

She was alone, left with the sound of the door slamming closed on the rest of her life.

JAKE HAD LEFT THE ISLAND hours ago. He hadn't even said goodbye. Cora heard the helicopter land as she was setting the table for lunch. She moved to the window to watch as he ran across the wet grass and climbed in. He never even turned to look at her. The chopper lifted off and he was gone.

A short time later Amanda and her guests returned, and Cora found herself going about her chores mechanically. At one point, she realized she hadn't cried once. But then, she knew it wouldn't have made a difference if she had. Jake was gone, and crying wouldn't bring him back.

Of course, she didn't have much time to feel sorry for herself. Shortly before dinner, Mrs. Benson ran into the kitchen, shouting that they had to call the ambulance because William Mackenzie wasn't breathing right.

Surprisingly calm, Cora took the phone from the distraught housekeeper and made the call, contacting the Myst Inlet Fire Department and requesting medical help. While they waited for the paramedics to arrive, she hovered over William, worried about the paleness of his skin, his unresponsiveness and his shallow breathing.

When the paramedics arrived, they loaded him onto a stretcher, covered him with blankets and a plastic poncho to protect him against the rain that had started to fall. Amanda, Dr. Sheffield and Mrs. Benson followed the stretcher down to the dock, prepared to accompany him on his trip to Crouse

Irving in Syracuse. Amanda promised to call as soon as she knew anything.

Once they were gone, Cora went to the kitchen and did what had always calmed her. She made food. Several hours later she set the vegetable peeler down and stared at the pile of carrots stacked in front of her. How had that happened? There was enough to feed a small army of rabbits. She'd become so immersed in her concern for William that she had peeled the entire bag without even realizing it.

Although the clock over the stove told her it was past eleven, she knew she wouldn't be able to sleep. She needed to wait up until she heard from Amanda. Both Megan and Vivian had gone to bed shortly after nine.

She glanced at the clock again—11:30 p.m. She knew the helicopter taking William to Crouse Irving Medical Center in Syracuse had arrived hours ago and he was in the hands of competent doctors, but she wished Amanda would call and set her mind at ease.

The radio on the counter played some vaguely familiar pop tune, but every half hour, the station announcer had broken in to give a weather update, warning the inhabitants of the St. Lawrence River Valley to brace for an early winter storm.

Rain and sleet lashed the windows, and every once in a while, the room lights flickered ominously. Overnight, the rain and sleet was supposed to change to snow, blanketing the northeast with more than twelve inches of snow.

Grabbing a plastic tub, Cora scooped the veggies into the container and snapped on the lid. A quick glance at the clock over the stove told her it was well past her bedtime. She got up and stuck the tub on the bottom shelf of the refrigerator.

She wondered whether she should simply go on up to bed or wait a little longer to see if Amanda would remember to call.

She hoped Amanda had been able to get a hold of Jake. He wouldn't like not knowing that his father's condition was this grave. He'd want to be there, especially if his father wasn't going to make it through the night.

Wiping her hands on a towel, she deposited the vegetable peeler in the dishwasher, closed and locked it and then turned the dial to start. The gentle whirl of water spraying in the machine was comforting, almost, but not quite, drowning out the fierce howl of the wind whipping around the castle.

Amanda had reassured her before leaving that if the electricity went out, the castle's private generator would kick in. But if something happened to the generator, they'd be left making their way around the stone monstrosity by flashlight and candles.

It was frightening to realize that the three of them were essentially stranded in the middle of the St. Lawrence River until the storm passed. Even if she wanted to get to shore, the probability of anyone getting out to the island wasn't good. The Coast Guard patrolled the waters, but Cora was fairly certain that on a night like this, they were busy with other concerns.

She reached behind her and untied her apron, glancing at the rug by the fire. Caesar lay stretched out on his stomach, his giant head resting on his paws. As she headed for the stairs, his eyelids didn't even flutter, but as soon as her foot hit the first step he lifted his head and his body tensed.

He scrambled to his feet. As he loped over to her, his brown eyes glared accusingly at her. He didn't like the fact that she might have tried to get upstairs without him in the lead. He bullied his way into the stairwell with her, his big body pushing her up against the railing in the narrow space.

"Easy there, champ, one at a time," she grumbled.

He ignored her and pushed ahead. He'd gone three or four steps before he glanced back as if to say, You coming, slow-poke?

"I don't understand your attachment to me, Caesar. You're smart enough to realize that I'm not your typical dog-lovin' sucker. Cleo got that message loud and clear. You don't see her sniffing around me, do you?"

He looked at her as if smiling, letting her know that he understood her reluctance to forge a friendship, but also letting her know that he didn't give a damn how she felt about this odd partnership. The sleek muscles of his haunches bunched and rippled as he started up the stairs ahead of her. Cora followed.

She was halfway to the top when the lights flickered and then blinked out. Even in the stairwell, she could hear the raging wind hitting the outside wall of the castle. She waited, praying that the generator would kick in. Nothing.

She swore softly and ran a hand along the railing, guiding herself upward. Caesar nudged her when she reached the top, letting her know he was right beside her in the dark.

The hall was pitch-black, but she again used her hand to guide herself down the hall. A few seconds later her fingers closed over the cool metal knob of her bedroom door.

Relief flowed over her. There was a flashlight on her dresser, left over from her walk a few nights ago.

As she turned the knob, the lights flickered and then snapped on again. She heard the start-up whirl of the elevator.

She paused. Who would be using the elevator at this time of night? Especially after what had happened the other night. Jake had made it clear to everyone that the elevator was off-limits until he was able to have a repair crew in to take a look at it. And even worse, the power was going on and off. Didn't the person realize they could become trapped in the elevator if the power stayed off? Cora shivered.

But the elevator labored up to the second floor and came to a grinding halt. She waited, her breath trapped in her throat.

The inside gate of the elevator rattled back and then silence filled the hall. The overhead light in the elevator was off, leaving the inside pitch-black. It was a dark, empty hole of nothingness. Cora squinted, trying to see inside. But it was too dark.

Beside her, Caesar stiffened, a low threatening growl growing deep in his barrel. She reached down and touched his back, her fingers pressing into his raised hackles.

"What is it, boy?"

He growled again, the sound low and ominous. He pressed his big body against her legs, his muscles shifting and bunching beneath his fur. He was trying to keep her from walking down the hall.

The pulse in the side of Cora's neck kicked up another few notches. Something or someone was lurking in the darkened elevator.

"Who's there?" she called.

Her voice echoed in the hall.

Nothing.

"I've got a knife," she threatened, thinking of her paring knife sitting safely in its case in her dresser drawer. "You'd better not come any closer."

Nothing.

And then, a weak voice spoke from the depths of the dark elevator. "Help me. Someone please help me."

The voice was familiar. It was Vivian Sheffield's voice.

"Mrs. Sheffield? Vivian, is that you?"

"Help me," the voice cried out again.

Grabbing Caesar's collar, Cora headed down the hall. The dog stalked alongside her, his legs stiff, the growl rumbling even deeper in his chest. Whatever was going on, Caesar wasn't liking it one little bit.

She was almost to the end of the hall when the lights flickered again and snapped off, plunging the house into total darkness again.

Cora stopped. Should she go back for the flashlight? Why hadn't she gotten it when she was right there? She chewed her bottom lip.

But then Vivian cried out again, "Help me. Someone please help me."

In the darkness, Cora felt the narrow hallway widen into the main hall. She could feel the cold air sweeping up the stairs. As she turned in the direction of the elevator, she almost fell. Something or someone was stretched across the hall.

She bent down, and her hand touched hair and warm flesh.

"Vivian," she whispered.

"He's inside the house. He's here." Her voice was barely audible, the words strained. Fractured.

"Who's here? What's happened."

Kneeling down, Cora touched the side of Vivian's face, her hand slipping in something wet and sticky. Her heart thudded against her breast bone. She knew without seeing it that it was blood, the thick coppery smell choking her.

Fear raced through her veins, speeding along with the velocity of an arrow to her heart.

She reached down and shook Vivian's shoulder. "Vivian, talk to me. What happened? Who's here?"

She didn't answer.

The lights flickered wildly and then snapped on. Cora screamed.

Vivian lay stretched out on her back, a gaping wound cut horizontally across the width of her neck. Her eyes stared blankly up at Cora. Her hands trembling, Cora pressed her fingers to the side of Vivian's neck. Nothing. No flutter. No pulse. She was dead. Erik had gotten to her, taken her life and was now stalking her.

A whimper slipped from between Cora's lips and she scrambled backward, her hand covering her mouth. "Oh God. Oh God, he's here."

Her chest constricted and she gulped air, but it was if her throat had closed up on her, preventing her from ever breathing again.

Caesar licked her face, his brown eyes concerned. His body was tense. He didn't know how to help her.

Desperate, Cora scrambled to her feet. She needed to get to a phone. If the lights were back on, then perhaps the phone line had been restored, too.

She ran to the head of the stairs. The hall below was empty, the shadows deep along the edges. The windows flashed with lightning and the wind howled. Rain drummed against the stained-glass panes.

The library. She would hole up in the library and try to get a call out to the mainland from there. At least there she knew where the secret passageway was located. She could push something up against the panel and keep anyone from entering.

She started down. Halfway down the marble steps, lightning lit up the huge stained-glass window over the front doors. A second later, a crack of thunder split the air, seeming to shake the stone walls with its force.

The chandeliers overhead flickered off, again plunging the castle back into total darkness. Cora grabbed the banister with both hands and crouched down, making herself as small a target as she possibly could.

The frantic beat of her heart throbbed in her ears. Caesar leaned in to lick her face, his breath hot against the side of her face. She buried her head in his fur for a minute, trying desperately to take strength in the dog's size. He would guard her. He wouldn't let anything happen to her.

Remaining in a crouch, she continued downward, her steps cautious. Tentative.

She had to make it to the library. Had to make it to safety. If she could reach Jake by phone, she could tell him to send reinforcements. He wouldn't let her die, no matter how angry he was at her for lying about her identity. He would come and take her off the island. He would get her to safety if she could only reach him.

RAIN POUNDED a thunderous beat on the roof of the limo. In the front seat, the wipers swept across the windshield, beating a frantic tattoo. They were having a hard time keeping the sleet from building up.

Twice the driver had been forced to pull over to scrape the buildup from the glass. The storm was so bad that when the corporate plane had landed at Ogdensburgh airport, his pilot had said there was no way he'd take the chopper out in this weather. Determined to get to the island somehow, Jake had called for the limo.

He leaned forward and pressed the button that lowered the partition. "How's the driving, Ernie? Are the roads getting too slick?"

"It's pretty tough going, Mr. Mackenzie. But we'll be in Myst Inlet in less than ten minutes." Ernie nodded at the dashboard. "The local station is telling everyone to brace for

the main part of the storm to hit any minute now. Hard to believe it isn't already here, but they're talking about this all
changing over to snow. Lots of it. I'm betting we get there
before it hits."

Ernie put on his turn signal and pulled out into the left lane,
maneuvering around a slow-moving snowplow. As he eased
back into the right lane, the back wheels skidded a bit. With
practiced ease, he applied a touch of the gas and the car
straightened out.

"Nice save," Jake said.

"Thank you, sir." The driver paused for a moment and
then added, "I'm not sure you'll be able to get out to the island tonight. The winds are pretty bad. Might be next to impossible for Gracy to dock the boat, let alone navigate the
river."

Jake glanced out the window, but it was too dark to see the
river running parallel to Route 12. But he knew it was out
there, black, fast and wild. "Just get me to the marina. I'll take
it from there."

The chirp of his cell phone cut through the tense atmosphere of the limo. Jake sat back and flicked open his cell.
"Jake Mackenzie."

"Jake, it's me, Marty."

"Where the hell have you been? I've been leaving mes-
sages for you all over the place."

"I know. I'm up here in San Francisco, and I've been a busy
little beaver."

"San Francisco? Why there?"

"Why not?" Marty laughed and Jake knew from the tone
of it that the man was onto something. "Are you sitting
down?"

"Yes, just tell me what you've got."

"Tyler Connery and some guy out here by the name of Erik Dubane, who by the way, was arrested for a rather sensational murder, are one and the same person."

Jake sat forward, jamming his elbows onto his knees as he pressed his cell to his ear. "What are you saying?"

"Apparently Connery has the habit of changing his name. In fact, he changes it so often that the authorities out here aren't really sure *what* his real name is. They're still digging around in his background. But whoever he is, Connery is also Erik Dubane."

"Holy sh—"

"Hang on, buddy, that isn't even the good stuff," Marty interrupted.

"There's more?"

"Oh, yeah, lots more. This is going to blow your ever-loving mind. Guess who has been out here to visit Dubane?"

"Who?"

"None other than your beloved stepmother, Amanda."

Jake sat back, his shoulders hitting the posh leather of the seat. He frowned. "Why would Amanda want to visit Dubane?"

"Good question, and one I don't have all the answers to yet. But apparently she hooked up with Dubane's lawyer and visited him. Remember that little trip she took a few months ago. The one when she seemed to simply disappear and you and I got a little curious?"

"Sure."

"Well, from what I can figure out, Dubane's lawyer told the guards that Amanda was his secretary and he brought her in to meet privately with Dubane."

"This doesn't make sense. What would be the reason?"

Jake tried to wrap his brain around the puzzle. None of it made sense. "If Amanda knew that Dubane was Connery, do you think she was trying to find out what happened to Natalie?" Jake felt like he was grasping at straws. Amanda hadn't cared that Natalie took off. Amanda only cared about herself and the money.

"Your guess is as good as mine. I have a few other leads to follow up and I'll get back to you when I have some answers. But you need to know that there's more to all this than just Connery and Dubane being one and the same person."

"Such as?"

"The D.A. out here, Greene, says that he's worried about the safety of his key witness against Dubane. He thinks she's in danger. Her name is—"

Understanding hit Jake like a bolt of lighting. "—Cora. Cora Shelly is Greene's witness, isn't she?"

Fielding's voice held a hint of admiration, "You guessed it. Cora Sheldon, aka Cora Shelly, is scheduled to testify against Erik Dubane. According to Greene, Dubane killed Cora's roommate and then tried to murder her. Greene says that it was a pretty bad scene. Dubane brutalized her before she was able to escape."

"Damn, Marty." Jake raked a hand through his hair. How could he have been so wrong about Cora? How could he have pushed her away when she needed him so much? "I hurt her. I couldn't see straight after you told me that she wasn't who she claimed to be. I told her I couldn't handle a person who lied to me like that. That I couldn't handle the deceitfulness. I pushed her away and never gave her a chance to explain why she was keeping her identity a secret."

"Don't start blaming yourself. You had reason to be suspicious. Connery took you to the cleaners. He seduced your wife and took off with a lot of your money. Probably killed Natalie from the sounds of things. If Cora is the person you think she is, she'll understand."

Jake shook his head. He could only hope she'd understand. He had a lot of explaining to do when he got back to the island. Why hadn't she simply told him what was going on? Why couldn't she have trusted him?

"From what Greene told me, Dubane was Cora's neighbor for a year before he attacked. He played mind games with the two girls—did little things to torment them. Apparently they couldn't get anyone to help them, to believe them."

Jake shifted restlessly, trying to peer out the window to determine where they were. "Look, I need to get off. I've got to try and reach Cora."

"Wait, don't hang up yet."

"What?" Jake was impatient now, eager to call Cora and convince her that all that had been said between them was a mistake. That he cared for her more than even he realized. He needed her. Needed to hear her voice and feel the touch of her small hand in his.

"You haven't heard the worst part yet. Greene told me that this guy Dubane escaped during a pretrial hearing last week. They have no idea where he is. But Greene's worried about Cora. He said she freaked out when he told her that Dubane had escaped. She hung up on him before telling him where she was hiding."

"Did you tell him she's on Midnight Island?"

"No, I wanted to wait and talk to you first."

"Call him back and tell him. And Marty, tell him I'm on my way to get her to safety right now."

"You think Dubane might be on the island?"

"I don't know. Beatrice is dead and the police have ruled

her death as suspicious. I originally thought she had just fallen on the rocks. But now I'm not too sure. Cora has had a couple of weird things happen to her lately."

He thought back to the weird dreams and the talk of drugs. Could someone have been drugging her? Had Amanda been gaslighting her with the help of Sheffield? He couldn't rule it out. Something was terribly wrong.

"I need to make sure Dubane didn't get out onto the island somehow."

"But why would Dubane go there?"

Jake scrubbed his palm across his face, a feeling of dread pressed down hard on him. "She's a witness for the prosecution. He might be looking to eliminate her. We also know that Amanda saw him in prison and shortly afterward she hired Cora to work for us. We can't rule out the possibility that for some reason she and Dubane are working together."

"But why? What would be Amanda's motivation?"

"That's your job. Find out! Now I'm getting off. I need to get a hold of Red. I need to let him know what's going on and have him pick up Amanda and Sheffield for questioning."

Jake clicked off and immediately started dialing a new number.

"Myst Inlet Police Department," a woman's voice said.

"I need to talk to Red. This is Jake Mackenzie."

"One moment, please."

"LaPlant."

"Red, it's me, Jake."

"Where are you? Amanda has been trying to locate you. They had to take your father up to Crouse Irving in Syracuse. He isn't doing so hot. They want you there pronto."

"I have another emergency that needs my attention first."

"What?"

"I need you to take me out to the island."

Red's laughter rumbled over the cell. "You're kidding, right? Have you looked outside?"

"No, I'm not kidding. I'm almost at the marina. Meet me there."

"Not a chance, Jake. No one is going out on that river tonight. Not even the Coast Guard."

"You and I are."

"You can't be serious."

"I am. I think there might be a killer loose on the island."

"What?"

"I don't have time to explain right now. Meet me at the dock in five minutes."

"Okay, but this better be good." Red hung up, and Jake leaned forward again, his eyes straining to see out the sleet-encrusted front window.

"We're here, Mr. Mackenzie," Ernie said, pulling the car into the large lot adjoining the Hidden Harbor Marina.

"Keep the motor running. I have one more call to make," Jake said as he turned up the collar of his jacket with one hand and keyed in the number of Midnight Castle with the other.

A few seconds later Cora's sweet voice warmed his ear. "H-hello?"

"It's me, Jake."

He could hear her take a shuddering breath on the other end of the phone, and then her fear seemed to rush through the receiver in a flood of words, "Oh God, Jake. He's here. He's here in the castle. He's killed Vivian and he's going to get Megan and me. You've got to help us. We're alone. No one else is out here. They're all gone."

He didn't need to ask who *he* was. He already knew. "I'm coming, Cora. I'm at the marina. I'll be there as quickly as I can. Where's Megan?"

"She's right here. The dogs are with us, too. We're hiding in the library, but I can hear him. He's playing with us, Jake. He's done this to me before. I know who he is."

"I know who he is, too, sweetie. But you've got to hang on. I'm coming for you as fast as I can."

She must have put her hand over her mouth, because suddenly her sobs were muffled. He knew she didn't want him to know how frightened she was. Didn't want him to know how afraid she was that he wouldn't get there in time.

"Are you there? Cora?"

"I'm here," she said, her voice strained.

"Good girl. Do you know where he is right now?"

"I—"

The line clicked off in midsentence.

Jake's fingers tightened on the phone. "Cora? Cora, answer me, sweetheart!"

The cell lay silent.

It felt as though his heart might punch a hole through the center of his chest, it was beating so hard. He hit the redial button. He swore softly. The numbers seemed to take forever to run.

Finally the phone rang. And then it rang again.

No one picked up.

He jammed the cell in his pocket and yanked open the car door. He paused and yelled back over his shoulder to his driver, "Call the hospital. Somehow you need to get a message to my father. Tell him to hang on. Tell him not to let go until I get there."

The wind hit him full in the face with a freezing blast of rain and sleet. It lashed his cheeks and neck.

A patrol car with its flashing lights on swung into the marina parking lot, coming to a stop next to him. Red jumped out, his bulky frame covered in an ankle-length slicker and hood. He threw a second one to Jake.

"Your cell phone must have gone out!" he shouted. "Your man Marty called. He said to tell you that he's pretty sure after talking to Connery's lawyer that Amanda lured Cora to the island to discredit her testimony. To paint her as unstable. Crazy. If she did that she must have figured that Cora would never be able to testify against her son."

Jake stared at him. "Amanda's son?"

Red nodded. "According to Marty, the records just came through. Erik Dubane aka Tyler Connery is really Amanda's biological son. He was taken away from her when he was seven. Guess the kid was pretty disturbed and spent his entire childhood in institutions. Pretty violent."

Red's explanation went a long way to explaining the beginning of his original investigation of Amanda—the one his father put a stop to. It explained her involvement with the Child Welfare system.

"Well, it somewhat explains why she did what she did to Cora…if there is such a thing as an explanation for such cruelty. I think when we do a search of the castle, we're going to find drugs—hypnotics or some type of hallucinogens. I think Amanda was drugging Cora with something. Probably something she got off Sheffield."

"We'll have those two in custody in no time. A little pressure on that fat shrink and he'll be singing like a canary on a sunny day."

Jake pulled on the slicker and nodded toward the police cruiser. "Let's go! I don't think we have much time."

He headed for the docks, not waiting to see if Red was following. A hard knot of anxiety churned in his stomach. He needed to reach the island, and he needed to get there in time. He needed to make sure Cora was safe.

Chapter Thirteen

Cora sat on the floor, her back braced against the door.

She took a deep, shuddering breath and whispered a desperate mantra to herself. *Stay calm. Don't panic. You can hold him off until Jake arrives.*

Outside, the wind howled and the snow and sleet lashed the windows. Unlike four months ago, when the police arrived at the last minute to sweep her to safety, there wasn't much chance of that happening this time.

This time she was alone on the island with only Megan and two dogs at her side. Jake was separated from her by a monstrous winter storm and a raging river. It looked as though she was going to have to handle this alone.

She tried not to think about how cold and scared she was. She needed to stay calm for Megan.

She glanced around. They'd jammed a heavy door stopper under the bottom of the secret panel behind the desk and then pushed the heavy desk up against it. She was pretty sure it wouldn't stop anyone from getting in if he knew where the secret passage was and he really wanted in. But at least she'd hear him forcing his way in.

Megan sat next to her, humming softly, her arms wrapped around herself, rocking back and forth, oblivious to everything. Cora figured Megan'd gotten so confused she had simply withdrawn. Perhaps that was best right now. Cora hadn't much energy left to comfort Megan even if she wanted it. It was all Cora could do to keep from rolling into a ball and whimpering.

A candle sat on the floor between them, throwing a flickering circle of light around them, and the fire behind the iron screen kept the room reasonably warm. Cora had some concern that their supply of wood would run out before the heat came back on, but then Erik might reach them before that happened. They had a long night ahead of them.

Megan's rocking intensified and her hum turned into a singsongy chant. "He's home. He's home. He's home."

"Who's home?" Cora asked, her brain finally registering what the woman was saying.

"My brother's home. My brother's home."

Cora's head snapped up and her heart surged with sweet relief. She got to her feet and ran for the window. Jake was home? Had he somehow gotten across the river to them? She wanted to weep with relief.

Outside, rain whipped across the landscape and the light down by the boathouse, powered by a separate generator, swung wildly in the wind. Huge waves washed over the wood planks of the dock, swamping it and the shore. There were no boats docked, and Cora knew there was no way a helicopter could land.

She turned back toward Megan. "There's no boat out there, Megan? Jake isn't home."

Megan lifted her head and scowled. "No, silly, not Jake. My real brother. My real brother is home."

"Your real brother?" She slowly walked back to the

woman. "What are you talking about, Megan? Who is your real brother?"

Megan smiled smugly. "Tyler. I'm talking about Tyler. He's my *real* brother. He's the one who's come back."

Cora frowned, trying desperately to understand what Megan was trying to tell her. Whatever it was she was trying to say, Cora instinctively knew that it was critical.

"Are you talking about the gardener who used to live here? Is that the Tyler you're talking about?"

Megan nodded, her braid bobbing up and down like some kind of demented tail. She giggled. "Yes, Tyler is my real brother." She looked panicked for a moment and added, "But no one is supposed to know that. No one except Mommy and me." She pressed a finger to her lips. "Don't tell, it's a secret."

Cora crouched down and cupped Megan's hands in her own. Somehow she needed to break this crazy code and understand what Megan was talking about. "Why is it a secret? William loves you. He loves your mother. He'd love your brother, too."

Megan looked puzzled for a minute but then said, "Mommy says no one could love Tyler. She said he's bad. She said that no one would understand. She said I wasn't to tell anyone he's my brother, not even William."

"What was Tyler doing here at the castle, then? Why did he work as a gardener?"

Megan seemed to have lost interest in the conversation and she slowly rocked herself, humming softly.

"Megan, concentrate," Cora begged, her voice sharp. "Why did Tyler come here?"

"Mommy says he wanted to see us. He hadn't seen Mommy since he was a little boy. I don't remember him because I was a baby when he went away." Her eyes clouded slightly. "Mommy said that the bad people came and took him away when he was only seven. They took him to live somewhere else—in a big hospital with lots of doctors. Mommy didn't get to see him anymore." Her eyes filled with tears. "Mommy was so sad when they took him. She couldn't stay there anymore and she moved away."

"Do you know the name of the place they took Tyler to live in when he was a little boy?"

Megan shook her head. "No, but Tyler told me it was an awful place. A place where the people were mean to him all the time. He said they hurt him there."

Suddenly Megan's face crumpled and her eyes widened with alarm. She clamped a hand over her mouth. "Oh no!" she whimpered around her hand. "I just told you the secret, and I promised Mommy I wouldn't tell."

Megan's blue eyes stared at Cora in alarm, and the intense color of the eyes sent a terrifying chill through Cora.

Her hands tightened into fists.

Oh God, how could she have not noticed the color of Megan's eyes? The similarity? A sob fluttered in the back of her throat, and she raised a fist to her mouth, trying desperately to hold the sob back. Megan's eyes were the same brilliant sapphire blue as Erik's.

The terror had come full circle. The woman sitting in front of her was Erik's sister.

They both jumped when a light knock hit the library door.

"Oh, Cora. Little Cora Bora, where are you?" Erik's taunt filtered through the thick, paneled door, sending a chill of fear so sharp and so painful through Cora that she thought she might pass out. "Come out, come out, wherever you are."

"*Please, Jake,*" Cora whispered as she sank to the floor and put her hands over her ears. "Please get here soon."

THE HEAVY BOW of the Myst Inlet Police's cruiser rose up on the crest of the wave and then slammed down the other side with a bone-jarring thud. Jake grabbed the dash and braced his feet to absorb the bulk of the toss. His body moved with the jarring motion.

He glanced over at Red. The police chief's eyes stayed fixed on the dark horizon. The wipers danced across the windshield, but they seemed to barely put a dent in the ice and snow lashing the front of the cruiser.

"It's pretty bad, huh?" Jake said.

"*Bad* ain't the term I was thinking of," Red said grimly. "Try out of control and life threatening. We've got to be nuts to be attempting this." Red glanced over his shoulder at the fading lights of the marina. "I vote that we turn around and go back."

Jake shook his head. "You don't get a vote. We're going to the island." He met Red's gaze. "They're out there alone. We can't leave them to deal with Connery on their own."

"What makes you so sure he's there?"

"Because when I was able to get through to Cora, she said Vivian was dead and someone was stalking her. They're holed up in the library, and we need to reach them before he does."

Red fought with the wheel as another wave hit them, rocking the boat with a bone-jarring shake. "We won't be much good to them if we're both on the bottom of the river."

"That won't happen," Jake said, trying to infuse his voice with a confidence he wasn't feeling at the moment.

CORA LIFTED HER HANDS away from her ears and listened. The pounding on the door and Erik's taunts had ceased a few minutes ago. But the silence was almost worse. At least when he was outside the door, shouting and pounding on the door,

Cora knew where he was. Now she wasn't sure what he was up to.

Getting to her feet, she moved to the window overlooking the marina. "Jake, please hurry," she whispered softly. "I don't think we have much time left."

Suddenly a heavy thud hit the library door, followed by the sound of splitting wood. Megan screamed, and Cora whirled around. Another thud hit the door and the door shuddered on its hinges.

Erik had gotten resourceful—he'd gone for an ax.

It would only take a few minutes for him to chop his way through the door. Cora turned back toward the window. What now?

Out on the lawn a wisp of white flitted across her line of vision. Standing on tiptoe, Cora struggled to see through the thick snow and sleet.

Sure enough, the outline of the Lady became visible. She was looking up at the window, beckoning to Cora, telling her to come outside. Without further consideration, Cora unbolted the window and pushed open the sash. A bitter wind swept in through the open window, blowing snow and ice into the room.

The cold seemed to revive Megan and she stood up, wandering over to see what was going on. "What are you doing? Close the window, Cora, it's cold outside."

Cora buttoned up her sweater to her neck. "We need to get down to the boathouse. But we're going to have to go out the window. Erik won't let us out the door."

Megan shook her head. "No, I don't want to go outside. Mommy would be angry. She wouldn't want me to catch a cold."

Cora wanted to shout, wanted to shake Megan and tell her

that she was going to catch more than a cold if she didn't co-operate. But she held her tongue. "It's okay, Megan, we're just playing hide and seek with Erik. See the Lady?" She pointed to the drifting outline of the woman out on the side lawn. "See how she's telling us to follow her?"

Megan looked out the window. She turned around, her face red from the wind whipping through the opening. "But it's cold out there." She backed away, shaking her head. "I don't want to go. Tyler won't hurt us. He's my brother."

"Tyler's sick, Megan. He wants to hurt us." She cringed as the ax hit the door with another thud. Thank God for the thickness of the oak door.

She pointed out at the lawn again. "Look, the Lady is try-ing to tell us to come with her. She wants to help us. She's telling us to follow her. Please, Megan, please come with me."

Cora gently pushed Megan toward the window, but the woman's face suddenly changed, becoming angry, almost sullen. "No! I want to stay. I want to talk to my brother."

Cora tried to hold on to her, but Megan pulled away and ran across the room. "I'm coming, Tyler! I'm coming!"

Cora watched in horror as Megan starting yanking the fur-niture pushed up against the door out of the way. "Don't, Megan! Don't let him in."

But Megan ignored her, her fingers already working the heavy bolts locking the door. Erik shouted through the door, urging Megan on, telling her to hurry. And Cora knew that she couldn't wait any longer. Saving Megan was no longer the issue. She had to get out, had to save herself. Erik was here to kill her, not Megan.

She threw a leg over the windowsill and scrambled over the side. The wind pulled at her clothes, making them billow, as her feet struggled for a foothold on the stone ledge. Her fingers cramped, already frozen from the bitter ice and wind hammering the castle.

Finally she let go, dropping the final few feet to the ground below. Her shoes skidded on the snow- and ice-encrusted grass and she almost went down, but she steadied herself against the side of the castle and looked around, trying to orient herself.

Caesar jumped out the window, landing next to her.

A few yards away, barely visible through the blinding snow, Cora could see the wavering figure of The Mournful Lady. She was still beckoning urgently for her to follow. Without a backward glance, Cora took off across the yard.

She'd only gone a few feet when she lost sight of the Lady. The wind howled around her, the snow heavy and wet, sticking to her clothes and soaking her with a chill so deep and relentless that she felt as though she couldn't go another step.

But she did, stumbling forward, peering through wet lashes, trying to find the figure who seemed to be her only salvation. She'd reached the thicket and the path leading to the boathouse. She paused in the shelter of the shrubs, unsure where to go. Should she head toward the boathouse? It was most likely the direction Jake would come from, but it was also a dead end. Once she went down the path, there was no way back except the way she came. Nowhere to go but into the river.

She hunched her shoulders and laughed softly, the sound slightly crazed. Who was she kidding? There was nowhere for her to go period. She was on an island. Her escape options were nil. If Jake didn't get here soon, she was dead.

She glanced back toward the castle, barely able to see the lighted window of the library through the driving snow. Shadows moved in the room and then the faint light from the candle was blocked as someone stepped up to the window.

Cora stared across the length of the yard, knowing without really being able to see the person that it was Erik standing there. He looked out at her, contemplating his next move. And then as she watched, he threw his leg over the sill.

Cora turned, her decision made for her. No time to backtrack. Her time had just run out.

She plunged down the path to the boathouse, the thicket of bushes momentarily sheltering her from the wind. Caesar trotted alongside.

Up ahead, she could see the Lady. She was still with them. She turned and beckoned to her again, her motion urgent. Cora fought the fatigue settling over her as her body combated the bitter cold.

A few seconds later they broke through the thicket onto the beach. The wind was worse here, the speed and drive of the snow incredible. Waves rolled up on the shore, washing over the docks and battering the sides of the boathouse. The wind howled and roared with the intensity of a runaway tanker.

Cora staggered backward, her hair whipping into her eyes. Caesar nudged her leg, turning her in the direction of the boathouse.

She turned in time to see The Mournful Lady glance over her shoulder as she melted through the side of the structure. She motioned again for Cora to follow before she disappeared.

Stumbling and tripping over the icy rocks, Cora made her way to the building. As she opened the door, the wind caught it and flung it wide. She stepped inside and used the full weight of her body to close the door again.

The inside was damp and cold. Colder even than the outside temperature. Water lapped at the boat slips, splashing up onto the wooden docking. Jake's collection of antique Adirondack boats bobbed up and down with the flow of the river, each securely tied. No doubt Gracy had anticipated the storm, securing them before leaving with Amanda.

On the other side of the structure, she saw the Lady seem to melt into the wood flooring. She ran after her, aware that Erik was close behind her.

Caesar clawed at the floorboards, growling and sniffing. Bending down, Cora pulled up one of the boards, the wood splintering her fingernails. Beneath the deck was a small crawl space.

"Oooooo, Cora!" Erik's voice carried on the wind.

"Come on, Caesar, get in," she ordered, frantically trying to shove the big dog into the crawl space. He dug in his toes, but when she climbed in first, he quickly followed.

The space was cramped and dark. Cobwebs pulled at her hair and tangled in her fingers. Cora tried not to think of the spiders crawling around overhead.

"Lie down," she ordered, reaching up to pull the boards back into place. Caesar lay down with a grunt, and Cora settled next to him, hugging his big body for warmth.

As she shifted onto her side, something jabbed her hip, and she reached around to move it aside. Her fingers closed around something smooth and hard. Turning on her flashlight for a brief second, she shone it in the corner.

A scream rose in her throat. She clicked off the light and shoved a fist against her mouth to muffle the sound. She rested her forehead against Caesar's thick fur. "Oh God, oh God, please tell me that's not what I think it is," she whispered softly.

Turning over onto her back, Cora turned on the light again.

A skull, attached to the skeletal remains of someone, stared across the tiny space, the eye sockets eerily empty.

Cora's head dropped back against the floor with a dull thud, and she switched off the light again. Darkness filled the small crawl space.

"I think we found Natalie, Caesar," she said, squeezing her eyes shut. "She never even got off the island."

Caesar nosed her neck, trying to comfort her.

Suddenly the door to the boathouse swung open and someone stepped inside.

Caesar growled but Cora grabbed his muzzle and buried her face in his neck. "Be quiet, puppy," she begged softly.

He nuzzled her again, and although his hair stood on end, he didn't growl.

"Oh, Cora! Come out, come out, wherever you are!"

Cora held her breath as Erik passed overhead, his heels striking the floorboards with a heavy thud.

"Come on, Cora. I know you're in here. Don't make this hard on me. You know how angry I get."

Her fingers tightened in Caesar's hair, and she felt the rumble of a growl shake deep within the big dog's body. "Please, baby dog, please don't growl," she whispered softly in his ear.

Erik walked back again, pausing directly over them. She held on tight and sighed when he continued on.

They lay silent for several minutes as Erik searched the boathouse, calling out to her every few minutes tauntingly. Finally she heard the door open and close again. But still she lay quiet, holding on to Caesar.

Time passed. She thought she might have actually fallen asleep because every muscle in her body was cramped.

There was no sound from above. Even the wind seemed

to have quieted. Perhaps he was gone, retreating to the house and warmth.

Her legs were cramped and cold and she knew Caesar wouldn't be able to stay still too much longer.

She sat up and cautiously pushed the boards aside. She popped her head up and looked around. The boathouse was empty. She climbed out, reaching down to grab Caesar's collar and pull him out, too.

She cautiously made her way to the door and peeked out. The storm had lessened some, but it was still snowing. She glanced out at the river and almost wept with joy when she made out the shape of a boat making its way toward the dock.

Caesar bounded out of the boathouse and onto the dock, barking a greeting.

Cora stepped out onto the walkway and raised a hand, but it was then that Erik grabbed her from behind. She yelped and Caesar whirled around, bounding back toward her. But he was too late.

Erik pulled her backward into the boathouse, slamming the door and locking it against the dog as he threw himself against it.

"Guess you thought you'd fooled me, huh, Cora?" he said, throwing her onto the deck.

She got to her hands and knees, scrambling backward away from him. His face was twisted with a crazed hatred, the blue of his eyes so painfully familiar that she thought her heart might split with fear.

He picked up the flashlight that had fallen from her hands, and hefted it in the palm of his hand. "Nice weapon you've got here, Cora. I think this will finish the job nicely."

She got to her feet and ran, but he was on her in a second. Someone was pounding on the boathouse door, calling to her. It was Jake. He'd come. He'd come for her just as he said he would.

Erik slipped an arm around her throat and tightened.

"Jake!" she screamed, struggling to get away. She tried to yell again, but his arm cut off her air. Nothing came out.

She felt the world going soft around the edges. She fought harder, but he was too strong. She slipped into darkness.

JAKE POUNDED on the door, but it was bolted from the inside.

"I'll get a crowbar!" Red shouted over the wind, heading back to the cruiser at a dead run.

Jake knew there wasn't time. He ran to the end of the dock and jumped into the water. The shock was unbelievable. Freezing water surrounded and pulled at him as he swam for the door to the first boat slip. He ducked beneath the water and swam into the boathouse.

His head throbbed from the cold and his entire body went numb. The waves battered his body and threw him against the wooden pilings. He swam harder, grabbing the ladder nailed to the side of the dock.

He pulled himself up the ladder, hand over hand, falling onto the inside deck. He scrambled to his feet and searched the inside. A few feet away, a man held Cora against him, her tiny body limp in his big hands.

"Connery, you son of a bitch," he yelled. "Put her down!"

Connery whirled around, a crazed grin on his handsome face. "Did you come for this, Jake?" He grabbed a hunk of Cora's hair and threw her down. Her body crumpled into a heap, and she didn't move, her face pale.

"You have a hard time keeping your women, don't you, old boy?" Connery mocked him.

With a roar of rage, Jake charged, hitting the man in the

middle of his body. They toppled over backward, hitting the decking with a bone-jarring thud.

Jake drew back a fist, but Connery swung the flashlight, hitting him across the bridge of his nose. Blood spurted and Jake reeled in a haze of pain. The world around him tilted crazily. He shook his head, trying to clear it.

The flashlight hit him on his left temple this time, but Jake rolled with it. He couldn't see through the veil of blood covering his face, but he could hear Connery coming for him.

He slammed the heel of his hand up against the man's chin, sending him over backward. He used his sleeve to wipe away the blood. When Connery started to get up, Jake hit him again, sending him over the side of the dock. His head crunched against the side of the boat with a sickening thud, and he sank from sight into the cold, dark water below.

Jake turned and ran to Cora. He dropped down beside her and cradled her against him. She felt so small and fragile in his arms, her weight barely noticeable. She was still, too still.

He reached down and gently smoothed back several strands of wet hair, his fingers brushing her cold cheeks. She was so pale.

His heart squeezed tight; fear rose up into the back of his throat. Was he too late? Had Connery won?

The thought was so painful he pushed it aside. She couldn't be gone, couldn't be lost to him. He couldn't bear the thought of it. Couldn't bear the pain.

She moaned and her dark lashes, damp and spiked, fluttered on her cheeks, and she stared up at him, the warmth and depth of her cinnamon-brown eyes touching him with something indescribably beautiful. She was alive. She was safe.

"I thought you'd never get here," she whispered, her voice low and raspy.

"I thought I was too late." He leaned down and gently

kissed her forehead, her nose, her cheek and then finally her mouth. Her lips were cold beneath his, but she kissed him back, her arms reaching up to encircle his neck, holding him tight.

He held her close, his grasp protective, loving. Finally he raised his head.

"Where is he?" she asked, her voice trembling slightly.

He didn't need to ask who she meant. "He won't be bothering you ever again, Cora. He's dead."

Her small frame stiffened in his arms and her eyes filled with tears. "Is Megan all right? Did he hurt Megan?" Several tears rolled down her cheek, spilling onto his hand. "I...I didn't want to leave her, Jake, but she wouldn't come with me. Sh-she let him into the library. She said he wouldn't hurt us, but I knew he would."

Jake's arms tightened around her and he held her close. "It's okay, sweetheart. Everything is okay. Megan's fine. The phone started working again and she called us. She's up at the house. Connery didn't hurt her."

Cora sighed in relief and sagged against him. "I thought he'd hurt her. I didn't want to leave her."

"In all his craziness I guess Connery saw Megan as his sister. He didn't hurt her at all. He just left her up at the castle and came after you."

Cora pulled back a little, staring up at him. "H-how did he knew I was here?"

"As far as Red and I can figure out, Amanda told him."

"And he came here after me?"

Jake nodded.

Cora's lower lip trembled slightly. "He's been here for a while, hasn't he?"

"I think so. I believe that he's been playing a sick game of cat and mouse, hiding out in the tower room and using the passageways to get around."

Cora shuddered. "He could have killed me at any time." She glanced up at him. "He was the one that pushed me into the tub and tried to drown me, wasn't he?"

Again Jake nodded, his arms held her tighter, trying desperately to impart some feeling of safety into her slender frame. But something told him that it would take her a while to recover from this new trauma.

"Why did Amada bring me here?"

"I don't think she was trying to kill you. I think she recruited you for the job thinking she could discredit your testimony. Make you seem unstable. Crazy."

"She drugged me, didn't she?"

Jake nodded. "We think so. We won't know for sure until the police lab runs some tests on that tea mixture she was giving you. But Red and I are pretty sure it will come back showing she put something—some kind of hallucinogen—in it. It would go a long way to explaining things."

"But why? Didn't she realize how dangerous Erik, I mean, Connery was?"

Jake shrugged. "I don't know. Red put a call into Syracuse and the police department there have both Amanda and Sheffield in custody. We'll know more when they are done questioning them."

"Sheffield was involved, too?"

Jake nodded. "Probably. The man would do anything for a buck."

"But why would Amanda protect Connery? She had to know how sick he was. How violent."

"I figure that she never got over him being taken away from her. When he came back and found her here on the island, she must have thought she could help him. That she would keep him safe by keeping him near her." He drew a hand through his hair. "She convinced me to hire him to take care of the gardens. Maybe she thought if he lived on an island away from everyone, he'd be able to stay out of trouble."

"Do you think she knew what he was up to when he started working on Natalie to run away with him?"

Jake shrugged. "Who knows. I'm guessing that she decided to stick by him no matter what. Maybe her guilt over losing him the first time was too much for her to even consider him being lost to her a second time. Whatever happened, she looked the other way—allowed the blame to get deposited at my doorstep—when Natalie disappeared."

Cora reached up to touch his face, her eyes searching his, the sadness in them so intense he could feel the pain in his gut. "Connery killed Natalie."

"How do you know?" he asked.

She took his hand and gently led him over to the crawl space she had hidden in. The soft sympathy in her eyes cut him deeply.

The bleached white skeleton stared up at him, the gauzy white dress a familiar sight.

"Oh God, she never even got off the island," he said. "Never even escaped what she saw as her prison."

"I'm so sorry, Jake. I know things weren't good between the two of you, but no one should have to lose someone they loved like that."

Jake was about to tell her that it was all right, that he'd gotten over the shock before he'd even met her, and knowing now what happened to Natalie seemed to be taking some of the pain out of things. But he didn't get a chance to tell her because she glanced over his shoulder, and he saw her eyes widen in shock.

He turned, his hands tightening protectively around her slender body.

On the other side of the boathouse, near the crawl space Cora had pointed to stood a pale woman dressed all in white.

She lifted her head, and her dark hair fell away from her face. She smiled sadly and Jake sucked in a startled breath.

"Natalie," he whispered, his voice barely audible.

"That's the woman, Jake. That's the woman who has been appearing to me," Cora said. She lifted her eyes to him, her expression transfixed. "It's Natalie?"

Jake nodded, unable to speak.

For a moment the figure of the woman seemed to hover over the floorboards of the crawl space. Her shape was almost transparent, as the first rays of dawn seeped through the cracks in the old boathouse wall and surrounded her in a warm yellow glow. She faded to the color of pale ivory within the glow.

As they watched, she lifted a hand in a sign of farewell. And then she rose upward, her body floating. Jake watched in total astonishment as she seemed to melt up through the solid structure of the roof, her body disappearing like a wisp of gentle wood smoke.

"What the hell was that?" he mumbled, the hair on the back of his neck standing on end.

He stood up, reaching down to help Cora to her feet. He wrapped a protective arm around her narrow shoulders and they walked arm in arm to the spot where the woman had stood a few moments ago.

"Where did she go?" he asked, glancing up toward the rafters.

"She's gone, Jake. I think she only stayed long enough to say goodbye. She wanted you to know that she was finally at peace."

Jake shook his head. "This is ridiculous. I don't believe in ghosts."

Cora laughed softly and tightened her hand around his waist. "It doesn't matter what you believe. It's what we saw that counts. And we both saw it." The relief in her voice was evident. He knew how much it meant to her to have someone other than Megan see the apparition.

She laid her head against his chest. "She saved my life, Jake. She saved me by leading me to the boathouse. She wanted me to find her body, but I think she also knew you'd be coming by boat. She wanted me to be here when you arrived."

He could hear the emotion in her voice, and he tightened his arms around her. "It's okay, you're safe now."

She nodded. "But I'm safe because of Natalie. I think Connery would have gotten to me if she hadn't shown me where to hide. She must have known that he wouldn't go back to the spot where he hid her body."

They stood over the crawl space, gazing down at the skeletal remains of the woman in the white gown, the delicate white turning gray with dirt and dust. Jake reached across and lifted down a canvas tarp. He gently laid it over the opening. "Thank you," he said gruffly. "Thank you for saving her for me."

They linked arms and walked out of the boathouse together into the light of the dawn. The storm had passed, the winds had died and early sunlight bathed Midnight Island's beach with a sparkling array of crystallized white. It was a new day for both of them.

Epilogue

Fresh, newly grown blades of grass bent beneath Cora's feet. Overhead tiny buds of green leaves pushed upward off the bare branches of the trees, threatening to burst forth into full bloom at any moment.

She turned and glanced over her shoulder, marveling at the beauty of Midnight Castle in the golden hew of sunlight, a sunlight that announced the dawning of a new spring. The stones of the castle shone polished and strong, the windows inviting with a strange and wondrous warmth. It was a warmth she hadn't noticed when she had first arrived on the island.

She smiled. Five months ago the place had seemed desolate and forbidding. She had viewed it as her prison, and now she called it home. Now everywhere she looked, she saw new beauty and something else to be in awe of.

They'd only been back on the island for a few days. The trials had taken time, and they had traveled back and forth. But now they were here to stay. She breathed in the smells of fresh earth, the river and life.

As she gazed at the castle, two huge black beasts rounded the edge and streaked across the lawn toward her. They were followed close behind by their master. Her lover. Her husband. At the sight of him, a love so strong, so poignant that it seemed about to burst up through her chest and into her throat, overwhelmed her. She could not look away, could not take her eyes off of him. She watched him stride across the lawn toward her, his steps eager, confident.

The wind off the river, cool and gentle compared to the fierce bitterness of the winter wind, brushed back his long, dark hair and allowed her to feast her eyes on the beauty of his chiseled features. What had she ever done to deserve such a man? Such passion? Such sweetness and trust?

She smiled somewhere deep in her soul, and realized they both had gotten a gift. A gift of a new life. A new beginning. Even from a distance, she could see his smile of devotion. The look of anticipation on his face. She knew it mirrored the one on her own face.

Caesar and Cleo reached her first, jumping up with their muddy paws and marking her barn jacket with brown stains. She laughed and pushed them down, bending down to pat their huge heads, surprised at her lack of fear. Jake had changed all that, helped her to realize her own inner strength and determination.

"Have you been waiting long?" Jake asked, coming up and slipping his arm around her.

She stepped easily into the circle of his embrace, savoring its warmth and protectiveness. "Waiting any period of time for you seems like an eternity."

He laughed softly and pressed a hand to the center of her back, bringing her up against him as he kissed her passionately.

After a moment, she drew back and smiled up at him. "But when I get a greeting like that, it makes it all worthwhile."

He reached down and tenderly touched her belly. "Still not showing, are you?"

Cora felt her cheeks flush, but she placed her hand over

his, pressing him against the core of her being. "But he's in there and he's growing every day."

"My dad would be proud to know him if he had lived."

Cora stroked Jake's cheek, trying to impart some sense of comfort and understanding of all he had lost in recent months. "He would have been a wonderful grandfather, Jake. I've been thinking, laddie, that William Jacob Mackenzie would be the perfect name for our wee one. What thinks you?"

Jake grinned. "Well, I think you have a lousy Scottish accent, but I like the name a lot."

They were quiet for a moment, reveling in the thought of the event to come, but then Cora asked, "Are you ready to do this today?"

Jake nodded. "I've been ready for a long time."

They linked hands and walked across the lawn, the dogs bounding alongside them. They stepped onto the path leading to the point.

"I got a call from Red today," Jake said.

"The verdicts are in?"

Jake nodded. "Yes, guilty on all counts. Both are going to jail. Amanda for much longer than Sheffield, of course, but the D.A. said that your testimony was right on the money. You were calm, composed and very convincing."

"Only because you were there every day to be my leaning post. My support."

Cora leaned her head against his arm. "How do you think Megan is going to handle all this? She's been so quiet these past few days."

"It will be difficult for her. But we'll help her through it."

They walked through the thicket and stepped out onto the point. The wind was stronger here, and it whipped through Cora's hair and stung her cheeks.

To the left in a sheltered spot sat a small white headstone. The words Natalie Mackenzie Beloved Wife and Daughter stood out in stark relief.

For a brief moment, Jake stared out at the ships passing on the river. "I think she would have liked being put to rest here. It was her favorite place. A place she'd come to dream and fantasize about escaping to wild and exotic places."

Cora bent down and against the newly carved stone gently placed the bouquet of pink tulips she'd bought. "It's funny how different people are. I dreamed all my life of a quiet, peaceful place like this and Natalie wanted adventure and wild excitement. I never even knew something like this could exist for me."

"And now it all belongs to you."

"Well, not exactly mine, Jake. It's your land and home."

"What I own—every piece of dirt, stone and gem is yours, Cora. You are my salvation. My peace. You are what I have been searching for my entire life."

As they slipped into each other's arms again, one of the ships on the river blasted its horn as if in celebration, but neither one heard it or lifted their head. They were too involved in proclaiming their love and commitment. Entering into a world of eternal togetherness.

like a phantom in the night comes
a new promotion from

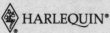
HARLEQUIN®

INTRIGUE

GOTHIC ROMANCE

Beginning in August 2004, we offer you
a classic blend of chilling suspense and
electrifying romance, starting with….

A DANGEROUS INHERITANCE
LEONA KARR

And don't miss a spine-tingling Eclipse tale each month!

September 2004
MIDNIGHT ISLAND SANCTUARY
SUSAN PETERSON

October 2004
THE LEGACY OF CROFT CASTLE
JEAN BARRETT

November 2004
THE MAN FROM FALCON RIDGE
RITA HERRON

December 2004
EDEN'S SHADOW
JENNA RYAN

Available wherever Harlequin books are sold.
www.eHarlequin.com

HIECLIPSE

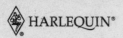

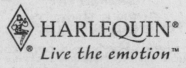

If you enjoyed what you just read,
then we've got an offer you can't resist!

Take 2 bestselling love stories FREE!

Plus get a FREE surprise gift!

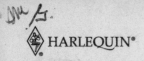
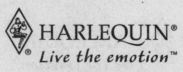